THE ROOF OVER OUR HEADS

BY NICOLE KRONZER

AMULET BOOKS • NEW YORK

Cataloging-in-Publication Data has been applied for and may be obtained from the Library of Congress.

ISBN 978-1-4197-5456-8

Text © 2023 Nicole Kronzer
Book design by Deena Fleming

Printed and bound in U.S.A.
10 9 8 7 6 5 4 3 2 1

Amulet Books are available at special discounts when purchased in quantity for premiums and promotions as well as fundraising or educational use. Special editions can also be created to specification. For details, contact specialsales@abramsbooks.com or the address below.

ABRAMS The Art of Books
195 Broadway, New York, NY 10007
abramsbooks.com

*For Bethany and Kristyn, my sisters
and permanent friends*

CHAPTER ONE

Three items remained on my to-do list: check in costumes, finish prepping dinner, and empty buckets in the attic.

Jade arriving four hours early was not on my list. It was not on anyone's list. Yet here she was.

"Why?" I asked when I pulled open the front doors and found Jade standing on the carriage step in jeans and a white tank top, a small suitcase at her feet.

"That's no way to greet someone donating two weeks of her life to help out your family, asshat," she said. She looked good in that tank top. Her dark skin—"bronze" was the word she always used to describe it—all glowy now that it was June. Her curly hair pulled back from her face. The other parts of her body doing their other parts things—not that I noticed. Or cared.

Five years ago in sixth grade, when Jade learned that I, a white guy, had one white mom, one Black mom, and two biracial brothers, she double high-fived me. Right in the middle of math class. Instead of dividing fractions that day, she told me about her white parents, and we exchanged stories the whole hour and became friends.

But a lot had changed since then.

I forced my eyes to stay trained on hers. "My family does not need you here until five."

She raised an eyebrow. "I thought you might want help setting up."

"No, thank you."

"But—"

Our argument paused as a blue Honda Civic pulled into the circular drive. Whoever it was hadn't been here before—I could tell because of how slowly they were approaching the house. Gaping, probably, unsure if number four Summit Avenue really meant this five-story, red sandstone mansion.

It did.

Smiling, I sidestepped Jade and jogged down the steps. Unless someone had ordered food, this person was here to deliver costumes. Including mine.

A bewildered-looking woman in her forties stepped out of the car. "Is this—"

"Probably?"

She laughed a little. "I'm supposed to be delivering costumes from Beauregard Costume Rental?"

"Nice! Kathy and Mandi send you?"

"Yes! I'm—"

"New," I finished.

"Oh, god. That obvious?"

I laughed. "No worries. You've come to the right place."

"I'm Jade," Jade inserted herself. "And this is Finn."

I rolled my eyes at Jade as the woman keyed open her trunk, revealing a mountain of long dresses and suits on hangers enclosed in plastic dry-cleaning bags.

"Finn," Jade warned me as I piled the bags high over my arm. "Victorian costumes are really heavy."

I added three more to my stack. "Good thing I'm really strong." In her defense, I didn't used to be. But like I said—a lot had changed.

"What *is* this place?" the costume deliverer asked, following us under the carriage porch and up the steps.

I glanced at Jade and adjusted the costumes I was holding so I could open one of the front doors but didn't respond right away. There was the easy answer: the Jorgensen House. Originally built by Swedish lumber and railroad baron Karl Jorgensen in 1891 for his family, consisting of his wife, Anna, and their eight daughters.

But even the easy answer led to more questions. Who owned it now? Who was I? And the one this person was sure to add: Why did we need all these costumes?

It was a long story. And a complicated one. And I didn't feel like going into it with a stranger.

Jade piped up. "Let's just hang the costumes on that Z-rack."

Back in sixth grade, when we were best friends, I would have flashed Jade a grateful smile. But we weren't in sixth grade anymore.

Kathy and Mandi's new hire shrugged and looped the hangers over the rolling rack I'd set up in the reception room.

"Whoops—be careful of the plaster," Jade said. I glanced up in time to see the costume rental lady remove her hand from the burgundy wall. "It's over a hundred years old—super delicate."

Dammit. Another reason to thank Jade.

After our third round trip, the woman waved at us, climbed into her car, and drove away.

"So. How are your lines?" Jade asked as we stood side by side on the carriage step. I stretched my spine. Jade was three and a half inches taller than me. These days, basically everyone was taller than me, but Jade's extra inches somehow irritated me the most.

"My lines are fine."

She gave me side-eye.

"They're *fine*," I repeated. "'Sir, you're needed. Cook has been murdered.' See? Twenty-five more like that. In here." I tapped my skull. "And you?"

"Lockbox."

"Then the show's going to be fine."

A squirrel chased after another squirrel and they skittered up a tree, chattering at each other. The leaves shook.

"So you're really not going to let me inside?" she asked.

"You've been inside." I knew I was being childish, but I didn't care.

"I'm going to go in there," she said. "And I'm going to find your moms, and I'm going to offer to help."

"Do what you want. I've got dinner to prep." And the buckets to empty. But for some reason, I didn't want to tell her that part.

"I will. See you later."

Then the warmth of her body beside me was gone. And even though it was seventy-five degrees out, I rubbed my arms.

If only Alexa would show up early, too. I'd be happy to let her help me. But no. Of course it was Jade . . .

I was still standing there, staring at the tree the squirrels had darted up, when one of the front doors swung open.

4

"Dude, get inside," my older brother Andre said. "There's, like, a million things left to do."

"Right. Sorry." I elbowed through the door and followed him across the entryway's looping mosaic tiles.

"Guess who told me you were outside?" Andre asked, playfully slapping my cheek with one hand as he opened the interior door with the other.

I batted his hand away. "Why? Was she trying to get me in trouble?"

"Two correct guesses," he smirked. "It's like you share a brain."

Ignoring him, I pulled out my to-do list, flattened it on the L-shaped desk underneath the portraits of stern Karl and proper Anna Jorgensen, and crossed off *check in costumes.* "Okay. What do you have left? And is Kendrick moping or is he actually doing things?"

Our other brother, Andre's identical twin, was in the throes of missing his latest boyfriend. Kendrick claimed to have found "the one" three to five times a year, but none of them ever lasted more than a few months.

"He's mostly moping," Andre reported, retrieving his own battered list, "but I got him to promise to put on a brave face in public and in front of Lula and Nomi." Our moms are actually Laura and Naomi, but Andre and Kendrick named them Lula and Nomi when they were learning to talk. "This thing has too many moving parts for them to worry about how Kendrick is feeling about it."

"Good," I said.

"Yeah. But best-case scenario would have been sending Kendrick off to lover boy's hometown to get him out of his system before the show," Andre joked.

"No kidding," I agreed. "Two weeks of doing this play and living like it's 1891 is going to be tough enough. But with Kendrick 'in love' and not allowed to use his cell phone—"

"It's going to be hell on wheels."

"Worse—hell in a horse-drawn carriage."

Andre laughed. "Yeah, well—we've got each other."

"Always," I said. I tugged him into a quick hug. "I'm really glad you're home."

"Me too, kid." Andre thumped my back. "You feeling ready? Lines good?"

I bristled but nodded.

"Then I need your help with one thing. Lula's got me making all the beds with hospital corners, which I can only do at the rate of, like, one every fifteen minutes. I tried to argue they probably weren't invented yet, but—"

"They totally were?"

"Damn Victorians," Andre said. "Making my life all hard."

Living like Victorians one hundred and thirty-some years later was going to be hard for all of us. But fun, too. And we were doing it for a good cause—to pay to fix the leaking roof. And a bunch of terrific people were helping out, and Nomi had written the play—*A Midsummer Night's Art Heist Garden Party Escape Room Murder*—and it was ridiculous and wonderful and—

I laughed. "This is going to be great," I told Andre.

He folded up his to-do list and tucked it back into his pocket. "Totally great. Ready?"

"Ready."

CHAPTER TWO

Four hours later, I clutched the back of one of the heavy dining room chairs and searched the crowd for my parents.

The cast had arrived—Mr. Hoyt, our school drama director, was chatting with Andre and Kendrick by the secret entrance to the silver safe while wearing his trademark bow tie. Birdlike Joan Dooley, a local historian, and Martin Lord, who was playing the butler, were peering up inside the fireplace. Maddie McGlynn, Lula's ginger-haired college-aged assistant, was smacking the hand of her friend who played the organ to keep him from messing with the pocket door into the art gallery. My friend Noah, his younger sister, and—my mouth went dry—Alexa Murphy, with her peaches-and-cream complexion and light brown hair woven into a braided crown, were hovering over the buffet.

Alexa had transferred to our high school in St. Paul at the beginning of second semester from Chicago and was immediately cast in our production of *Drowsy Chaperone.* Normally, our drama director put new people in small roles to make sure they were nice to everyone and could memorize and take direction without complaining. But Alexa had been given the part of Trix, who had a huge solo, right out of the gate.

Alexa was special. Onstage and off.

Unlike Jade, who was mostly a pain in my ass. What was she doing tugging at the trim by the butler's screen?

I released my grip on the chair and took a few steps closer to her to tell her to knock it off, but that's when I finally noticed my parents: Lula in backstage black, her short blond hair spiked up, Nomi in a yellow top and jeans, her dark brown straightened hair tucked behind her ears. Their heads were tipped together in fervent conversation.

"Lula! Nomi!" I called, ignoring Jade for now.

"Hi, Finn!" Lula said when I reached them. Nomi slipped her arm around my shoulder. "Excited?"

"Totally. But—" I lowered my voice. "I didn't get to the buckets. I was going to do it after lunch, but—"

"It's been a busy day," Nomi finished for me. She smoothed my hair. As an almost-senior in high school, I knew I should be shaking off that kind of parental preening, but after the year we had, I didn't care who saw that I leaned into her a little more.

"Is it okay if I slip away during the tour and do it?" I asked. "If someone else heads up dishes?" The buckets wouldn't take too long, and then maybe I'd have another chance to review the script. Better safe than sorry.

"Of course," Lula said. "Okay. I'll quickly pass these out, then—"

"I can do that for you." I took the stack of papers from her hands.

"Great. Thanks, honey. Then I guess all that's left to do is save—" Lula cut herself off, and her face froze, but just for a quarter of a second. At the same time, Nomi squeezed my shoulder hard. *Save what?* The roof? I already knew about that. And so did everyone else. Why were they being weird?

But then they both relaxed and Lula smiled and kissed my cheek and Nomi turned me loose.

I looked over my shoulder as I began setting a packet of information at each chair, but now they were talking to Maddie McGlynn and everyone was laughing.

I'd imagined that weird moment, right?

I glanced at the top packet in my hands and skimmed the first page.

VICTORIAN GUIDELINES

1) When you wake up tomorrow, it will be 1891. In addition to putting on the play, we are testing out the concept of hosting Victorian Immersive Experiences here at the Jorgensen House, so no vestiges of modern times (except medication and eye correction) will be allowed. This includes, but is not limited to, electronic devices, modern snacks, books printed after 1891, modern toiletries, any of your own clothing or shoes, or anything invented after 1891.

2) You are expected to fulfill your assigned role, operating to the best of your abilities with the social norms of the late Victorians. (See page 3.)

3) People shall be referred to by their character names with respective statuses in mind. (See page 4.)

I was smiling when I finished my trip around the table and claimed a seat near the buffet. But then Jade appeared out of nowhere and tugged at the dining room chair next to mine. I swallowed a groan. There were sixteen chairs to choose from. She needed to be *right* next to me? I had been hoping Alexa would sit there.

Back during *Drowsy Chaperone* rehearsals, Alexa and I kept finding ourselves next to each other for notes. At first, it was accidental, but then we made a point of it, fake pretending otherwise. "Finn!" she'd say after squeezing into the formally nonexistent spot between me and another actor on the edge of the stage, "fancy seeing you here!" I'd scoff in surprise, "Alexa Murphy! As I live and breathe!"

I liked her so much—I'd wanted to ask her out for months. But my plate had been more than full with my responsibilities here at home; I couldn't add another thing. Even if that thing was dating Alexa. And anyway, we'd had time to become friends. Flirty friends. Flirty friends who might become . . . more than friends.

I tried to catch Alexa's eye to invite her over, but then Andre and Kendrick plopped down into the chairs on my other side, and Nomi and Lula walked past and wiggled their eyebrows at us, and I let it go. There would be plenty of time to connect with Alexa later. After all, she was going to be staying here for two weeks.

"Welcome, everyone!" Lula called from the head of the table, and the excited chatter quieted. I shifted in my chair, struggling to contain my excitement. I wasn't sure if it was about the play finally starting or Alexa or about Lula being okay and in charge, but whatever—it felt so good to feel happy again.

"I'm Laura Turner, many-hat-wearer here at the Jorgensen House, but for the next two weeks, your director. Please accept my heartfelt gratitude for taking all of this on. Agreeing to rehearse a play for only four days, put on twenty performances the following ten, all while living here full-time like Victorians? You're magical unicorns, every one of you."

Laughter filled the room with an energy usually absent from this giant, rambling house. I leaned back a little. I could get used to this.

"Here's the schedule for tonight," Lula said, her cheeks flushed with pleasure. "After dinner, I'll give you an overview of living like a Victorian, then my assistant Maddie will take whoever wants it on a tour of the house." Maddie McGlynn saluted us all from her seat near Lula.

"We'll get everyone settled in their rooms," Lula continued, "then hopefully you'll sleep like babies on your extremely Victorian IKEA mattresses."

More laughter.

"Tomorrow when you wake up, it'll be 1891. Since the cook won't be here until tomorrow afternoon, we'll have two more delicious Finn meals after this one. Let's give Finn a round of applause, both for stepping up and for these sure-to-be-outstanding tacos!"

I was perfectly happy to just smile and move on, but Andre elbowed me, and Jade hissed, "Stand up, Finn!" So I half-rose out of the chair and offered a stupid little wave.

But it was only tacos.

At first, I'd been daunted at the prospect of making a meal for so many people. But that feeling swiftly passed. My foods teacher always said, "If you can read, you can cook." Compared to the work of acting, making dinner—even for this many people—hadn't been that hard for me.

It probably helped that I really liked cooking, though. I just started learning how this year. When Kendrick and Andre came home from their freshman year of college, they lost their minds over my Welcome Back Chicken Cacciatore.

"When did we start eating like royalty?" Andre had asked between mouthfuls.

"After you two moved out and there was actually food left in the house to *make* things!" I'd said. But really, it was because of Lula. She'd been diagnosed with kidney cancer and gone through surgery and chemotherapy this winter and spring. Feeding Nomi and Lula (but let's be honest—mostly Nomi) had felt like one of the only things I could do to help.

"Do you have any instructions for us, Finn?" Lula asked after the applause died down.

"Yes," I said, blinking quickly to return myself to the present—and to my rosy, very much alive, cancer-free mom. I gestured to the waist-high hutch against the wall on the butler's screen side of the dining room. "Everything's over there on the buffet. The meat is ground turkey, and there are also black beans. Oh—and the salsa spiciness levels are well labeled for those with Scandinavian palates."

Beaming through the group's laughter, Lula held up her hands. "All right then! Let's dig in!"

Amid hums of appreciation, the cast queued up, and I stepped back to let everyone else go ahead of me.

Jade hung back, too. "That's the original fireplace hood, right?"

"Uh, yeah?"

She nodded once. I squinted at her as she joined the line. What did she care about the fireplace hood for?

"I'm starving," Noah said, sidling over to me and tucking his pale, freckled hands into his pockets. "If those brownies you made for closing night of *Drowsy* are any indication of how this meal's going to be, I can't wait."

"Glad you liked them, because I made them again for dessert."

Noah did a dorky celebration dance. Laughing, I followed him to the stack of floral scalloped dishes on the end of the buffet.

"What makes them so magically transcendent?" he asked, selecting the top plate.

I took the next one and stage-whispered, "There's a secret ingredient."

He considered this and stage-whispered back, "Is it passion fruit?"

"*Passion* fruit?"

"Yeah!" We each grabbed a few flour tortillas. "On those British baking shows—" He affected a believable British accent. "They're always using passion fruit."

I laughed, ladling into the black beans. "Nope. Just espresso powder."

"Well, maybe—"

"Finn, these are *so* good!"

I whirled around at the sound of Alexa's voice, and my newly bean-filled taco slipped off my plate and landed business side down on the hardwood floor. "Uh, thanks!" I called, my heart whacking around in my chest as I scooped it into some napkins. *Smooth, Finn.*

"Who knew you were such a talented cook?" Mr. Hoyt called out. "Well done, Finn!"

I popped up. "Oh! Thanks, Mr. Hoyt!"

"Three cheers for the best cook I know!" Andre shouted. "But since he's not here, three cheers for Finn! Hip hip—"

I flushed, shaking my head as the cast joined in on *hooray*. Even Jade, though a half-smirk accompanied it. But I had to admit it felt nice to be appreciated, even if it was just for making a meal.

CHAPTER THREE

"Victorian Deep Dive in one minute! Last call for dessert!" Lula announced.

"And the built-ins are all original, too?"

I spun around in my chair at the dining room table. *Jade.* She was a human mosquito. "Yes. Why are you—"

But she marched off before I could finish my question.

Then Alexa caught my eye and pointed at the brownie she was lifting off the buffet. "This is my third!" she mouthed.

I grinned and thumbed at the empty chairs next to mine, but as she started to weave my way, Kendrick flopped into one of them.

"Ugh," he grumbled. "Do I have to stay for Victorian Deep Dive if I've lived like a Victorian my entire life?"

"Be cool," I muttered, whacking his arm.

"Why?" he asked and whacked me back.

Alexa set her plated brownie on the table and tucked a leg underneath her as she sat. "Hi," she said to Kendrick. "I'm Alexa. I'm playing Margaret Jorgensen."

"Kendrick," he said. "I'm Simon Pendercast." And he smiled.

I let myself relax a little.

"Simon Pendercast," Alexa repeated. "You're one of the gentleman suitors."

"Indeed," he said, bowing slightly.

Alexa giggled and reoriented her plate. "So . . . this house is amazing. Jade said your mom fixed it up?"

I nodded, distracted momentarily by Jade tugging open a door in one of the curved glass built-in cabinets. What was she looking for? I cleared my throat. "The renovation's mostly stagecraft and paint and theatre magic."

"Well, it's gorgeous," Alexa said.

"The fire alarm goes off every time it gets humid, and the roof leaks," Kendrick said. "So don't get too excited."

I shot Kendrick a look. "Mom's the dramaturg for the Beauregard Theatre—"

"That's, like, a theatre historian, right?" Alexa interrupted me.

I nodded. "And when the old lady who owned this place died twenty-five years ago, she left the house to the theatre with the intention they'd sell it and keep the money. But the artistic director loved it and kept poking around for some way to keep it. Mom was fresh out of college and suggested she live here and rent Beauregard sets and props out of the basement and use the money to fix up the house so they could host Victorian immersion weekends," I said. "It's taken a really long time, but it's pretty much done now. That's part of what we're all doing living like Victorians during these two weeks—to see if it works."

Kendrick put on his best Lula voice. "Imagine staying here for the weekend, dressed in Victorian clothing, playing Victorian parlor games. Having Victorian meals! This house has so much to teach us—about the Gilded Age and its extravagances, but also its influence on who we are today! Plus weddings. We can totally make a crapload of money hosting weddings."

Alexa and I laughed.

"Still," Kendrick drawled. "Why she insisted on test running Victorian immersion on *top* of putting on this play, I mean . . ."

I shot him another look. Luckily, Alexa didn't seem to notice the shift in Kendrick's tone.

"The dark wood panels, all the fireplaces and chandeliers— someone said the wallpaper in here is *leather*? It's like a Victorian family could walk in any minute." Alexa took a bite of her brownie. "I can't believe this is where you live."

Before I could explain that we lived in only a tiny part of it and offer a personal tour, Lula called for everyone's attention.

"Feel free to keep enjoying Finn's brownies," she said, "but we'll get started . . . Now, you all should have received our Victorian Survival Guide and schedule via email, but here it is again on paper. I'll highlight a couple things and then answer questions."

I skimmed my copy to see when I might have some downtime to hang out with Alexa.

REHEARSAL SCHEDULE

Servant Breakfast: 7 a.m.

Family Breakfast: 8 a.m.

Rehearsal: 9–noon

Servant Luncheon: noon

Family Luncheon: 12:30 p.m.

Victorian Etiquette (or rehearsal as needed) : 1–3 P.M.

In-Character Break: 3–4 P.M.

Victorian Dance: 4–6 P.M.

Servant Dinner: 6 P.M.

Family Dinner: 7 P.M.

In-character evening activities: reading, games, music, etc.
Note: Equity actors, please see your exceptions on page 6.
On show days, mealtimes will be adjusted.

Since I was cooking *and* acting tomorrow, it was going to be a tight day for me. I did some mental math. Between getting dressed and lighting the wood-burning stove and boiling water for tea and coffee before making any actual food . . . I was going to have to set my alarm for *four forty-five a.m.*

My face must have looked deeply pained, because Alexa flashed me one of her crooked smiles that said, *Hey, you. Cheer up!*

The last time she'd shared one with me was when we ran into each other on the day the Acting Lab list had gone up without either of our names on it.

Auditions for seniors-only Acting Lab had been held during the last week of school. I'd only made it through the opening line of my monologue before a void opened up in my brain, sucked the rest of the monologue into it, vaporized all the words, then sealed itself shut. It wasn't the first time something like that had happened to me—lines I was sure I had memorized betraying me when it counted the most—but boy had that sucked. With the chaos around here plus the stress of the end of the school year, I probably hadn't prepared as much as I should have. Still.

"I feel like punching something," I'd said.

"Aw, don't do that." Crooked smile. "Because then you might break your hand, and I'll feel like I have to do something to help, and I was not paying attention during that unit in health class."

I'd actually laughed.

"Mark my words, Finn. It'll be our names on that list in September."

Mr. Hoyt always left two slots open for transfers or for anyone who improved over the summer. The fall would be a better time for me to audition anyway—I'd have months to prepare. But if I wanted to follow in my family's footsteps—Andre and Kendrick were in exclusive college acting programs and cited their year in Lab as the reason—I needed to get my act together. Literally.

Between convincing Mr. Hoyt I belonged in Acting Lab and Alexa I was boyfriend material, I had a lot to prove over the next fourteen days.

Jade elbowed me. "We're on page two."

Ugh. Why couldn't a void suck Jade into it, vaporize her, and seal itself shut?

I flipped the packet over and took steadying breaths as Lula spoke about wealthy Victorians believing poverty was due to laziness and not the result of capitalism and multigenerational wealth. Also, a lot about men being breadwinners and a young woman's main job being to "protect her virtue."

I finally found where Lula was reading and followed along.

Despite how we as individuals might feel about these norms, we are not here to judge. Instead, as we step into the Gilded Age, we can look inward to our own society, reflect on how past choices have made us who we are, and how, in turn, our choices might affect future generations.

These norms will manifest themselves in this house in several key ways:

1) No unmarried woman shall be in a room alone with an unmarried man without a chaperone.

2) With the exception of the housekeeper and butler, servants should not speak to the family unless spoken to first, or be seen by the family at all unless they are serving a meal.

"Uh," Magnus the organist interrupted Lula, "so what happens if we break these rules?" Magnus had lived on Maddie McGlynn's floor this year in the University of Minnesota dorms. I'd said hello when he'd arrived but hadn't really spoken to him yet.

Lula looked up from the guideline sheet. "What happens if you . . . *break* the rules?"

"Yeah, like, what if you're . . ." Magnus consulted the packet, a smirk spreading across his face. "An unmarried man, and you're caught with an unmarried woman in your room, for example?"

Maddie's voice was sharp. "Then I imagine this won't *count* for the thing it's supposed to *count* for."

Count for? What was she talking about? Plus, her tone seemed harsh, considering how hard she'd lobbied for Magnus to get this role back in May.

Magnus leaned back on two legs of his chair and said, "It's just, according to this, Victorians sound pretty strict. But Maddie said this was going to be fun."

In one swift movement, Maddie shoved his chair forward, reconnecting all four legs to the floor.

"I—" Lula faltered. Nomi stepped in. "We hope it will be fun, but that we'll all learn something, too."

"Well, it sounds like a lot of fun to me," Alexa said.

Mr. Hoyt adjusted his bow tie. "I entirely agree."

Mr. Hoyt and Lula were friends from college, so he'd offered to recruit the teen actors. That was how we'd ended up with not only Alexa but also Noah, his sister, and Jade, too.

I was initially surprised by everyone's willingness to take on this weirdly intense thing, even though it included performing a great show, but then I realized that they signed on well before Acting Lab auditions. Maybe that was it—signing on to this project showed Mr. Hoyt they were team players. Even though Jade and Noah had made it into Lab, maybe now they were hoping face time with Mr. Hoyt might influence the shows he chose for next year. He'd built *Blood Brothers*, a musical about twins separated at birth, around Andre and Kendrick, after all.

I guess we all had things to prove to Mr. Hoyt.

Lula read out the rest of the Victorian rules and then pointed at the cast list. "After tonight, please address each other by the names and titles listed here."

THE JORGENSENS:	
Mr. Jorgensen (formal) Karl (informal)	Fletcher Hoyt
Mrs. Jorgensen (formal) Anna (informal)	Naomi Turner
DAUGHTERS:	
Helen (age 21—married)	
Margaret (age 19) *Miss Jorgensen (formal) *Margaret (informal)	Alexa Murphy
Elizabeth (age 17) *Miss Elizabeth (formal) *If elder sister is absent, Miss Jorgensen (formal) *Elizabeth (informal)	Jade Montgomery
Florence (age 15—at the lake)	
Lillian (age 15—at the lake)	
Alice (age 12—at the lake)	
Dorothy (age 10—at the lake)	
Millie (age 1—at the lake)	

SUITORS:	
James *Mr. Pendercast (formal) *James (informal)	Andre Turner
Simon *Mr. Simon (formal) *If elder brother is absent, Mr. Pendercast (formal) *Simon (informal)	Kendrick Turner
MALE SERVANTS:	
Butler *Mr. Lord (formal) *Martin (informal)	Martin Lord
Footman Always addressed by first name: Jeremiah	Magnus Torvald
Footman Always addressed by first name: Tobias	Finn Turner
Coachman Always addressed by first name: Henry	Noah Peterson
FEMALE SERVANTS:	
Housekeeper *Mrs. Dooley (formal) *Joan (informal)	Joan Dooley
Lady's Maid *Logan (by the family) *Miss Logan (by other servants) *Grace (informal)	Maddie McGlynn
Scullery Maid Always addressed by first name: Bridget	Lindsey Peterson

My eye caught on my own name: *Finn Turner. Footman. Always addressed by first name: Tobias.*

When she told me I'd be playing a footman, Nomi apologized up and down that she hadn't written a larger role with me in mind specifically—it was just that she'd written the play as a romp while she was on tour to distract herself from missing us. She never intended to actually stage the thing.

I wanted to believe *that's* how I ended up with only a handful of lines and not because of the reason I suspected: She didn't trust me with a bigger part.

In fact, at first, she'd asked me to be the cook. My job would have been to prepare the meals and lie dead in the silver safe for the entire play like a piece of furniture. But one look at my disappointed face sent her backpedaling. If the cook had lines to deliver, that would have been one thing. But Mr. Hoyt already knew I could just sit there, speechless.

Lula peered at the cast through her fingers. "Is everyone totally memorized?"

Every cast member's head bobbed up and down—even Magnus's. I joined in the nodding a second late.

"My blood pressure and I are so glad to see everyone is prepared," Lula said, and everyone chuckled. "Theatre is such an important part of who we are as a family, and we're so grateful to you all for being here."

I smoothed my handout on the table.

"Now, the last page has a few Victorian slang terms listed that might be fun to try and work into your vocabulary. For example, Victorians called the bathroom 'the necessary.'" Lula smiled at the group's delight. "Over the next few days, Maddie will teach us all how to play a popular Victorian card game called faro, or if you prefer, Andre has plans to set up croquet on the back lawn. But right now, it's time for a tour of the house. So if you already know your way around, will you help Finn with the dishes? We'll be in our proper roles tomorrow, but tonight, it's all for one and one for all. Any questions?"

"Uh, actually . . ." I raised a hand. "I can't help with the dishes, remember?"

Lula quirked an eyebrow.

I jerked my chin toward the attic a couple times, but she just squinted at me.

"Buckets?" I mouthed.

"Right! . . . Say, Joan?" As Joan Dooley agreed to lead dish duty, I avoided Jade's prying eyes. I knew it was killing her, wondering what I had to do. But that was just too bad.

CHAPTER FOUR

As everyone broke into the tour group and the dishwashing group, I slipped out of the dining room into the grand hall. Taking the sage-green carpeted steps two at a time, I climbed the wide central staircase up to the landing, peeling off to the left fork up to the second floor. A half dozen steps across the hall led me to the narrower flower staircase. "Flower staircase" wasn't its official name or anything, but the newel post on the second floor featured a flower bud carved into the top of it. Then, as you ascended the steps, the flower opened up a little more on each post until you reached the top. The third floor's post was in full bloom.

In some ways, this whole house was like those flower carvings in reverse. The first floor was all showy with its draperies and wood carvings and high ceilings—the public rooms in full bloom. The second floor's flower was still open, but less so. The family rooms. Two guest rooms. Narrower, less expensive wood trim. Up on the third floor, the ceilings were lower. The wood even less ornate. That's where the schoolroom was. Where the female servants lived. And through the servants' wing, up the final flight of stairs, was the fourth floor. The attic. Where the flower bud was firmly closed up.

Closed up in terms of beauty, though—not containment. Because the roof leaked. A lot.

At the top of the attic steps, I threw open the door and slammed it shut. Totally unnecessary, but when we were little in this house, learning rules like "Don't touch the walls!" and "Stay away from the gas lighting!" our parents knew there had to be some places where we could tear around.

I remember them taking us up here when we were five and seven. "You have free rein in the attic," they told us, gesturing to the enormous, echoey, wood-paneled room. "You can run, jump, put on plays—Hey! Maybe the Jorgensen treasure is up here!"

"Can we touch the walls?" Kendrick asked.

They laughed. "Yes."

"Can we slam the door?" Andre wanted to know.

"Yes," our moms agreed. "You can slam the door as many times as you want."

I still loved slamming the door. After flinging it closed behind me one more time for fun, I scooped up an empty five-gallon Home Depot bucket and surveyed my forest of receptacles. Currently, a dozen pots, five Tupperware containers, ten empty paint cans, three sand pails, and Kendrick's old goldfish bowl dotted the attic floor, collecting plinks and plonks of water from our leaking roof.

A slate roof can last a long time. Like, two hundred years, apparently. But at the ripe old age of one hundred and thirty, ours started misbehaving. I was so glad I happened to come up here to grab the record player for *Drowsy Chaperone* in March, because after one hundred inches of snow this winter, all that snow was starting to melt. And that melt was coming inside.

Lula was still recovering, and Geoffrey Thatcher, the beloved Beauregard artistic director who had approved Lula's plan to turn the Jorgensen House into Victorian Disney World, had just passed away. So I didn't tell Lula or Nomi about the roof. They had enough to worry about. Instead, I found buckets. And spike tape to mark where those buckets lined up under their particular drip so as to easily replace them in the right spot after being emptied. I decided I'd tell them when Lula was feeling better.

I kept using that word—"when." Even though I didn't always trust it. *When* she could handle things again. *When* this was all over.

Because theatre people believe in the power of the spoken word.

Belief in that power was probably what also kept me from telling anyone at school about how sick Lula was. I worried that if I gave voice to the sentence *My mom has cancer*, I would be inviting something dark and terrible into an already dark and terrible situation.

So during those months, I said *when,* not *if,* and transferred the unwelcome water into two orange five-gallon Home Depot buckets and hauled them down four flights of stairs several days a week, where I watered Nomi's plants under the eaves.

I could have poured the bucket water down the sink—there was one in the attic. But—and I would never admit this out loud—it didn't occur to me for, like, a month. And by that time, I was starting to get decent muscles from all that lifting. So the Voyage of the Buckets continued.

Until Andre caught me the night he came home from college.

"You *have* to tell them!" he exclaimed in the servants' wing, shaking me by the shoulders. Doing a double take, he squeezed my biceps. "Geez—I guess that's where these muscles came from." Then, perhaps to prove he still had the upper hand, he jammed his arms under my armpits from behind and laced his fingers around the back of my neck, lifting me off the ground. "Finn!" he reprimanded me as I squirmed. "Why are you keeping the leaking roof a secret?"

"Because of Lula!" I shouted, kicking him in the shin.

"She can handle it," he insisted, releasing me. He shoved me, then rubbed his leg. "Together, our parents can handle anything."

I wanted to tell him he hadn't seen the two of them fold into each other this year like I had. Lula had been diagnosed when Andre and Kendrick were away at college. She had insisted there was nothing they could do at home—they'd just worry—and told them to stay at school. So they'd stayed.

I'd wanted them home. I hardly knew who I was without them, anyway. And with Lula being sick on top of that? But when I talked about it with Nomi, she teared up and said Lula did not need the guilt of them missing school on top of everything else.

So I didn't tell anyone about the roof.

When I finally did—under duress—Lula and Nomi sobbed when they saw what I'd done.

"You saved the house, Finn," Lula whispered.

"There's a spot that's leaking into the west servants' bedroom," I said, following her with my eyes as she picked her way around the buckets. "That's the only one I haven't been able to find. The ceiling plaster has turned a super gross color down there. I put a tarp on the floor? But—"

"Finnster," Nomi interrupted, wrapping me in her arms. Her voice was thick and dropped low so only I could hear her. "Look at you, darling," she murmured into my hair. "Look at everything you've done. All those meals. Keeping up with school and shows. You made it so I only had Lula to worry about. And this whole time, you've been protecting everything she's worked for—what we've all sacrificed for, too?" She tightened her grip on me. I tried to resist the tears welling in my eyes—I hadn't cried in front of them once this whole time. But Nomi kept holding me. And holding me. And then—well.

I'm not a robot.

So my family learned about the buckets. And Lula predicted the money we were going to bring in from the play would be enough to fix the roof. But the extent to which the roof was leaking still didn't feel like something that needed advertising. I worried it made us seem negligent somehow. Or it took too much explanation, involved too many untold secrets.

So until the roof was repaired, I was a one-man bucket brigade.

CHAPTER FIVE

I avoided Maddie McGlynn's tour of the house by slipping down the servants' staircase. But in my hurry, water sloshed over the side of one of my buckets onto the second-floor landing.

Wood and water are a recipe for disaster! Lula always said. So I set the buckets down and opened the door into the family part of the house. Then I jogged down the hall to get a towel.

The Jorgensen House was designed to be fireproof—it was built with steel I-beams and curved brick. So even after a hundred and thirty-some years, the only movement that caused creaking was when people climbed up or down the stairs. A person could walk on the carpeted hallway all day without anyone knowing they were coming.

And that's why my parents didn't hear my arrival in the Turner Wing.

What we called the Turner Wing (after us, the Turners) used to be four bedrooms, two bathrooms, and a largish walk-in closet. In the 1970s, Millie, the final Jorgensen daughter, converted the rooms into an apartment so she wouldn't have to traipse around the mansion on her eighty-year-old legs. We divvied them up as Lula and Nomi's bedroom, my brothers' bedroom, a kitchenette, and Lula's office. I slept in the large walk-in closet off my brothers' room. So while my family technically lived in a mansion, most of the time it felt like we lived on top of each other.

But not this time. When I heard Lula say, "But you said you'd give us a chance!" I pushed myself flat against the wall. (Well, as flat as I could get without touching the plaster.)

"You said if we could prove the Victorian immersive experiences could work—"

"I know what I said, Laura—"

I squinted trying to place the deep voice made tinny through what sounded like speakerphone.

"But a new estimate came in from the roofing company," the voice continued, "and it's not pretty. You'd have to put on sixty performances to pay for it. Or charge a lot more. Or get a lot more exposure—"

"What if we do a VIP performance?" Nomi suggested. "For the final show? Feed the audience a real Victorian meal, charge a thousand dollars a plate—"

I nearly choked, which would have totally given me away. A *thousand* dollars? Plus—what was going on?

"Yes! And we have a connection at PBS!" Lula exclaimed. "Naomi—We could ask Georgia Periolat if PBS would be interested in . . . I don't know—something with the show, that VIP thing— Between the regular ticket sales, extra money, and the exposure . . . What do you say, Mark?"

Oh, no. *Mark* had to be Mark Lester-Dean. He was the brand-new artistic director at the Beauregard. And technically, our landlord. But I hadn't even met him yet.

His sigh crackled over the speakerphone. "I told you I wasn't crazy about this idea in the first place, Laura."

He wasn't? Lula and Nomi hadn't said anything about it. And I was so used to Geoffrey agreeing to basically every idea Lula had.

"Let me see if we can get Georgia on board," Lula insisted. "Don't make any decisions about selling until we hear back, okay?"

Selling? Cold washed over my body.

"Look," Mark said, "I told you I'd wait to call a real estate agent until I see how the run of this thing goes, and I'm a man of my word. But I'm also a realist. It's a beautiful house, but it's a drain on the theatre's already tenuous finances."

"But—"

"I know what you said about the prop and set rentals, but we can rent a warehouse for a fraction of what it costs to heat that place in January alone."

"But soon—"

"And I know it's on the state and national registers of historic places, qualifying it for grants and tax incentives. But—"

"The—"

"Immersive weekends. Weddings. I know, Laura. Your report was very thorough. The bottom line is Geoff Thatcher had a lot of expensive pet projects. This pet project is by *far* the most expensive. The Beauregard's financial focus has to be on growing new audiences. The average age of season ticket holders is seventy-three—"

I couldn't listen anymore. I tumbled out of our wing.

33

Mark Lester-Dean wanted to sell the Jorgensen House. If he did, we'd have to move. No way in three lifetimes could my parents afford to buy this place. But worse than that—what had the past twenty years been for if Lula had to leave now? Just as her dreams were becoming reality? *I can't imagine living anywhere else*, she always said. Well, the cancer was gone. She was going to live for a long, long time. And if she wanted to live here, that's where she was going to live.

I'd saved the house once. Somehow, I'd just have to do it again.

CHAPTER SIX

With the spill wiped up and Home Depot buckets emptied and returned to the attic, I descended the stairs to the first floor.

If we pulled off these two weeks—with the play, the VIP performance, proving Victorian immersion worked—it might be enough to keep Mr. Lester-Dean from selling the house. Might. We just had to be flawless. Unfortunately, while I was many things as an actor, flawless was low on the list.

I lifted the dry-cleaning bag labeled TOBIAS THE FOOTMAN off the rolling rack in the music room and flung it over my shoulder. I strode the eighty-eight steps from the front door of the mansion down the paved driveway, the reddish-brown sandstone brick of the two-story gatehouse looming larger as I approached.

The gatehouse was an ideal destination for two reasons: One, it was not on Maddie's tour, so I wouldn't be interrupted going over my lines. And two, as the younger male servants, Noah, Magnus, and I were going to be staying out there on our own. Back in Victorian times, male servants were separated from the female servants to avoid—I swear to god, Lula used this term—"fiddle-faddle." Arriving before the tour ended meant I could claim the best bed.

I pulled open the door with a practiced yank. It always stuck in the summer due to the humidity. Flopping my costumes over one arm, I sniffed twice. The air wasn't close and musty like it had been when Andre, Kendrick, and I played out here as kids. The street-facing window had been cracked open, and the almond scent of Nomi's blooming clematis wafted in with the breeze.

But the hardwood floor was still scuffed, and the four doorways on the first floor (leading to two closets, the bathroom, and the stairs) needed a fresh coat of cream paint. Still, there was a tidy little fireplace, its hearth made of the same marble tiles as the ones in the basement of the main house, and the cobwebs had been swept from the corners.

Painting the mauve and cream walls all one color would have gone a long way toward making the room stop looking like a failed attempt at an impressionist painting, but the bigger problems were the cracks and chunks of missing plaster. Cancer had prevented this last corner of the house from being renovated, but maybe Magnus and Noah would think it all looked kind of badass.

I eyed the twin bed Lula and Kendrick had jammed in front of the low window facing Summit Avenue. Partially blocking the stairs, it was by far the worst sleeping situation due to basically being in a hallway.

If I were a nicer person, I would have taken it, but instead I climbed up the narrow, twisting steps two at time and turned left into the room I wanted. It had chipped, light blue walls, brown floral tile, an in-room closet, and a large window overlooking the street.

Nothing special, really, but the room on the right had a creepy sink next to the bed that basically served as a convention center for spiders.

I opened the closet door. And then, my pitch matching that of a tiny child discovering said spider convention, I screamed. Clutching my chest, I stumbled back and bumped into the bed. My costume fell to the ground. "*Jade!*"

She picked the bag off the floor and hung the hangers on a closet hook. "Hello to you, too, asshat."

"What on *earth* are you doing in my closet?"

She picked at a paint chip on the door frame.

"I wouldn't do that," I said, pointing at her fingernail. "That paint probably has lead in it."

She pursed her lips. "I wasn't planning on eating it," she said, but stopped picking and crossed her arms. "Why are *you* here?"

I snorted. "I live here now."

"In this closet?"

I narrowed my eyes. "You're avoiding my extremely reasonable question."

She shrugged. "Maybe I was hoping you were someone else."

"Like who?"

"Hello?" a voice called from the first floor.

"Upstairs!" I called, glaring at Jade. This wasn't over.

Soon, Magnus filled the landing with his muscly frame. Up close, he was slightly taller, stronger, older, and better looking than me. Like a Hollywood actor cast as Finn Turner.

"Hey there." He chucked his chin in Jade's direction. "I don't suppose there's any chance you'll be the one living across the hall from me?"

"Uh, *no*," she said, smiling. *Smiling!* "I'll be inside the house."

"Too bad." He grinned and stuck out his hand. "Magnus Torvald, the organ-playing footman. I'm also available for any *other* needs you might have."

My eyes widened. Oh, this was going to be good. Jade was going to let him have it, and I was going to watch. But she laughed and took his hand. "Pretty sure I'll be okay. I'm Jade Montgomery. I'm playing Elizabeth, one of the Jorgensen daughters."

"That's right . . . Maybe we'll have some scenes together, milady." Magnus bowed over her fingers.

Maybe they'd have some scenes together? He'd said he was memorized—but how was that possible if he hadn't read the script? Plus, *milady?* Wrong century *and* continent, pal.

But again, Jade didn't seem to notice. She just chuckled and reclaimed her hand.

Magnus pushed past me while I continued gaping at Jade. He let a green duffel fall to the ground. "Maddie told me I'd be sleeping in the gatehouse. Okay if I take this room?" He pulled out a bag of Marshmallow Mateys breakfast cereal, a tub of cheese puffs, and a jumbo box of condoms. "I slipped away from the tour to stash my contraband before it's too late." He opened the closet door. "Oh, cool. They brought my clothes in already."

"Those are—mine, actually," I stammered.

"Whoops. They're in my closet. Here you go, buddy." Magnus tossed me the bag. To my surprise, I managed to catch it, but not before one of the metal hangers scraped my hand.

I tried not to wince. Instead, I opened my mouth to claim this room and tell Magnus he should move into the one across the hall with the creepy spider sink, or better yet, downstairs, but I got stuck—mesmerized, actually—watching Magnus with that jumbo box of condoms under his arm. Size medium condoms.

Maddie said he'd just finished his freshman year of college. Did all college guys know their condom size? Was that part of the college shopping list? Mini fridge, extra-long sheets, and a box of condoms to fit your particular penis?

Good on him for being realistic, though.

Still. Who did Magnus think he was going to have jumbo amounts of medium-penised sex with here?

My eyes flicked to Jade. Had she been hoping *Magnus* would find her in the closet?

Suddenly it felt so hot in here.

Magnus kicked off his shoes, slid under the covers of the bed, and pulled them up to his chin. "Gosh. If only there was someone to tuck me in," he said, winking at Jade.

For a third time, instead of reading him the riot act, or better yet, punching him, she laughed.

My vision turned black at the edges.

CHAPTER SEVEN

The next morning, courtesy of my Victorian replica windup alarm clock, a shrill *ding-a-ling-a-ling-a-ling* rang impossibly loud and long. It had to be a joke—it was still pitch-black outside. Magnus had set my clock to go off in the middle of the night, right?

But after I dropped the clock on the floor twice, fumbling with thick fingers to silence it, I peered at my wristwatch. It really was the godforsaken hour of a quarter to five.

Well anyway, good work, Finn, I thought as I exited the bed and struggled into my cotton long johns. If I hadn't laid out my clothes the night before in the order I was supposed to put them on (long johns, trousers, white shirt, suspenders), I might still be staring at them draped over the wooden chair in the corner of my room. Instead, I had the brain space available to curse whoever hadn't invented the zipper yet. Because my god, the buttons. Everyone with stock in button manufacturing in 1891 must have been set for life.

My eyes fluttered closed, and when I opened them, I blinked at the sprung hardwood floor underneath my feet. It looked like I was in the kitchen. I squinted around the room through one eye to verify: gray-veined marble covered the bottom half of all the walls. Bars shielded frosted glass windows. Curved brick and steel beams painted white formed the ceiling above.

I rubbed my eyes.

Definitely the kitchen.

I'd either sleepwalked or teleported here. Both options seemed equally likely.

I trudged to the far end of the room to light the stove.

First things first: Open the flue. Through the fog of my brain, I reached for the phrase the docents had taught me at the historic Ramsey House: *Back to begin, front to finish.* I twisted the handle on the far side of the stove top away from me. That would open the flue and create a draft for the fire to catch.

Then, it's just like building a campfire! the Ramsey docents had assured me. That part was easy—even this early in the morning—thanks to my Outdoor Adventures class this fall. I opened the door to the firebox on the left side of the stove, twisted a few sheets of newspaper and poked them inside, then laid a couple pieces of kindling on top.

I smiled as my match whooshed into flame on the first strike. Jade had been miserable at lighting matches in Outdoor Adventures, breaking most of them the second she struck them on the box.

I touched the match to the newspaper, and it caught fire immediately. Soon, the kindling began to burn, too. When I was sure the fire would take, I selected a length of oak, laid it on top of the burning newspaper and kindling, closed the door to the crackling inside the firebox, and mentally high-fived myself.

As the stove would need ten full minutes with the flue open before I'd pull the handle forward to redirect the heat into the stove itself, I turned around and braced myself over the two-tiered wooden prep table, staring at the meal plan in front of me.

Tea, the first item read.

My eyes drifted closed.

"Good morning!"

One hand skittered out from under me, and I nearly banged my chin on the prep table. Blinking several times, I pushed myself back to standing as the sound of hard-heeled shoes clapped on the floor toward me.

"Oh, no! Are you okay?"

The voice was unmistakable: high and clear—like that of an adorable fairy. It belonged to sixty-something Joan Dooley, historical researcher/author and now housekeeper. Mrs. Dooley stood barely five feet tall in a navy day dress that sported a little bit of lace at the collar. A white apron covered most of the front of her skirt and bodice.

"Hi, Joan—uh, Mrs. Dooley. Yes—I'm—it's—" I interrupted myself with a jaw-cracking yawn.

"Oh, honey. You look so tired!" Joan cooed. She squeezed my shoulder. "Let's make some tea and *wake you up!*"

"Good idea," I said. "But—" I protested as she retrieved the kettle from the shelf next to the wood storage room and set it on the stove top. "Uh—you don't have to be up yet. Lindsey—wait, Bridget is supposed to be here." Lindsey, Noah's little sister, was playing Bridget, the scullery maid.

"She's in the room next door to mine in the servants' wing." The lines on Joan's face deepened. "But when I told her it was time to wake up, and that technically, it was her job as the scullery maid to be awake first, she said—Well. I won't repeat it. But even for a teenager, it was rude." Her hand darted out as if to stop her words from reaching me. "Not that all teenagers are rude. *You're* not rude, Finn."

I was too tired to defend the teenage reputation. Plus, she wasn't wrong about Lindsey. Lindsey was in either seventh or eighth grade— I couldn't remember. And though I'd seen her when she came to shows and when I went to cast parties at Noah's, basically all I knew about her was that she whined a lot.

"Laura did a remarkable job up there," Mrs. Dooley continued, "in the servants' wing, I mean. It *does* break my heart that she chose historical accessibility over historical accuracy, but—" Joan shook her head, her white hair immobile in a perfect knot at her neck. "We all make choices. And it *is* very pretty to look at. Even though none of it is real."

Joan had been working on a book about nineteenth-century historic homes in St. Paul when she met and interviewed Lula. Lula gave her a tour of the house, and Joan had been appalled when she learned what Lula was doing with theatre magic. She'd even given Lula expensive archival tissue paper as a thank-you gift with a note that said, "It isn't too late to choose restoration over renovation!"

"Well . . . thanks," I said, pivoting back to the large cast-iron wood-burning stove. "Let's get this beast heated up." Grabbing a thick hand-knit washcloth from a drawer in the prep table, I folded it in half, placed it over the handle, and twisted it *front to finish*.

Although the kitchen historians from Villa Louis and the Ramsey House had given me pointers, and I'd watched a dozen YouTube videos, I was still a little nervous relying on this stove for our meals. I'd practiced a few times in the past week, baking several loaves of serviceable bread. But there were several disaster loaves in there, too.

"What now?" Mrs. Dooley asked.

"Can you fill the teakettle?" I asked her. While she was busy at the white enamel sink, marveling at what good shape it was still in, I picked up my meal plan:

SERVANTS' BREAKFAST:

Tea

Coffee

Oatmeal (raisins, brown sugar, maple syrup to add)

Sausages

FAMILY BREAKFAST:

Drinking chocolate

Tea

Coffee

Poached eggs with asparagus tips

Toast

Cheese

Sausages

Fresh fruit (raspberries and strawberries)

I pushed down another monster yawn and blinked several times. My stomach rumbled.

"Did you know," Mrs. Dooley said, thunking the filled teakettle onto the stove top, "that Victorians hated food preparation sounds and smells? They believed if they could smell their food before the meal, it would ruin their appetite, so they put their kitchens and eating areas as far away from each other as they could. A downstairs kitchen like this one masked those sounds and smells, but all that stair climbing certainly made things inconvenient for the servants!"

Between the two of us, Nomi and I called Joan Dooley "Mrs. Did-You-Know." But I was thankful for her help this morning, so instead of telling her I *did* know, I just said, "Interesting!"

"Now what?" Mrs. Dooley asked. "Should I chop something?"

"Sure . . ." It was awfully nice that she was willing to help, even if she wasn't one hundred percent in Camp Lula. "Actually, can you slice the bread and cheese? They're both in cold storage down the hall. Third door on the right. Ignore the flats and props and stuff. We couldn't figure out a place to put them. It was bad enough clearing out the kitchen."

"Wait," Mrs. Dooley said, her eyes wide. "Cold storage. So Laura used my source for block ice?"

I nodded. "She's determined to make this experience as authentic as possible. She loves that old movie with . . . uh . . . the guy who was also Superman I guess? And the time travel . . ."

"*Somewhere in Time*?"

"Yeah! Remember how he sees the modern penny and the whole time-traveling spell is broken, and he gets whisked back to the current day? Mom wants us to disappear into the 1890s as much as possible. Especially after we get the show on its feet. So our mantra has been 'Victorian in every way except for laundry.' But even there she went so far as to see how much bluing and a mangle would cost."

"I could have helped her source those things if she'd asked." Joan Dooley tapped the table. "We'd have needed a whole team just to do laundry, though. Did you know that the washing machine is perhaps the single greatest liberator of women?" Joan spun on her efficient heels and called over her shoulder, "I commend her choice of modern laundry. This is all very exciting!"

It *was* exciting. It was stupid early in the morning, and the only thing I'd managed to do so far was light the stove, but even so.

I glanced at the meal plan and realized I should have asked Mrs. Dooley to get everything we needed from cold storage all at once. I took a few steps out of the kitchen to call after her, but as soon as I passed through the door, thumping sounds drew me to the servants' dining room.

Someone poking around where they shouldn't? It had to be Jade.

"What are you doing down here?" I asked, taking two quick steps into the room.

A tall girl in a sturdy, dark gray day dress with a pinafore and a mop cap glared at me. "I belong here. I'm playing Bridget the scullery maid."

"Right. Sorry—I thought you were someone else."

"Well, I'm not." Lindsey squinted. "This is supposed to be the servants' dining room, so where's the food? I'm starving. And that old lady woke me up *singing* this morning." She released a huge sigh. "This is so stupid. You know this is stupid, right?"

I narrowed my eyes. "No one's making you be here."

"Yeah, they are. My mom and her boyfriend are on an Alaskan cruise for two weeks. Which is super bad for the environment, by the way. But Noah gets whatever he wants, so they were like, 'Yeah, you can be in a weird-ass play in a weird-ass house and live like a caveman for two weeks as long as'"—here, she punctuated with jazz hands—"'*Lindsey* goes.'"

I said a silent thank-you that I wouldn't have to deal with Lindsey once the actual cook showed up. "Well, come on into the kitchen. The more hands we have, the faster we can get breakfast on the table."

"*Servants'* breakfast. *Real* breakfast happens after that. What's up with those guys not having to help?"

I was starting to wish I'd stayed in the kitchen. I stepped back into the hall. "That's what they pay us the big bucks for."

Lindsey rolled her eyes but followed me. "Didn't you make out with my brother once?"

I coughed.

I *had* kissed Noah. At a theatre party back in ninth grade when I thought since my parents were gay and my brothers were gay, I should probably see if I was, too.

I wasn't. I was a little disappointed, to be honest. It was just another thing about me that made me different from my family. Noah had been really nice about it at the time, saying maybe it wasn't all guys, maybe it was just him. But not even that deep down, I knew the truth. I liked girls.

Noah hadn't been weird afterward, and he'd said he was pretty sure he was bi and didn't care if I told people we'd kissed. But he wouldn't tell anyone unless I said it was okay.

He was just a really nice guy all around. But he'd told *Lindsey*? "How did you—"

Lindsey smirked. "I didn't. But Noah kisses everyone."

I couldn't swallow. Even though I wasn't into Noah, I still felt a little bad that I wasn't—what? More special?

Dammit. I hadn't even had caffeine yet.

"Can I have breakfast now?" she asked.

"Yeah," I said. "Let's go."

Joan Dooley was standing at the work table, cheerily slicing cheese. "You made it, Bridget!"

Lindsey just stared at her.

Mrs. Dooley's smile faltered, then recovered. "Did you know in the Victorian era male cooks were very expensive? That's why cooks were often ladies—you didn't have to pay them as much. And did you know taller male servants got paid more than shorter ones?"

I hauled a pot to the sink to fill it up with water for the oatmeal. "That sucks." More short-guy injustice.

Joan Dooley raised her voice to be heard over the sound of the water filling the pot. "If you were a woman, you would have been called 'Mrs.' and your last name. But since you're a man, we simply call you 'Chef.'"

I perked up a little more at that. "Chef. I like that."

Mrs. Dooley beamed and continued her slicing.

"Linds—*Bridget*," I said, "can you go get the oatmeal out of the pantry?" I pointed to the door across from where she was standing. "It should be labeled."

Lindsey sighed and followed my finger.

"She's certainly not a morning person," Joan said in a low voice.

I wasn't sure she was an *any*-time-of-the-day person. But I didn't want to risk Lindsey overhearing me. I needed her help if I was going to pull off two breakfasts and two lunches plus participate in the read-through before the cook showed up. So I made a noncommittal sound and lugged the pot filled with water over to the stove, shoving it onto the burner next to the teakettle.

"I can't find it!" Lindsey whined from the pantry.

As I strode across the kitchen to help her, I found myself wishing Lindsey had slept in and it had been Jade poking around next door after all.

CHAPTER EIGHT

I held my breath while I piled sausages onto a platter that Maddie was holding. I'd almost pulled the whole morning off—with help—and all that was left was delivering the family meal upstairs. Then I could return to my main role as Tobias the footman. But I had to admit, between tacos for fourteen the night before and breakfast for fourteen this morning, I felt . . . good.

I covered the sausages on Maddie's platter with a silver topper and then laid down my tongs. "We're running a little late, everyone," I said, addressing the five members of the servant staff, "so we need everyone's help hauling the food up to the butler's pantry. But then Magnus and I—"

"Jeremiah, you mean," Magnus said, shooting finger guns at me. With precision, Magnus blew the "smoke" off each finger gun, sneaking a look at Maddie, whose eyes bulged in annoyance.

As the lady's maid working for the women in the family, Maddie had shown up right before servants' breakfast in a green plaid day dress, fresh from styling Alexa's, Jade's, and Nomi's hair. She'd dragged Magnus behind her, who'd slept in.

Noah had arrived not long after his sister, and even though he was technically in charge of (our nonexistent) horses, he offered to "chop whatever needs chopping." I had accepted his help but hated Lindsey a little for making me feel awkward about meeting Noah's eyes.

"Yes. Sorry. *Jeremiah.*" I forced myself not to shove the platter of sliced bread into Magnus's hands.

"I've decided my footman was an orphan," Magnus declared, the platter slipping a little due to his white gloves. "And he was rescued from the streets by a young, hot nun because he could sing like an angel. And—"

"*Jeremiah,*" Maddie hissed, elbowing him. "We're running late, remember?"

Thank you, Maddie. I nodded at Noah, who was holding my black uniform jacket. I took off my apron and slid my arms into the sleeves of the narrow-fitting square-cut tailcoat, and Noah tugged it up over my shoulders. He turned me around and pulled down on my lapels to straighten out the coat.

"Sharp," Noah whispered, and I huffed out a laugh, and whatever Lindsey-induced awkwardness I was imagining between us evaporated.

"Then *Jeremiah* and I," I continued, adjusting my cuffs, "plus Mr. Lord, as the butler, will deliver all the food to the sideboard in the breakfast room."

"Do you need help plating?" Noah asked.

"No, but thank you. Traditionally, breakfast is served buffet-style." I donned my white gloves. "Ready, everybody?"

"Ready, Chef!"

Joan Dooley had informed each person as they came into the kitchen that I was to be referred to as "Chef," and every time they did so, my smile widened a little more.

I lifted the vat of warm drinking chocolate off the stove and led everyone through the maze of basement rooms up the servants' staircase into the large staging area that was the butler's pantry.

The drinking chocolate was heavy, but I was pleased to note that thanks to all the bucket work, my arms weren't shaking when I set it on the counter.

"Why didn't *we* get chocolate for breakfast?" Lindsey demanded, sniffing the pot as she deposited her platter of fruit next to it.

"Maybe there will be some left over," Noah said. He set down a silver pot of coffee and hip-checked Lindsey.

As I transferred the chocolate into a carafe, I marveled at Noah's generosity with his sister. I was annoyed by her and it had been only a few hours. I couldn't imagine being related to her.

"I call climbing the ladder!" Magnus shouted.

A two-story china cabinet spanned the entire length of one wall of the butler's pantry. A rolling ladder was attached to a landing so servants could access a second story of dishes.

Before I could respond, Magnus had scampered to the top. "I'm the king of the world!" he shouted.

"Magnus!" Maddie hissed. "Get *down* from there!"

"We don't need any more plates!" Joan Dooley added, like being helpful had been Magnus's intent.

"I'm, like, the emperor or something!" Magnus continued, flipping his coattails and gliding back and forth.

"I thought he said he was the king," Lindsey muttered.

"Magnus—" I began, hoping I could shut him down before Lula had to intervene.

"Young man, come down from there this instant!" Butler Martin Lord's crisp British voice chilled the room. "You are a footman, sir, not an orangutan!"

Magnus reversed his trip, leaping down the last few rungs. "Just joking around," he said to no one in particular.

"Then you should have joined the circus," Martin said, tugging at the fingertips of his glove to remove it from his hand. Using tongs, he began transferring slices of cheese to a silver platter with precision.

Everyone else, even Lindsey, exchanged glances. But while it wasn't a secret, I might have been the only one in the room who knew that while my family had mourned the passing of Geoffrey Thatcher as the Beau's artistic director and our friend, Martin was mourning the loss of his husband. My parents had worried it was too soon for Martin to be in a show—especially one here, a place Geoffrey had loved. But Martin had readily agreed. "It's just the thing," he'd told us. "Thank you for thinking of me."

My brothers always described Martin as a British Mr. Rogers. But as nice as Martin Lord was in real life, this butler version of him was certainly going to keep us all in line.

I took a quick inventory of all the dishes ready to be carried into the breakfast room. Was it enough? Too many? I bit my lips as I peeked under the silver topper at the asparagus tips. Were people even going to want vegetables for breakfast?

"Everything looks delicious, Chef," Noah said.

I replaced the topper. "Thank you." Noah was right. It was going to be fine. I nodded to Magnus and Martin Lord. "Ready?"

Gloves in place, Mr. Lord picked up the silver pot of coffee and cleared his throat. "As the butler, I lead the way. Then the first footman, followed by the second."

"Who's the first footman?" Magnus and I asked in unison.

"Traditionally," Joan Dooley offered, raising a tiny hand that matched her tiny voice, "the taller footman is first."

"First footman!" Magnus exclaimed, adding some biceps flexes that were noticeable—even through the sleeves of his tailcoat— making me feel foolish for ever having admired my own. "Sorry, little dude," Magnus said, his gloved hand producing a muffled clap on my shoulder. "Better luck next time."

I breathed through *little dude* and picked up the carafe of drinking chocolate, gripping it extra tightly. "It's fine," I said out loud.

Coffee in hand, butler Martin Lord led the way back through the door we'd entered at the top of the stairs, across the landing, and then through the opposite door into the breakfast room.

The breakfast room was one of my favorite spaces in the house. As in most of the first-floor rooms, carved dark wood panels ran up the wall from floor to chair height. But from chair height up to the crown molding at the ceiling was a sort of thick, seafoam-green embossed wall covering. It gave the room a bright, cheerful atmosphere. Add in the morning sun streaming through the lace curtains Lula had hung from the three large windows facing east, plus the light bouncing off the cut glass chandelier and the mirror above the fireplace, and the room just seemed to open its arms and say, "Welcome!"

Waiting less-welcoming at the dark wooden oval table was a frowning Mr. Hoyt, who, dressed in a brown gabardine three-piece cutaway suit with a navy ascot tied at his throat, was reading the paper. "An earthquake in Italy . . . Shame," he muttered.

Lula had managed to reproduce two weeks' worth of June 1891 issues of the *St. Paul Daily Globe* on actual newsprint. The first thing Martin Lord had done after servants' breakfast was heat up an iron on the stove in the kitchen and press that morning's newspaper.

"Did you know butlers did this every day?" Joan Dooley had asked as we all stared at Martin ironing the newspaper. "The heat got out the wrinkles *and* set the printing ink so it didn't stain the reader's fingers!"

As Mr. Hoyt flipped the paper open, I caught a front-page headline proclaiming "Thirtieth Drubbing." What on earth was a drubbing? And did you, or did you not want thirty of them? I decided you probably didn't.

On my third (and final) trip into the breakfast room with a jaunty arrangement of strawberries and raspberries, Alexa entered dressed in a long lavender gown with puffed sleeves, her hair swept up in a high floofy bun. She didn't look remotely like a teenager anymore. I swallowed to find my voice to ask her something—how she slept, or if she liked her costume, or even if she wanted to hang out later.

But when I set the fruit on the buffet, a familiar face peered up at me from her position crouched between it and the wall.

"Jade!" I exclaimed. "What are you—"

"That's 'Ms. Elizabeth' to you, Tobias-the-footman," Mr. Hoyt reprimanded me.

I looked up. "Sorry, she surprised me. I didn't—"

"And I'll remind you not to speak to the family unless spoken to first." He shook out his newspaper. "Mr. Lord, kindly school your footmen in proper address. There was also excessive noise coming from the butler's pantry."

Was he kidding? I knew we were supposed to be in character, but this was the first morning. Rehearsal hadn't even started yet. Plus Jade was the one who—

Butler Martin Lord puffed up his chest. "I do apologize, Mr. Jorgensen. Come along, Tobias. Jeremiah, please prepare a tray for Mrs. Jorgensen and send Logan up to her room with it."

"Why does *she* get breakfast in bed?" Magnus complained, not moving.

I shot a worried look at Mr. Hoyt, who was now glowering at Magnus.

Magnus didn't seem to notice. "And why are you 'Mr. Lord' but Maddie is 'Logan' and Finn and I are called by our characters' first names?"

Joan Dooley popped her head into the breakfast room. "Married women get breakfast in bed. Butlers use the title mister. Lady's maids are referred to by last name only. Footmen, first name only."

Martin Lord nodded once. "All of this was explained in your packet *last night*."

Then, before I could exchange a look with Alexa, Martin Lord frog-marched Magnus and me back into the butler's pantry. If this was how it was going to be for the next two weeks, I had no idea how I was going to talk to Alexa. And I'd certainly gotten off on the wrong foot with Mr. Hoyt.

CHAPTER NINE

Ten long minutes later, I banged open the back door.

Martin Lord had lectured Magnus and me in the servants' dining room for what felt like an hour—a serious drubbing. My cheeks still burned from embarrassment. Even worse than Martin Lord's lecture, though, was being yelled at in the first place by Mr. Hoyt. If only Jade hadn't been crouched down in that corner. Why hadn't anyone yelled at her?

Now I had only a half hour to review my lines before it was time to wash the breakfast dishes. While I didn't have a good solution for talking with Alexa, I knew I could at least get back on the right foot with this in-character version of Mr. Hoyt if he saw I was prepared for rehearsal.

I stormed across the kitchen porch, my slick shoes sliding a little on the tile floor. After clattering down the steps, I beelined up the path toward the gatehouse. But even though clouds blocked the sun, I squinted when it came into view.

An unfamiliar woman stood in front of it, her back to me. She was dressed in a light pink, high-necked gown. The sleeves weren't as puffy as Alexa's had been. There was also a small bustle. This woman was so sophisticated. Beautiful, even. Who was it? Had the cook arrived early?

At my approaching footsteps, she turned around. "Geez. Finally."

I stumbled on a bump in the asphalt. "*Jade?*"

"We need to talk," she said. "You're becoming a liability and—"

"You—look—*good*," I interrupted her.

"Oh! Well, this corset's murder, but . . ." Jade smoothed her skirt. "I clean up okay I guess."

Her dark, curly hair had been rolled back and pinned up, achieving a similar look to Alexa's. The corseted dress gave her an hourglass shape. I guessed she had been dressed this way when I saw her in the breakfast room, but she was crouched down, and it was so fast, and I was too surprised to notice her clothes.

It wasn't that Jade was a mess in real life. Nomi had once described her style as "fun." I wasn't sure what she meant by that. The thing I usually noticed about her was her hair.

It had taken a turn for the awesome our sophomore year after the *Blood Brothers* cast party. Jade had offered to help Nomi with the food table in the parlor, and as they'd arranged store-bought cookies on plates, Jade had haltingly asked Nomi if she had any hair products to recommend, because her white parents had straight hair and didn't really know how to help her with her curls.

Nomi had abandoned the cookies immediately and pulled up a website on her phone. They'd looked at pictures of textured hair together and decided what type of curls Jade had.

I knew their conversation wasn't for me—that I shouldn't be

listening. But I couldn't help it. I'd stayed around the corner in the hall, a jug of Hawaiian Punch under each arm, and just listened to them talk. Their shared experience made me both happy and a little jealous at the same time.

Now, I always noticed Jade's hair. But I never knew what to say.

But her hair *plus* this costume? I *super* didn't know what to say. There was something about the way she was holding herself. She was elegant. She was mature.

She waved a hand in front of my face. "Greetings from planet Earth, asshat."

I recoiled. She was a jerk. "Can you knock it off with 'asshat'?"

She leaned back, surprised. I was surprised, too. Maybe it was the lack of sleep or the stress, but I'd just been honest with her. Super honest.

"I call you 'asshat' all the time," she said. Her voice had lost its edge. "You've never said anything—"

"Well . . ." I looked down and tugged at the sleeves of my tailcoat. "I guess I'm saying something now."

Jade started to fold her arms over her chest in her classic annoyed-Jade move, but the tightness of her dress prevented it. Instead, she clenched her fists. "Fine. Then you have to stop double-checking my classwork."

"I don't double-check your—"

She put on a voice, which I swiftly realized was an impression of me. "'Wait a minute, Jade. *That* can't be correct.' 'Jade, let me look at that again before we submit it—'"

"Well, you're always right! It's infuriating!"

The sides of her mouth twitched. "I'm always right? Can I get that in writing? Maybe signed by a notary?"

I drove my heel into a crack in the driveway. "Don't push it, *Miss Jorgensen*."

Even though I was looking at the ground, I knew she was smiling.

"Stop double-checking my work, and I'll stop calling you asshat." She held out her hand. I eyed it for a moment, but then I shook it.

Then something weird happened: My thumb, of its own accord, passed over the back of her hand. Tenderly. We froze for a second, neither of us speaking.

Then we jerked apart.

"So. You wanted me?" As soon as the question was out of my mouth, my face burned up like the newspaper I'd lit in the stove.

"I—um—" she stammered, pausing long enough for me to know we were both regretting the double meaning. "I . . . have a proposition for you. A project, of sorts. For the two of us."

A breeze blew up, shifting the clouds. The perfume of clematis wafted in, and I smiled—its almond scent always made me think of Nomi.

Jade smiled back, and I realized she thought I was smiling at her. And that we rarely smiled at each other anymore. And that when she smiled, her nose scrunched up like a tiny accordion.

"Okay," she said, still smiling, "So. I was going to do this on my own, but you keep drawing attention to me—"

"Because you're sneaking around!"

"Just—*listen*. If you help me . . . I'll get Alexa to go out with you."

My cheeks flushed. "Wait. What?"

She put a hand on her hip. "If you were hoping to have some CIA-intrigue-level crush, you have failed. It's clear you're obsessed with her."

"I'm not—obsessed," I insisted, scrubbing at my cheeks. "We're friends."

"Fine. Then whatever."

She picked up her skirts to leave, but I grabbed her by the crook of her elbow. "At least tell me what this is about." Then I dropped her arm. Superfast.

"Okay," she said, her eyes twinkling the way they did when she explained a particularly difficult proof. "Remember in sixth grade when you and I searched the entire third floor for the missing Jorgensen treasure?"

"That was what we did after school for basically an entire year? So yeah."

"I'm setting the stage here, Turner. You can ditch the sarcasm. What actual thing did you think we were looking for?"

I shrugged. "Pirate gold?"

Jade laughed. "*Pirate* gold?"

"Well, what did *you* think we were looking for?"

She bit her lip and let it go. Then she met my eyes. My heart thudded.

"If I'm honest . . . probably pirate gold."

Another strong gust of wind blew Jade's dress around her ankles, and the dappled clouds gave way to clear sky. We blinked in the bright sun.

"To be fair," I said, "Anna and Karl Jorgensen's letters don't specify. They just say 'lost treasure.'"

She tapped her nose twice with her pointer finger. *Spot on.* "So here's where things get interesting. Did you see that letter from the disgruntled scullery maid in Joan Dooley's book?"

"Yeah—it surfaced when Joan called out for previously unpublished nineteenth-century letters from St. Paul for her research. Wild, right?"

"Remember what it said?"

"You know, this conversation would go a lot faster if it wasn't in the Socratic style, Jade."

She raised her eyebrows, and I sighed. "*Yes*. The maid was so mad at Mrs. Jorgensen that she hid her emerald necklace. The one in the portrait in the reception room."

"Exactly. The maid hid it in the house where 'Mrs. J would never find it.'"

"I read the—I *know*, Jade."

She ignored me. "Now. There was another interesting primary resource in Joan Dooley's book: the careful documentation of how Mrs. Jorgensen's jewelry was divided among her daughters after she died."

"A list we've known about for years."

"Okay, but did you notice that the emerald necklace . . . wasn't . . . on it?"

I narrowed my eyes and reached for my nonexistent phone in my pocket to double-check.

"Trust me," she said, her voice dry. "It's not there."

I blushed a little. "What are you suggesting?"

"That the Jorgensen House treasure isn't pirate gold—it's Anna's emerald necklace from her portrait." She spread her hands. "And now that we know what we're looking for . . ."

My heart flip-flopped. "Oh."

"Oh?"

"Yeah, I mean, Jade, that's . . . great detective work. But even if you're right, and the necklace is still in the house, and we find it, it would belong to the Beauregard Theatre, since they own the place." Treasure hunting had been fun when we were younger, but . . . I kept my voice gentle. Jade's face was so vulnerable. "It's . . . kind of a waste of time now, isn't it?"

Time I didn't have if I was supposed to be using these two weeks to save the house. Not to mention impress Mr. Hoyt and woo Alexa.

Jade set her jaw. Vulnerability gone. "Not everything's about money, you know."

"Uh, yeah. My family is all *theatre* people. I definitely know."

"So why won't you do this with me?"

I blocked the sun with my hand. "Why do you want to find the necklace so badly?"

She huffed. "Because I'm applying to a bunch of Ivy League schools, and they all have this essay question that's like, 'Every applicant has excellent grades and extracurriculars. What sets you apart?'"

"What sets you apart? You're Jade," I blurted.

Her hands fluttered in front of her face. "No, but have you *seen* what some of these kids do? They dig wells in developing nations. Invent apps for drones to deliver groceries to shut-ins. Cure cancers. Meanwhile, I went all in on grades and theatre. My parents tried to tell me for years I needed to diversify my interests, but—"

"Jade—"

"This is my ticket," she said, her eyes drilling into mine. "If we find a *literal hidden treasure*, that would definitely set me apart."

"Why don't you just volunteer in a soup kitchen or something?"

She threw up her hands. "Volunteer hours are in the community service section!" If she could have lit me on fire with her eyes, she would have.

"Fine, fine," I placated her. "What if I just promise not to get in your way?"

She swept an arm toward the house. "You saw Mr. Hoyt and Martin Lord! They're not messing around with those Victorian rules! I'm family and a woman. You're a servant and a man. Between the two of us, we have the whole house covered. It's a perfect plan."

"Jade—"

She pressed her lips together. "If you're going to get anywhere with Alexa with all these gender and class separations, you're going to need my help."

I rolled my eyes. "If worse comes to worst, I'll talk to her when these two weeks are up. In fact, why not wait until after the show when you can search the whole house by yourself?"

"Because . . . I wouldn't be invited."

I didn't know how to respond.

She barreled on. "Look. Do this with me now and not only will I fast-track things with Alexa, I'll also get you ready for your Acting Lab audition."

I took in a sharp breath. "You'd . . . do that for me?"

The corners of her mouth dipped. "You should be in Lab, Finn. Just because you struggle with stage fright doesn't mean you aren't a great actor."

"Oh—" The sun was beating down. I tugged at my collar. "I don't have stage fright."

She drew her eyebrows together. "Sure you do. You write all your lines on your props."

My face blanched. She'd noticed that? "That's just . . . insurance."

"Then is it a memorizing problem?"

"No."

"Well, what happened at the *Drowsy* audition? And the Acting Lab audition? And—"

I waved her away. "I was busy with other things. I didn't have enough time to prepare."

She studied my face like she wasn't sure whether to believe me or not. "So? What's the bottom line? Are you in or out?"

I definitely wanted her help preparing for the audition, but— "Let me get this straight: I search the male and servant spaces, you search the female and family spaces, I go out with Alexa and get into Acting Lab, you get into an Ivy, and the Beauregard gets the necklace when we find it?"

"Yeah. I'm sure the Beau would be happy to have all that money."

Money. My mouth went dry. A priceless emerald necklace had to be worth at least—how many performances had Mr. Lester-Dean said it would take to save the house? Sixty?

I sighed and squinted my eyes, trying very hard to make it sound like I was doing *her* the favor. "Ugh, Jade, *fine.*"

She threw her arms around me in a tight hug that was over before I had a chance to register it was happening.

"We should have a system to keep track of the search," she suggested. "A notebook maybe?"

"Y-yeah, there's probably something up in the schoolroom." I couldn't help it—I smiled. The schoolroom had been Jorgensen Treasure Hunting HQ back in sixth grade. Before I could stop myself, I said, "Remember that crack in the wall we were convinced was the edge of a secret hiding place—"

She smiled back, and I felt like I was looking into the face of my best friend again. "But you wouldn't touch the plaster because of the oils in your hands—"

"Yet jamming a screwdriver in there seemed like a great plan?"

She laughed. It was so contagious, her laugh. My chest lurched with the memory of it even as I laughed along with her. "Lula was so mad . . ."

"Well, you did stab out a six-inch chunk of priceless wall."

"I did. But you took the blame." I'd been both surprised and unsurprised. I'm not sure I ever thanked her.

"Of course," she said. "We were friends."

Were. Past tense. The air felt thick.

Dropping her eyes, she tugged at her bodice. "Anyway. We should probably just keep this between us, yeah? Simpler that way?"

"Yeah . . . definitely."

We arranged to meet in the coat closet under the stairs to discuss our progress well before curfew, as the creaky steps in the gatehouse made post-bedtime sneaking around a nonstarter for me.

"Noah would never rat you out, though," Jade said as she walked me toward the gatehouse. "And Magnus wouldn't say anything if he thought you were meeting a girl. After all, this is the dude who sneaked in a jumbo box of condoms."

"Right!" I laughed. "Talk about overly optimistic."

Jade cocked an eyebrow at me. "I mean, I know he says dumb things, but he's *hot*. And funny. And it's also strangely sexy that he plays the organ."

But *she* wouldn't—would she? I pretended to throw up.

Jade laughed, her nose scrunching even more, which made me want to make her laugh even more.

"Hey," she said suddenly. "I'm sorry about what happened with Mr. Lord and Mr. Hoyt yelling at you." She tugged on my coat sleeve. "That was totally unfair."

I stared at my sleeve where she'd touched it, the thank-you stuck in my throat.

"Oh, and breakfast was *magnificent.* I'm serious. I didn't think I even *liked* asparagus. And that drinking chocolate? And aren't, like, poached eggs really hard to make? Anyway, great job. See you at rehearsal." She turned toward the house, her steps poised and certain. "Seven thirty under the stairs!" she reminded me over her shoulder. "And don't forget the notebook!"

"Okay!" I managed to call back, adding a late wave she didn't see. As I yanked open the sticky door to the gatehouse, I replayed the actually semi-nice conversation between us in my mind. Martin Lord and Mr. Hoyt had transformed into very different Victorian versions of themselves. Had 1891 changed Jade and me, too?

This version of us was nice. But I wasn't holding my breath.

CHAPTER TEN

I sat on my bed in the gatehouse and reviewed all twenty-six of my lines.

I read them out loud, then wrote them down, then wrote them down again. The words were clear in my head. Still, I'd felt comfortable with my lines before my Acting Lab audition and had tanked that one big-time.

When I burst into the butler's pantry to do the breakfast dishes, all the downstairs people except Magnus had already shown up to help. But even without Magnus (or maybe because of his absence), the cleanup went quickly.

Noah volunteered to go find him, so I stuck my pruney hands in my pockets and hurried up the servants' stairs, down the grand hall, and into the music room, my footman's tailcoat and script under my arm. Maybe if Mr. Hoyt and Mr. Lord weren't there yet, I could sneak in a conversation with Alexa.

When I stepped across the threshold, Andre and Nomi were sitting on the pink brocade settee across the room with a script between them, Kendrick perched on the arm, all three deep in conversation. Martin Lord and Joan Dooley chatted in folding chairs that were arranged in two semicircular rows a few feet away from me. Maddie perched on the edge of the seat of one of the pink wingbacks by the reception room door, working Lindsey's hair up into a poofy bun.

But no Alexa.

Someone tugged on my tailcoat, and when I twisted to see who it was, Alexa wiggled her eyebrows at me as she, Jade, and Mr. Hoyt wandered over to the fireplace. I grinned as she tucked her hand into Jade's arm. But . . . what was Jade doing? Her eyes were fixed on Mr. Hoyt's as he yammered at them, but something weird was going on.

I wandered nonchalantly in a wide circle until I could see Jade's gloved fingers behind her back pushing on the carvings of women in togas holding harps on the fireplace surround. Was she testing for secret compartments? A smile twitched at the corners of my mouth.

Lula strode in from the grand hall, clipboard under one arm and a pencil over her ear. "Good morning, everyone!"

"Good morning!"

Noah and Magnus slipped in behind Lula. Magnus darted over to Maddie, who had bobby pins clamped between her teeth. Upon seeing Magnus, Maddie's lips pursed the bobby pins even more. But then he blinked those puppy eyes of his and she caved, offering him a seat on the arm of her wingback. I tried to share a look with Noah, but he was busy joining his sister on the floor.

"I trust you slept and ate well." Lula winked at me, and I winked back. But then it dawned on me—I hadn't seen her at either breakfast. Had she eaten? I'd been so careful about her meals since her diagnosis. I hoped she'd sneaked in and grabbed some food while I was out of the breakfast room. I'd have to remember to ask her later.

"We'll start rehearsal by reading and walking through the script," she explained, "so you can see what the whole thing would feel like from beginning to end if we weren't doing multiple scenes at the same time."

I was really excited about this part. Instead of acknowledging the audience and leading them from room to room like Nomi had written in the first place, Andre had suggested running several scenes simultaneously, telling the audience they were "invisible guests." Audience members might follow their favorite character or be drawn into a room by what was happening.

"Please experiment with blocking as we go, and feel free to keep your scripts for this first read/walk-through, even though I know you're all off book."

If I was being paranoid, I could have sworn several pairs of eyes swiveled my way. But when I looked around, no one was watching me.

"If you're not in a scene," Lula continued, "come along anyway, and you can pretend to be the audience. Why doesn't everyone have a seat and we'll get started?"

Mr. Hoyt led Alexa and Jade away from the fireplace to the front row of folding chairs. I slid into a chair behind them.

"Hey," I said, trying to hit the right volume so Alexa could hear me and Mr. Hoyt couldn't.

"Hey," she whispered, twisting a little to face me.

"Fancy seeing you here," I whispered back.

She covered her mouth with her hand. Then, in the quietest voice, breathed, "Someone said you *made* the drinking chocolate?"

I nodded, and she pretended to swoon.

"Margaret," Mr. Hoyt said to Alexa, "kindly switch places with me."

Seriously? I tapped Jade's shoulder as a distracted Alexa and Mr. Hoyt traded seats on either side of her. "Help," I mouthed.

She jerked her chin in Mr. Hoyt's direction. "Later," she mouthed back.

"Okay," Lula said as everyone settled into their chairs. "Mr. Lord, after my announcement, the whole thing starts with you as the butler. The audience will come in, and—oh! Hello, Mark."

Everyone's heads whipped toward the door leading in from the reception room.

"This is our artistic director," Lula said, gesturing at the tall, broad-chested man in the back of the room who I swear must have been a draft horse in a former life. "Mark Lester-Dean." Her eyes darted over to Martin Lord.

Of course, I thought. *It can't be easy meeting his husband's replacement.* I glanced at Martin, too, but couldn't read the back of his head.

Mr. Lester-Dean held up a hand in greeting. "Happy first day, everyone. How are you liking Victorian living so far?"

I inhaled, preparing to say that we loved it and that I was sure future immersion weekends would be super successful. I planned to lay it on extremely thick. But Magnus beat me to it.

"Dude, there are *so* many rules."

Oh, no.

"There *are* a lot of rules," Mark Lester-Dean acknowledged, and he leaned against the wall. I cringed. What was a polite way to tell your mom's boss and your entire family's landlord to stop touching the plaster? "What's your favorite?"

"Favorite rule?" Magnus asked, looking around at everyone like, *Can you believe this guy?*

Housekeeper Joan Dooley's birdlike voice chimed in. "I'm enjoying exploring old ways of doing things I take for granted now. Like washing dishes together instead of loading a dishwasher. We share conversation and stories. It's been so nice to remember how the older, slower ways bring us together."

"When everyone shows up," I muttered to myself, shooting a look at Magnus.

"What else?" Mark Lester-Dean folded his arms and *rested his foot against the baseboard.* My whole body tensed. Lula tugged on her earlobe but said nothing.

Jade raised a hand to shoulder height. "I'm enjoying rewriting history."

"Say more about that," Mark Lester-Dean said.

"Well, most of the actors playing the wealthy family are people of color. And the servants are white. This is not what Victorian America looked like. I think seeing us in these unexpected roles in the play asks the audience to consider the role that race plays in their own lives."

I wasn't sure the casting had been done that way on purpose. Especially since a lot of the teenage parts had come down to who responded to Mr. Hoyt's call for actors.

But rewriting history. Challenging racial expectations. That was really interesting. I smiled at Jade, and she smiled her scrunchy-nosed smile back.

"What an astute observation," Mr. Lester-Dean said. "I like the way you think, young lady. If anyone has additional astute observations after I leave, Laura, make sure to pass them on."

"Of course!" Lula said, strain lines forming above her eyes.

I could tell she was worried about Mark being here. I wished he hadn't come until we got the show on its feet. Today's version was going to look rough. What if he pulled the plug before we even had a chance to get started?

"Now don't mind me," he said. "I'm just a fly on the wall."

Fly on the wall? More like elephant in the room.

"Wonderful," Lula said, gripping her script. "From the top!"

CHAPTER ELEVEN

"Hello, everyone," Lula said, reading the house manager's speech in the script. "Welcome to the Jorgensen House! Tomorrow, Mrs. Jorgensen is hosting a large midsummer garden party. Today, a pair of young potential suitors of two of the Jorgensen daughters have been invited a day early to get to know the family. You, too, have been invited as a silent, invisible guest."

"Why would anyone want to be a silent, invisible guest?" Magnus whispered. "If I was going to a party, I'd want to *party.*"

I sneaked a glance over my shoulder at Mark Lester-Dean, but his eyes were on Lula and luckily he didn't seem to have heard Magnus.

"You are free to travel about the first floor of the house," Lula read. "Please do not move up or down stairs, or try to enter closed doors. There is some seating on the edges of the rooms, but you are also welcome to stand. It is impossible for you to attend all of the scenes, as there are up to three going at a time, so follow the scenes or characters that most interest you."

"Three scenes go on at the same time?" Lindsey whispered, probably to Noah. "I've never seen a play like that before. How are we going to do that?"

I bristled and resisted the urge to see how Mr. Lester-Dean was reacting. Hadn't Lindsey read the script?

"You may laugh or gasp or react vocally," Lula read, a little more loudly, "but please do not talk to each other or try to touch or interact with the actors. Kindly avoid standing in doorways."

"Dude. It would be *so* weird to be touched by a silent, invisible guest," Magnus muttered.

My chest felt tight, and I willed Magnus to stop talking.

"The Jorgensens don't know it yet," Lula read, "but there has been a murder and an art heist. Your collective job as silent, invisible guests is to solve both crimes. Different scenes will offer different clues, so it's best to spread out and gather as much information as you can."

"Seriously? That sounds *fun*, I'd see that show," Magnus said, no longer whispering.

"Did you even read the script?" Maddie asked, rounding on him and finally giving voice to what everyone was probably thinking. (Except maybe Lindsey.)

"I read *my* part," Magnus retorted.

I pretended to pick at a paint scratch on the back of the folding chair next to me, but really, I was studying Mark Lester-Dean's increasingly deep frown out of the corner of my eye. I scowled at Magnus and Lindsey (for good measure), but neither of them noticed.

"There will come a moment," Lula persevered, "when I will call you all back here, and you will have a few minutes to put your clues together and make your best collective guesses as to who committed the murder and who stole the painting. If you are correct, you as an audience will see the final scene of the play. If you are incorrect, the murderer and art thief both go free, and you will all be asked to leave the house."

"Are you *kidding* me?" Lindsey asked. "The audience has to solve the crimes or they don't get to see the end of the play?"

Lula pinched the bridge of her nose. "Yes. That's the escape room part of *A Midsummer Night's Art Heist Garden Party Escape Room Murder*."

Lindsey shook her head. "What's going to stop people from posting who did it all over the Internet?"

"Everyone has to sign an NDA," Mr. Lester-Dean said.

"A nondisclosure agreement," Lula translated. "In order to see the show, they have to promise they won't tell anyone the ending, or they have to pay a big fine."

"Information that was also *in the packet*," Martin Lord breathed to Joan Dooley.

Lindsey's mouth dropped open. "That's a really messed-up idea. Like, in a good way."

I glanced again at Mr. Lester-Dean. His forehead crease was gone, and I could tell he was trying not to laugh. That was good.

"Wonderful," Lula said in the same tone she used to use when my brothers and I were little and offered her dead cicadas as presents. "Almost done here." She took in another breath. "Any questions? Then while Mr. Lord, our butler, cannot see you because you are a silent, invisible guest, he is on his way to the art gallery. Please follow him. Good luck."

As the playwright, Nomi stood. "Does this explanation seem clear?"

"Extremely," Alexa said, shooting a hand up. "I've always thought it was really, really clear. Super well-written. Like, the—It's, like, crystal." Alexa's ears reddened.

What was that all about?

"I'm glad," Nomi said. "And those of you who have just heard it for the first time?"

"Yeah, I get it," Magnus said, leaning forward with his elbows on his knees. "Watch the play, gather clues, solve the crimes."

"Except there's more than one scene going on at once," Lindsey said. "Is the audience going to, like, decide who follows who ahead of time?"

"Different audience members will enjoy different parts," Mark Lester-Dean explained. "I saw a show at Windy City Playhouse in Chicago kind of like this, and it really just works itself out."

"What if no one watches your scene?" Lindsey asked.

"You still have to perform it with the same gusto and commitment," Nomi told her. "You never know when someone might wander in during the middle."

Lula clutched her clipboard to her chest. "All right then. Andre and Kendrick, places, please. Everyone else: Shall we follow Mr. Lord?"

We stood and filed into the grand hall, passed under six cut glass chandeliers as we walked all the way down to the other end, and finally pivoted into the airy, two-story art gallery.

I loved the way the light shone through the gallery's high, south-facing windows. Wood panels ran hip-high around the room, and a polished brass railing separated curious art-goers from the cream slotted walls, which were once packed two stories tall with Mr. Jorgensen's art collection.

"Come see my favorite fireplace," Jade said in a low voice to Alexa as they darted past me. Jade pointed out the hearth made from a muted rainbow of mosaic tiles and the back panel of an iron lion that revealed itself only when the fire was lit. By the time they reached the fireplace, I couldn't hear them anymore, but I hoped maybe Jade was working in something about how cute I was. Or funny, or something.

"Yeah, baby!" Magnus shouted. "Does she work by manual pump, or is she electric?" Magnus spread his arms wide in front of the pipe organ's double-decker keyboard, then leaned back to appreciate all one-thousand-and-six pipes above. Lula explained that the electric pump would be turned on later, and he could test *it* out. I smiled to myself at the pronoun correction.

With an honest-to-god two-story pipe organ in our home, Lula and Nomi had tried to convince all three of us to learn how to play, but even after multiple viewings of *The Phantom of the Opera*, a musical that features several powerful organ-heavy songs, none of us had been into it.

If I'd learned, however, *I'd* be playing the other footman role—which was a much bigger part than mine. I tried not to be bitter. But my jealousy was hard to shake off entirely as I leaned against the brass railing and focused on the rehearsal in front of me.

Kendrick stood near the fireplace and mimed taking a drink from Mr. Lord's mimed tray. "I say, James," he said to Andre, indicating a painting with a nod of his head, "I do like this one with the boat."

Andre mimed taking a drink of his own. "That's all well and good, Simon, but if I wanted to marvel at aquatic transportation, I could have avoided a long train ride and stayed in St. Louis! I thought we were coming to spend time with the Miss Jorgensens."

"You *want* to spend time with Elizabeth and Margaret?" Kendrick as Simon asked.

"Not particularly," Andre as James replied. "But they're rich. And Margaret's not *terrible* to look at."

I sneaked a look at Alexa/Margaret, who was fake batting her lashes at Jade/Elizabeth.

Kendrick/Simon continued. "Lord knows after Father's series of bad investments, and Mother's falling-out with Grandfather, our family needs an infusion of money."

"Even new money . . ."

"Yes, well, desperate times . . . Now where is Mr. Jorgensen? The old man was supposed to meet us a quarter of an hour ago."

Andre/James sighed. "Perhaps he's preparing a list of questions to ensure we're 'young men of quality.'"

"And aren't just fortune hunters? Which is what we actually are?"

Even though everyone had read the script (well, everyone except Magnus and Lindsey), the group chuckled. It was amazing the way my brothers could capture an audience.

Mr. Hoyt as Mr. Jorgensen crossed into the art gallery. "Sorry to have kept you waiting, gentlemen, but I see Mr. Lord has wet your whistles!"

Jade subtly pulled on a knob that opened a long, narrow panel on the side of the pipe organ. She glanced around to make sure no one was watching her, caught my eye, and mouthed, "Necklace?"

I shook my head. I'd crawled all over the insides of the pipe organ as a little kid. There was nothing in there except pipes, dust, and mouse poop.

"Finn?" Lula asked.

I snapped to attention.

"Your line?"

I inhaled. Mr. Hoyt looked resigned. "Sorry," I said, mostly to my teacher. Irritation from Jade distracting me burned in my brain as I scanned my script for my first highlighted line. "Mr. Jorgensen, sir, I am sorry to interrupt, but you are needed in the dining room."

"Why don't you go where you think you'll stand when we block it?" Lula suggested.

I scurried over to the pocket door leading into the art gallery from the dining room. "Again?"

Lula nodded.

"Mr. Jorgensen, sir, I am sorry to interrupt, but you are needed in the dining room."

"Not now, Tobias," Mr. Hoyt said, not even looking at his script. "Can't you see that I'm busy?"

"But it's urgent, sir," I said.

"The only people of note in this house are my wife and two of my daughters! What urgent business could three women possibly have that isn't fripperies and gossip?"

"Rude," Lindsey muttered under her breath.

I couldn't help but smile a little. "The housekeeper requires you in the dining room, sir."

"I cannot possibly—"

"Sir, you're needed! Cook has been murdered!"

Mr. Hoyt, Andre, and Kendrick gasped theatrically. I smiled again. Tobias the footman was a small part, but at least he got to deliver the news about the murder.

"You're not going to smile when you say that line, are you?" Lula asked. "It's a silly play, but to the characters, that moment is very serious."

"Right. Sorry."

"Okay. Then you'll lead everyone into the dining room."

"When do the multiple scenes start?" Lindsey asked.

"Everyone will see the opening scene in the art gallery, then the second scene in the dining room," Nomi told her. "Then the multiple scenes begin."

As the group funneled into the dining room through the pocket door, I looked over at Alexa, her arm tucked into Jade's. One side of her mouth raised a little higher than the other when she saw me, and I grinned. Maybe I could just pop over and talk to her about the next scene or something. Mr. Hoyt was twenty feet away—he probably wouldn't notice.

But then I overheard Mr. Lester-Dean say in a low voice, "Laura, not everyone seems as prepared as we were hoping for. Are you going to be able to get this show on its feet in time?"

I couldn't help it. I faced him, and with more confidence than I felt said, "Absolutely, sir."

CHAPTER TWELVE

Mr. Hoyt/Mr. Jorgensen stepped into the dining room. "Mrs. Dooley! What happened?" he demanded.

"Mr. Jorgensen, sir!" Joan Dooley called as the housekeeper. "It's Cook! She's—" Joan looked around. As herself, she asked, "Where's the silver safe again?"

I was standing right there, so I inserted my finger into a small hole in the center of a carved wooden star and triggered the switch. A secret panel swung open, revealing a door-sized safe, complete with old-school combination lock. I smiled at the gasps from the cast. Jade caught my eye and mouthed, "Necklace?" again. I shook my head.

Inside, the silver safe was the size of a large bedroom closet. It had always been strictly off-limits when we were little, but I had still managed to be inside of it enough to know the only hidden panel was the one I'd just exposed.

"That's like magic!" Alexa exclaimed.

It *was* pretty cool. I winked at her as the cast continued to chatter about how they'd had no idea the compartment was even there.

"The silver safe will already be open during the play," Lula said from her perch on one of the hardback chairs. "You'll just have to pull open the door so Mr. Jorgensen and the brothers can see inside."

Kendrick peeked behind the panel. "Dear god!"

"What is it?" Magnus demanded, flinging his arms out.

"No," Kendrick chuckled. "That's my line. 'Dear god.'"

"Oh." Magnus looked a little sheepish. Then he stood up straighter. "Wait. Is there really going to be a person playing a dead body?"

Nomi and Lula exchanged a look. "That depends on how willing the cook is to play ball," Lula said.

It depends on how willing she is to play furniture.

"Why didn't you notice she was missing earlier?" Mr. Hoyt/ Jorgensen asked his housekeeper.

"She's been nursing a terrible cold," Joan/Mrs. Dooley said, "and I told her I would take over her duties for breakfast so she could sleep. But then I came here to collect the silver for the garden party and—oh!"

Jade was whispering something to Alexa. Was it about me?

"Finn."

My head snapped up.

"Your line," Lula said. Her voice was patient, but it was just patience-in-front-of-guests patience. Not real patience.

Cheeks hot, I jabbed my line in the script with my finger. "Shall I get my magnifying glass and start collecting clues, sir?"

"Don't be ridiculous, Tobias. Go get a constable. Avoid unnecessary detail—we don't need our dirty laundry aired about all over St. Paul. Just tell them it's an emergency. And Mrs. Dooley, alert the scullery maid that she's Cook's replacement for now. Can she prepare luncheon?"

I had one more line in this scene. No way was I—

Alexa and Jade were giggling. Together. They weren't looking at me, but—

"*Finn.*"

Oh, no.

"Can you give him the pickup again, Mr. Jorgensen?" Lula asked.

Mr. Hoyt nodded. "I'll stay and search for clues."

I skimmed the script, finding my line just in time. "Do you want to borrow my magnifying—"

"Go!" Mr. Hoyt/Jorgensen instructed me.

My faced burned with shame. We were only on the second scene, and I'd already missed my cue three times. And that was with the script in my hand. I didn't dare look to see Mr. Lester-Dean's face now. Or Lula's. Or Nomi's. Or Mr. Hoyt's.

Instead, I walked around to the far end of the dining room table near the fireplace and slumped into one of the tall hardback chairs. Jaw clenched, I flipped through the script. My next appearance wasn't for a while. Hopefully it was enough time to get my head in the game. Because I had to get it there.

"You okay?"

I glanced up at Jade. "Yeah. Fine," I lied. "Have you mentioned me to Alexa yet?" A little good news would be extremely welcome right now.

Jade squinted down at me. "Already?"

"Well, you were talking to her."

She let out an exasperated sigh. "Uh-huh. Because we're friends, Turner. Friends whose lives pass the Bechdel test."

"I *know* that, but—"

"Look, I'll talk to her when the time is right. I'm sure you can agree that the time is *not* right just after you've missed your cue three times in two scenes. And in the meantime, will you please make yourself useful?"

"What's that supposed to mean?"

"Elizabeth!" Mr. Hoyt demanded in his booming Mr. Jorgensen voice.

"I'll be there in a sec," she promised.

"In a *what*?" Mr. Hoyt asked, face stern.

"Sorry—in a *moment*, sir."

"Rough places for the top of Scene Three A, please," Lula called from the grand hall.

Mr. Hoyt coughed. Jade began to follow him but over her shoulder whispered, "Look for the—" her voice dropped out and she mouthed, "necklace!"

"Elizabeth!"

Jade's skirts swished as she hurried away.

The necklace. That's what had gotten me into trouble, distracting me in the first place. Well, plus Alexa. But the Alexa distraction had been Jade's fault, too, for talking to her when she was supposed to be paying attention to the play.

I scowled. While I couldn't control what Jade or Alexa did, I could control other things. Like keeping my nose in my script.

New plan: Be so on top of things that everyone forgets about the first two scenes. More stuff like opening the safe. "Magic," Alexa had called it.

I followed the others into the grand hall. I could be magic.

CHAPTER THIRTEEN

When I took up a position by the carved wood paneling in front of the central staircase, armed with my new plan, my brothers had already begun the next scene on the steps.

Alexa pulled at my attention as she awaited her entrance with Jade and Nomi on the left wing of the stairs, but I forced myself to watch Andre and Kendrick. I knew if I even glanced at Alexa, Jade would either smirk at me, the subtext being, *Your crush is* so *obvious*, or she'd catch my attention and mouth, "Necklace!"

Out of the corner of my eye, Mr. Hoyt stood with perfect posture by the other potted fern. He pulled the pocket watch out of his vest, clicked it open, studied it, and snapped it shut, replacing it with two fingers into its little pocket.

The Mr. Hoyt I knew—funny, warm, bow tie–wearing—had been completely subsumed by the stern taskmaster Mr. Jorgensen. I'd been directed by Mr. Hoyt over and over, but I'd never been in a play with him. Was this how he always was as an actor? Totally, one hundred percent in character all the time?

Even if it was just for this show—with the immersive experience layered on top—it stood to reason that the shortest road to impressing Mr. Hoyt was following in his footsteps. One hundred percent Mr. Jorgensen? Meet one hundred percent Tobias the footman.

I stood up straight, gathered my hands behind my back, and let my eyes focus into the middle distance. *I am Tobias. Ready to serve a meal, run an errand, and make the household seem impressive in general. Because I am a man, and paying me is expensive. Even though I'm short.*

I stood. And stood. And stood.

Then, when I couldn't take it anymore, I sneaked a quick look at Mr. Hoyt.

But unless teachers really *did* have eyes in the backs of their heads, all this standing still was benefiting no one.

I suddenly felt every minute of my four forty-five a.m. wake-up.

Since I was wearing white cotton gloves and wouldn't harm the walls with the oils on my hands, I let myself sink back against the wooden panel to rest. My fingers curved around a sphere.

Huh.

Jade had been pressing the fireplace surround in the music room, searching for hidden compartments. So . . . who's to say there weren't hidden compartments here? I pressed the center of the sphere with my thumb.

It didn't give.

But that didn't mean another part wouldn't.

Plain wooden panels ran chair-high down the non-staircase side of the grand hall, but there were also occasional complex carved narrow panels that ran floor to ceiling. Those tall panels included intentional vertical cracks to allow for the wood to expand and contract in the wild swings of Minnesota weather.

Maybe they were also the edges of a hidden space of some kind. Maybe there was a trigger like the one in the dining room amid all these flowers, berries, ovals, and bellies of cherubs. My brothers and I had looked for the Jorgensen treasure in closets and cupboards on this floor, but I didn't remember us ever being purposeful about the carvings. Especially since we were warned a million times about not touching the walls.

I traced the panel behind me until my finger found the oval center of a complex floral carving. I pressed on it.

Nothing.

After glancing to ensure everyone else was paying attention to my brothers on the stairs, I pushed the center of a flower and three wooden berries.

All solid.

Stepping back, I gazed at the bits near the ceiling. I could get a ladder later . . .

"Wait, what?" Magnus was directing his rehearsal-interrupting question to Andre. "Did he just say, 'When you met the right *man*'?"

My stomach knotted up the way it did when a hostess in a restaurant asked if Nomi, Kendrick, and Andre were a party of three when Lula and I were also standing right there, or when, upon seeing I had two mothers, a parent-teacher conference turned into the teacher spending the whole time talking about their gay nephew/ lesbian neighbors/bisexual aunt and how close they were.

I stepped away from the panels, hackles raised.

"Yup, that's the line, because James is gay," Andre said.

"He can't be," Magnus insisted. "It's the 1800s."

"People have been gay forever," Jade said in a patient voice from her position on the top of the stairs.

"But these are uptight Victorians with a million rules," Magnus protested. "There's no way they were gay."

My whole body jerked. I couldn't let him keep hijacking the rehearsal. What if he said something that hurt my family? "The Victorians were actually pretty fluid about sexuality," I said. "More than modern people realize." I knew intellectually that Magnus wasn't attacking my brothers or mothers, but his comments were still poking at something that burned in my chest. I'd seen a million times how quickly a seemingly innocuous question could turn into something harsh and callous.

"James and Henry would still have gone to jail if they were caught," Joan Dooley chirped, "thanks to cruel sodomy laws, but there is plenty of evidence of same-sex couples living their lives together throughout the 1800s."

"Yeah," I added, "especially by the 1890s. And especially in cities."

"Un*real*," Magnus said. "I mean, I'm not homophobic or anything."

Oh, god.

"It's just weird to think about. Gay Victorians. I mean, seriously."

My parents' faces were smooth. My brothers, unfazed, were palming something between them that looked like M&M's. Were they all really okay?

"You two certainly know your Victorian history," Mark Lester-Dean said, nodding at Joan Dooley and me.

"You mean they know their current events," Andre joked.

"Indeed!" Mr. Hoyt agreed.

Everyone chuckled—including my family.

"Shall we continue?" Lula asked.

The bank of stained glass windows above the stairs darkened. Then the rumble of thunder shook the panes.

CHAPTER FOURTEEN

I was being protective, but it wasn't without cause.

Two years ago—I can't remember where Andre and Kendrick were—Nomi and Lula and I were sitting on the couch in the common area, the space between the rooms in our wing that serves as our living room. We'd just finished watching a movie about a girl getting kicked out of her house because she didn't want to follow the religion the rest of her family did.

I said I didn't think it seemed realistic. Who would kick their own child out on the streets like that?

Then Nomi and Lula grew quiet. I said, "What?"

And Lula said, "He's old enough." And Nomi nodded.

"What's wrong?" I demanded.

"Promise you'll stay calm," Lula said, taking my hand. "This is an old story."

But something familiar and unsettling prickled at my neck.

"During my senior year of high school," Lula said, "I came home from the last day of school before winter break. My mother was sitting at the kitchen table clutching a baggie with two joints in it that she'd found in my sock drawer. She was furious with me. *I*, in turn, was furious with my brother. It was his—and I told her that. And she believed me. But when he came home from school and she confronted him, he outed me on the spot. He'd seen me kissing a girl. Wasn't that the bigger problem?"

When Lula didn't deny liking girls, her mother had made Lula choose: her family or "that lifestyle." Starting that night, Lula had couch surfed for a month until one of her teachers found out and quietly took her in.

My fists had clenched, and Nomi's fingers smoothed the furrows on my forehead. Luckily, Nomi explained, Lula had already applied for college, and back in the nineties, state schools were fairly affordable. So she still went, double majoring in theatre and history, and working two jobs to pay for it all.

Still—I was furious. I couldn't speak. Finally, I blurted, "I'm so mad that happened to you, Lula. No one should make you feel bad about being who you are. Ever. Especially not your *family*."

"I know," Lula said, and Nomi tugged my balled-up fist into her lap and held it between her hands. "That's why I left."

I shook my head. I was too full of rage to let it go. "Then what happened?" I asked, knowing the next part but wanting to hear it again.

Lula's face softened. After college, she landed the dramaturg job at the Beau—the perfect combination of her two loves: theatre and history. There, she found an even bigger love.

Nomi was in the first production she worked on, *A Raisin in the Sun*. They fell for each other when Nomi wanted to know even more about the work she'd done researching the African diaspora in the early twentieth century and—here, they both laughed—had she read these other twelve books on the topic?

Lula lived in the Jorgensen House for only a few months before Nomi moved in with her. The wealthy neighbors hadn't quite known what to think about this mixed-race lesbian couple settling in, but the family living next door had bonded with Nomi over her flowers, and other neighbors followed. Several even joined the theatre people who witnessed Lula and Nomi's commitment ceremony in the art gallery—the first room Lula renovated.

Two years later, Nomi had Andre and Kendrick. Two years after that, Lula had me.

At this point telling the story, my moms were smiling. I usually smiled, too. But this time, I did the math. Lula was twenty-nine when she had a wife and three sons and the job of her dreams. She lived fifteen minutes away from her mother and brother, but no one in her family had been in contact with her since she was eighteen. And now she was in her forties. More than half her life without them. They'd missed out on so much for no good reason at all.

It occurred to me to ask Lula and Nomi why they hadn't moved us all to Chicago to be near Nomi's parents and sisters after we were born—they adored us.

I didn't ask, though, because I knew the answer: It was because of the Jorgensen House.

That night, I'd hugged my moms and told them I loved them, and they'd hugged me back and told me they loved me, too.

But as I lay in my bed unable to sleep, staring out the window, hating Lula's mom and brother, suddenly something slotted into place.

There was this day in kindergarten when we went to a different Target from the one we usually went to. I was pointing out that *our*

Target had kitchen things where *this* Target had clothes when a man came around the corner and stopped cold. He shared Lula's short stature, white blond hair, and blue eyes. I was only six, but when she introduced us to him as her brother, I registered his hard stare and clenched jaw. Then he told Lula their mom was sick. Maybe Lula should try to see her. Bring her family.

So we'd gone a few days later, my brothers and me in brand-new shoes and button-up short-sleeve shirts. Lula's brother opened the door for us. Lula sat us all on the overstuffed couch, side by side by side. My new shoes lit up, and I perched on the edge of the sofa and kicked my heels into the peachy-tan carpet. I tried to tell Andre and Kendrick it was the same color as the carpet in our parlor, but they shushed me.

After what felt like the length of an entire *Sesame Street*, Lula's brother came back into the living room and said their mom wasn't feeling well enough to see us. Lula's face hardened—just like her brother's had. She thanked him for trying.

Then the five of us climbed into our minivan and went out for ice cream with any toppings we wanted, and I'd pretty much forgotten about it.

Now the whole story made more sense.

I closed my eyes and turned on my side, but I still couldn't calm down.

Another memory floated up. It was first grade, and I was sitting in the back of the minivan in the parking lot of my elementary school. Nomi was crawling in next to me. She'd come to pick me up because I'd gotten into a fistfight with a kid who told me I was lying—not only about Kendrick and Andre being my brothers but also about the three of us having two moms.

I was crying—I hated getting into trouble. "I'm sorry for hitting," I blubbered, reaching for her, "but Carson—"

Nomi tucked me under her arm. "Finn, no matter whose fault it is, you can't solve problems with your fists."

"I *know*, but—"

"Not everyone understands you only need two ingredients to make a family," she'd said, stroking my hair. "People and love. You know who taught me that? Lula."

"*I* know that," I insisted, snuggling into her. "*I* know it's people and love."

"Of course you do. And so do Andre and Kendrick. And so do I. And Lula, of course. So really, Finnster, that's all that matters."

My family was all that mattered. The world might be full of jerks like Carson, but I was safe with my parents and my brothers in our wing in the biggest, safest house in the world. They loved me and I loved them, and just like Nomi said—that was all that mattered.

It was still all that mattered.

I'd promised Nomi in the back of the van that I wouldn't hit anyone else.

But even now, the things people said sometimes made it extremely hard to keep my promise.

CHAPTER FIFTEEN

I tracked my family for signs of unease for the next two scenes, but they all seemed fine. I knew their external behavior didn't guarantee they were unaffected by Magnus's eruption, but I felt pretty confident reading them. So I let myself relax a little as I followed the rest of the cast back into the grand hall for Scene Four A.

"Hoyt's talking to Mark Lester-Dean," Jade muttered, pulling me into the south alcove between the central stairs and the library. "We're safe here." I peeked around the column. Jade had picked a good spot—the column plus the fern would block us from view.

"What's up?" I asked.

She arched her back a little and tugged at her dress, tucking her script under one arm. "You're getting distracted by the play."

"Yeah, I know . . ." Despite our tentative peace treaty, I still didn't feel like confessing to her about how unsettled Magnus's comments about gay Victorians had made me. "I just got wrapped up in the action," I said, flipping through my own script. Half true.

"Uh . . . You've read the play before. Many times, I imagine."

"I've read *my* part," I joked.

She scanned the hallway again, and I followed her gaze. Magnus was way down at the other end, trying to juggle his shoes.

Jade dropped her voice even lower. "Unearned Confidence, thy name is Magnus."

I snorted.

"I mean, interrupting rehearsal to ask a million questions plus admitting that he's done zero work to prepare? Who *does* that and isn't worried about getting kicked out of a show?"

"You mean besides—" I nodded at Lindsey, who was lying flat on her back on the ground twenty feet across the grand hall by the library.

"Yeah," Jade agreed as Joan Dooley crouched down next to Lindsey, "but she's basically a kid. Magnus should know better."

Jade and I watched Mr. Lord give Magnus a talking-to that looked significantly less gentle than the one Mrs. Dooley was giving Lindsey.

"Why do you think Magnus agreed to do the show?" I murmured.

Jade's shoulder tapped mine as she tipped her head to whisper, "He's fulfilling community service hours for his minor."

I leaned in closer. "His what?"

"He drank underage and got a ticket. It's called a minor."

"Aren't *we* suddenly a hardened juvenile?"

"Well, Maddie told me what that meant. But in general, yes. I'm very hard-core." The script still tucked under her arm, she thumped a fist into her open palm. "You don't want to know what I'm capable of if you stop looking for the necklace."

I laughed, and a little lightness returned to my chest. "Consider me warned," I said. "But like you said, I missed three cues in two scenes. You can help me prepare all you want, but if I keep that up, you could throw a pro-Finn parade with stilt walkers and elephants and the mayor chucking candy out of a convertible, and it wouldn't matter. I have to show Mr. Hoyt I'm serious." That was a much better reason to give her than that I was swept up by the show. And bonus, it was true.

"Sure, but—" She retrieved her script and flipped through it until she reached the current scene. "We're here—" More flipping. "And you don't come in again until *here*." She pinched the stack of pages between her thumb and forefinger. "You have this much time to poke around before you're needed. I'll even give you a one-scene warning. You can totally tune the show out."

"Unless Magnus needs another history lesson first." I hadn't meant to say it out loud, but something about Jade was making me let my guard down.

She made a face, then peered around the fern, and I peeked between the railings. Mr. Hoyt and Mark Lester-Dean were still discussing something.

"Do you think Magnus thinks our generation invented homosexuality?" Jade asked.

I released a tight sigh. "I want a mute button for that guy in the worst way."

"For sure," she said. "But at least he wasn't malicious. I think gay Victorians were a legit surprise. Still. It was good you stepped in."

I tugged at my jacket. "I just didn't want my family to feel—"

"I know," Jade said. "You're very protective of them."

I chewed on my lips, trying to find the perfect words. This was deep stuff. I wasn't used to talking like this to Jade anymore. Finally, I gave up on perfect. "It was easy when I was little—everything felt very right or very wrong. But it's more complicated now. I mean, back there . . . maybe I should have let my parents or brothers handle it."

"Trust me—it's nice not having to stand up for yourself all the time." She elbowed me gently. "There's unearned power that comes with a lot of your identities, Turner. I think it's good that you're trying to use them to help."

I considered this. Then I decided to confess something. Victorian Jade kept . . . surprising me. "I guess I'm not always sure when it's good to stand up, and when I'm . . ."

"Mansplaining? Or in this case, straight-splaining?"

"Yeah. And I'm not asking you to educate me, I'm just . . . blathering."

"Well," Jade said, "I think it's definitely not a great idea as a man to tell a woman how things are for women, or for a white person to tell a person of color how things are for them. You use your identity as a man to stand up to other men when women are being harmed. Same thing with being white. Or straight. But you know that."

I nodded.

"But other times? Big groups like this where people with the identities in question are present? I'm not always sure, either. But I think it's good you ask yourself that question."

We glanced at each other. I looked away, but when I glanced back, she was still there, eyes on mine. I blushed. "Well . . . while I wait for another place to maybe-or-maybe-not insert myself, I'll try to look for hidey-holes."

She snorted. "Hidey-holes?"

I pushed her a little and laughed. "Shut up." Now that I was really looking at her, I realized Jade had a tiny mole on her nose right where a nose ring might go. Had that always been there?

She pursed her lips. "Um, Finn?"

"Yeah?"

99

"Good morning, gentlemen!" Nomi said. The next scene was starting.

Jade shook her head. "I have to go," she whispered. "But—"

"I know, I know—look for the necklace. Leave me alone, you surly murderer."

She mock-gasped. "You *did* read the whole script!" Then, with a grin, she darted away.

CHAPTER SIXTEEN

I was making some necklace-searching headway in the library a few scenes later when Lula held up a quick hand. "We'll finish the lines in Six A," she called, making a note in her script, "but fight choreography is tomorrow."

"Aww, I wish I got to be in a fight," Magnus said. He fake punched the air like a boxer.

"Me too," Lindsey agreed.

Me three, I thought, eyeing Magnus. As I scanned the crowd to check on my family again, Noah put his arm around Lindsey's shoulder.

Lindsey shrugged him off. "You're not my brother right now," she muttered, and he gamely stepped aside. I knew Noah was nice, but I hadn't quite realized how patient he was until today.

"Miss Elizabeth? Have you thought about where they'll be when the lines start?" Lula asked.

Why was Lula asking Jade? I spun around to find Jade indicating an area next to the sofa. "I was thinking they would start around here," she said. Andre and Noah walked over to where she was pointing and Andre lay on the floor. Noah knelt above him.

Hold on. *Jade* was choreographing the fight? We'd taken that same stage-combat workshop at the Beau last summer—I should at least be co–fight choreographer. Plus, even though it had been in first grade, I was pretty sure I was the only one between us who had been in an *actual* fight. "Um—" I began.

Nomi touched my arm. "Later," she murmured.

I ground my teeth and stared at Jade, whose eyes were glued unnecessarily to her script. She was avoiding looking at me. I could tell.

"Noah—uh, Henry," Lula said, "take it from 'Permission to . . .'"

"Permission to slug him, madam?"

"No!" Nomi/Mrs. Jorgensen exclaimed.

Noah and Andre scrambled to their feet.

"James, are you all right?" Alexa/Margaret asked.

I wanted to stomp over to Jade and demand she tell me how she got the fight choreography job. But I didn't want to cause a scene like Magnus had. I exhaled sharply through my nose. *Later.*

"Okay," Lula was saying, sliding a pencil over her ear, "then James will punch Henry in the stomach, and they'll run out into the hall. But for now, let's move on to Six B in the dining room."

Pointedly ignoring Jade, I followed the crowd out of the library.

But Jade snagged my arm. "I know you're mad," she said, her voice low. "But I asked Laura if I could get some experience assisting with choreographing the fight because girls are always overlooked for those positions, and she said I could just choreograph the whole thing myself."

I tried to squirm out of her grip, but she tightened her hold. "Did you even *want* to choreograph the fight until you found out it was me who was going to do it?"

No. But I wasn't going to admit that. "It's just—we have the exact same amount of experience." I sounded whiny explaining it out loud—even to my own ears.

She dropped my sleeve. "You mean that class at the Beau last summer with the guy who thought he was teaching nine- to twelve-year-olds instead of ninth through twelfth graders?"

"He . . . adjusted on the fly."

"Uh-huh. Well, I took the class again for real with Micah Boldon this winter—"

"Micah *Boldon* taught the—"

"And I've done some more reading and watched some YouTube videos and—"

"Of *course* you have."

Her eyes darkened. "Hey. Here's an idea. How about you be happy for me for once?"

"For *once*?"

Magnus's voice bellowed from several rooms away. "But there's *so* much kissing!"

Jade and I exchanged a quick look that agreed, *This sounds more interesting than our argument,* and hurried out of the library down the grand hall into the dining room.

"What do you care?" Maddie's voice was ice, her spine perfectly straight, one hand on Kendrick's shoulder in front of the curved glass cabinet. "You're not the one doing the kissing."

"I—I—dude," he scoffed. "I'm just looking out for you!" He pointed at the stage directions and read them out loud. "'They leap at each other and start kissing. Still kissing, Grace pulls Simon out of sight lines and pushes herself against him near the wall. Simon. *Still kissing.*' What if someone . . . gets a cold is all I'm saying! So much kissing can't be sanitary!"

Kendrick raised an eyebrow. "Are you two together or something?" he asked.

"*No.*"

"But—" Magnus protested.

"Sorry, Laura," Maddie said, the flush in her cheeks matching the color of her hair. "Can you give us a sec?"

Jade and I scooted out of the way as Magnus and Maddie stormed past us.

"This is why reading the *whole* script is something I recommend," Mr. Lester-Dean said, mostly to himself.

This was not good.

Hugging her clipboard to her chest, Lula sighed and leaned against the dining room table. Was she overdoing it? My feet twitched to go over and check on her, but Lula was staring with purpose into the grand hall, where Maddie was pointing her finger at Magnus. His neck vein was pulsing.

"Why don't we skip ahead to Six C in the breakfast room?" Lula suggested.

As the rest of the cast drifted after her, Alexa slid herself in between Jade and me. "Can you believe Magnus?" she whispered.

My throat closed at her proximity. All I could do was shake my head.

"He'd better be some kind of organ prodigy," Jade said, "otherwise, what good is keeping that guy? And they're not together? Magnus totally acts like they're together."

"Yeah," Alexa agreed. "When Maddie was doing my hair this morning—"

Jade and Alexa gave each other an air high five. "Lady's maid!" they whisper singsonged in unison. I startled.

"She said she and Magnus really liked each other when they met at the U this fall," Alexa continued. "But he didn't want to have a girlfriend because he'd had a serious one all through high school, and he wanted to . . . She used that farming phrase that means have sex with lots of people?"

"Sow his wild oats?" I asked.

"Yeah. I guess he wanted to do that."

"Oh, god," Jade said. "But now?"

"Well, at first, Maddie was like, 'I'm not interested in partial membership of an oat co-op.' But then he, like, *domesticated* his oats? For two weeks in May. After finals. With some girl named Savannah."

"*No,*" Jade and I groaned.

Alexa nodded. "It's over with Savannah. They turned out to both only be in it for the . . . oat chasing? They got bored when the . . . planting happened—"

"As much as I love your dedication to this metaphor, Lex . . ." Jade drawled.

Alexa smirked. "Anyway, now he's all 'Maddie, my one true love,' and she isn't having any of it."

"Well," I said, eager to contribute to this enclave of secrets, "why won't she date him now if he's ready?"

Alexa and Jade gaped at me.

I took an involuntary step back. "What?" I'd definitely said something wrong. I just wasn't sure which part.

"Because she doesn't want to be his second choice," Jade said, like she couldn't quite believe she had to explain this out loud.

"Yeah. She's moved on," Alexa added.

"Well, who is she into now?" I asked.

Jade and Alexa exchanged another incredulous glance.

"Look," I pleaded, "I—I don't know, okay?"

They sighed at each other, then each took one of my hands. Even though theatre people touch each other all the time, my head filled with the sound of rushing waves, and I didn't hear the first few things either of them said. I blinked and swallowed and tried to concentrate.

". . . so even if she does like him," Jade was saying, "she's not going to say 'How high?' as soon as he wants her to jump."

"People want to be wanted right away," Alexa said. "Not after the person they like has decided no one better's going to come along. Plus, she's Maddie. She doesn't seem like one of those people who needs a boyfriend in order to . . . you know . . . like, survive."

Jade squeezed my hand and dropped it. For three seconds, it was just me and Alexa holding hands. Until . . .

"Ahem."

Alexa shook off my grip as I looked up to see . . .

Mr. Hoyt. Of course. He was still in his scene, but he held our gaze until I took several steps away from the girls. Then Mr. Hoyt nodded at us and came in on his cue without consulting his script.

Running a little, Maddie slipped behind Mr. Hoyt and sidled up next to Alexa and Jade.

"You okay?" Alexa asked her.

Maddie nodded. Then Alexa leaned in and whispered something to Maddie and Jade that made them laugh and shake their heads.

When I looked behind me to see the cause of all the disruptions, Magnus was gone.

CHAPTER SEVENTEEN

A few minutes later in the dining room, Seven A was ticking along, but Magnus wasn't back. The pressure built in my chest every time Nomi and Mark Lester-Dean glanced into the grand hall. Lula was trying to keep rehearsal going, but I knew she was worried—she kept tugging on her earlobe.

After Lula's third earlobe tug, I crossed over to Maddie near the butler's screen. "Are you going after Magnus?" I whispered.

"Nope," she said, eyes on her script.

Mark Lester-Dean glanced into the hallway again.

"It's just—" I protested.

"I'm not going, Finn," she said, flipping a page. "He has zero self-awareness. Plus, he doesn't respect me, he doesn't respect Laura, and he doesn't respect this house."

I could look for Magnus, but—I quickly counted the pages before my next entrance and winced. The scene was coming up soon.

Four seconds into my *should I or shouldn't I*, however, Nomi and Mark Lester-Dean glanced into the hall simultaneously.

That's it.

Even though Magnus didn't deserve to have someone go find him and massage his feelings, if someone didn't do it, the show was going to suffer, and we definitely couldn't afford that. I swept over to Lula at the head of the dining room table. "I'm going to go look for the oaf," I whispered.

She swatted my arm. "Thank you, Finn."

Jade shot me an inquisitive look as I left the dining room, but I ignored her. She hadn't told me about being the fight choreographer, so I didn't have to tell her everything, either.

After an unsuccessful first-floor search (butler's pantry, breakfast room, library, den, art gallery, coat closet, parlor, music room, and reception room), I stood in the front hall, stumped.

I'd ruled out Magnus going up or downstairs since I hadn't heard anyone on the steps. But should I check anyway? Maybe I hadn't been paying close enough attention to the sounds of his retreat.

Thunder rumbled, and I squinted through the decorative metal grate on the window of the penultimate door leading outside.

Magnus wouldn't have gone out in this storm, right?

Then lightning flashed, and in the momentary pulse of brightness, I saw that the door wasn't shut tight.

More thunder rumbled on the heels of the flash, but not before I'd plucked an umbrella from the stand, hauled open the interior door, and stepped through the entryway. Because where did I go when I was sulking? My bedroom. And where was Magnus's bedroom? Out in the gatehouse.

I twisted the handle on the right exterior door and pushed it open. The carriage porch overhead gave me a few seconds of protection from the rain to open the umbrella. Then I sprinted down the driveway and forced open the gatehouse's sticky front door. "Magnus?" I shook the umbrella outside and set it open on the floor in front of the fireplace to drip dry. "It's Finn!" I called as I shucked more rain off my coat and climbed the narrow, twisty staircase.

Magnus was lying on his bed, one hand scooping contraband cheese puffs out of a giant, Costco-sized tub, the other shoving them into his mouth. "Hey," he muttered.

I hovered in the doorway. "Hey. Your . . . next scene is coming up."

"Oh. Yeah, well." Magnus stared at the ceiling and chewed.

Despite my irritation with her, I should have asked Jade to come with me. She was so much better at this kind of thing than I was. My eyes flicked around his room. Everything was neatly put away. Even the huge bag of Marshmallow Mateys and the jumbo box of condoms were stowed out of sight.

"Want some?" Magnus tilted the cheese puff tub toward me.

"Oh! Sure." Thankful for a Mr. Hoyt–free moment, I tugged off my white gloves, tucked them into my tailcoat pocket, and scooped out a few. "Thanks. But then we should go."

"Yeah, okay." We crunched in unison.

I swallowed and licked the "cheese" off my fingers. But before I could say, "Ready?" Magnus asked, "Hey—how old are you?"

My shoulders tensed. "Uh . . . Seventeen. I'll be a senior."

"Oh!"

I waited for the rest—the exaggerated shock, the comments on my lack of height, how I'd be glad I had that face when I was forty. But all Magnus said was, "I thought you were going to be a junior."

We were silent for a moment. Then, gratitude at not being overly infantilized for once warmed me up enough to ask, "So—how long have you been playing the organ?"

He cracked a smile. "Two years . . . I mean, I've played piano forever. But then we went to this huge wedding, and there was an organ, and I was like, 'That thing's a *beast!*' and then I asked to try it, and they let me, and"—Magnus palmed more cheese puffs into his face—"the rest is history," he said through a full mouth.

"Does—" I paused, considering whether I should ask the rest of the question.

"Does anyone make fun of me for being an organ performance major?"

I half-nodded, half-shrugged.

"Yeah. Sometimes. People are mostly surprised, though. My dad's a corporate lawyer and he wanted to be an environmental lawyer, but he followed the money. He told me *I* should follow my heart, so—" More cheese puffs. "The organ it is."

"I appreciate a bold choice," I said, at first to be polite. But then I realized it was true.

"Thanks, man. I mean, I know I'll have to do something else to pay the bills, too, at least for a while, but I'm not afraid of that."

Magnus tilted the tub toward me again, and I hesitated. We needed to get back. But then my stomach grumbled.

"Okay, but then we really have to go," I said between bites. "Your scene is right after the one they're running now with Henry and James."

Magnus sat up, and the tub of cheese puffs nearly tumbled off the bed. "What happens in the James and Henry scene?" he asked, grabbing the tub at the last second.

"Uh, James tells Henry he's here to get him to come back to law school."

"Oh. That's it?"

"What do you mean?" I asked.

"Well," Magnus flopped back onto the bed and took to throwing the cheese puffs into the air and catching them in his mouth. "They're into each other, right?" *Crunch, crunch, crunch.*

"Yeah."

Fwoomp.

"And they tell each other that?" *Crunch, crunch, crunch.*

Where was this going? I shifted on my feet. "Eventually," I said.

Magnus had been catching cheese puffs with one hundred percent accuracy. But at this news, one fell on the ground. He sat up again and scooped it up off the floor, popping it into his mouth. "Good for them." *Crunch, crunch.* He swallowed, then looked at me with super serious eyes. "Are they dating in real life?"

I raised my eyebrows. "Andre and Noah?"

He nodded.

"No."

"But they're both gay, right? So they *could* date if—"

"Well, Andre's gay, but Noah's bi. But yeah. They could date. I don't think they're interested in each other, though."

Magnus sat on that one for a minute. I glanced at my watch. What was it that Magnus needed to say? Or hear? So we could leave?

"They could *get* interested in each other, though, right?" he asked. "That's, like, every Hollywood couple. Fake kissing inspires real kissing and then BAM. They're getting their picture taken holding hands, drinking Starbucks, and walking their rescue dog on a street outside a cupcake store or whatever."

"Sure," I allowed, suppressing a smile. "That happens."

"So what's to stop it from happening with Maddie and Kendrick?"

Ah. "Well, good news there. Kendrick has a boyfriend. He's not into girls at all."

"Really!?"

I laughed a little, not unkindly. "Really."

The wheels began to turn in Magnus's head. It was a slow process, but they *were* turning. "Hey," he finally said, "it's a good thing you aren't playing the coachman."

A fire in my stomach flared up. "Why not?" I demanded.

Magnus stared at me. "Because then—and I know it's pretend, but come on, man—you'd be kissing your own brother."

I smacked my forehead with my palm. "I didn't—yes. No, you're right. We draw the line somewhere, and that is the place where it is drawn."

Magnus snorted. "You're funny."

I huffed a laugh. "Thanks."

He stood up and crossed to the window. Rain still pounded on the glass. "I really . . . like her, you know. Maddie."

I wasn't sure how to respond.

"We met on move-in day. Same dorm. She was so—" Magnus shook his head. "She's everything, man. Like, she's really smart, and really funny, and well, you've seen her—she's *beautiful*. But I was like, 'I can't be meeting my person the first *minute* of college. I still gotta—'" He nodded at me.

I couldn't help myself. "Sow your wild oats?"

Magnus lunged at me and grabbed my arms. "*Exactly*, man. *You* get it." He flopped back onto the bed, and the cheese puff tub tumbled over. We'd eaten so many of them, though, that the remains

113

didn't spill out. Still, despite being a little stunned by his attack, I righted the tub and set it on the floor.

"But I was an idiot," Magnus continued, running his fingers through his slicked-back hair, breaking up the gel.

"You know . . . it *might* be—"

He studied me with such pure, hopeful eyes, it took my breath away. "It might be what?"

I thought back to what Jade and Alexa had told me. "It . . . might be that she feels like your second choice. After this school year when you wanted to . . . see lots of people. And especially after that thing with . . ."

Magnus's face fell. "Oh. Savannah. Yeah. I was such an idiot. But . . . you think Maddie likes me?"

"Well," I began, "she was excited to suggest you for the part back in May. But after this Savannah thing . . . I think she needs some time. And a little space. And she also wishes you respected Laura and the house more. And that maybe you kept some of your scene-stopping questions for later. Especially when they only concern you."

It was a lot, but I figured I should use the opportunity to try to get him to care about the play.

After a few moments of Magnus alternating between smoothing his pillow and punching it, he finally stopped manhandling the bedding. "Yeah. Yeah. That makes sense. I can give Maddie space," Magnus reasoned. "I mean, I'm basically her only option here, right? There are four dudes under forty besides me and two of them are gay, she thinks of you like a little brother—she told me that a long time ago—and the bi one's busy kissing a gay guy."

By the time I could formulate a response, Magnus was pulling me into one of those dude-bro hugs. All shoulders. Lots of back clapping. "We should go to rehearsal. Thanks, man."

"Yeah, yeah, of course." I followed Magnus down the stairs, brushing off the cheese puff dust his fingers had left on my coat.

While it would have been nice if Magnus paid more attention to the world on his own so he didn't have to be the central figure in every scene today, his heart . . . was mostly in the right place? At any rate, to my surprise, Magnus didn't entirely suck.

<hr/>

By the time we returned to rehearsal, a little damp thanks to huddling under the one umbrella, Mr. Hoyt was delivering the opening line from Scene Seven B. "Where? I don't see any painting!"

"There, sir!" Magnus called, leaping in front of me and barreling into the art gallery.

My moms and Mr. Lester-Dean caught my eye and nodded thanks, and I nodded back. I glanced over at Mr. Hoyt to see if he'd also noticed, but he was deep into the scene.

Which was where I should be. I grabbed my script and stared at my cue, "The intruder?" waiting for Nomi as Mrs. Jorgensen to say it.

"Intruder—"

I stepped into the room. "Mr. Jorgensen, sir?"

"Uh, Tobias, you stepped on my line," Nomi said.

"What?" I traced my finger down the script.

Nomi pointed at her own copy and showed it to me. "I say, 'The intruder?' after—"

"Oh, no. I'm sorry. I just—"

"It's fine. Let's go again from Mr. Jorgensen's line," Lula said.

I pursed my lips. Last time I was too late. Now I was too early.

But everyone knew I'd run off to find Magnus, and I'd returned him on time. It made sense that I'd gotten a little confused coming back into the scene.

At least I hoped Mr. Lester-Dean and Mr. Hoyt saw it that way.

CHAPTER EIGHTEEN

I slid my shoes along the carpet and followed Jade out of the art gallery after the rest of Scene Seven B. As we crossed through the pocket door into the dining room, she tugged at my sleeve and led me to the fireplace. "I know you're upset, but you found Magnus," she whispered. "I definitely think that outweighs the line mess-up."

I rubbed my eyebrow. "Yeah?"

"Yeah." As everyone transitioned into places, she flashed one of her old sixth-grade friend smiles at me.

So I did what a friend would do. "Look," I said, kneeling by the ceramic logs, pretending to tie my shoe in case Mr. Hoyt looked our way. "I'm sorry about getting on your case about the fight choreography thing—"

"Thanks, Finn, but I should have told you. I mean, I tried—I—" She let out a sharp breath. "I should have tried harder. I would have wanted to know. But . . ." I glanced up. She was playing with the cuff on her dress. "I just don't like it when you're mad. And I knew you would be."

I blinked. Then again. I stood. "Jade, I—"

She dropped her cuff and smoothed the front of her bodice. "Don't worry about it." The scene started. "Just look around," she mouthed, twirling a finger. "You're not on until Eleven B."

〜・〜

So for the next several scenes, I surreptitiously poked at panels and pulled out books and looked up fireplaces in search of Mrs. Jorgensen's hidden necklace while also trying to make sense of Jade admitting, *I just don't like it when you're mad.* Didn't she, like, *live* for making me mad?

But during Ten A, I stopped searching, because I couldn't take my eyes off Alexa's performance.

"How did you not get into Acting Lab?" I blurted to her after the scene as we passed from the den into the library.

"What do you mean?" she whispered.

"What do you mean what do I mean? You're so good!" Mr. Hoyt was way down the hall, but I dropped my voice anyway. "When you said, 'Elizabeth, don't *force* Father,' I'm not even Elizabeth, and I felt like I'd been slapped."

She laughed and side-hugged me, and my body tingled where we'd touched.

I made a mental note to compliment her acting more often.

"I hope Mr. Hoyt feels the same way . . . Not about being slapped, about thinking I'm good enough for Lab."

"He has to," I said.

"Places for Eleven B!" Lula called out.

"He has to change his mind about you, too," she said, waving a little. "Remember—it's our names on that list this fall."

Lula dropped in next to me, and my heart, which was already

thumping from the interaction with Alexa, started thumping faster. Was she going to yell at me for messing up so much?

"You have two lines," Lula reminded me.

I set my script on the bookshelf and tugged at my tailcoat.

"I won't start until I see your eyes on your script. You can do this." She gave my arm a bracing squeeze.

"Thanks, Mom." I was ready.

But then the fire alarm went off, the electricity zapped out, and we were plunged into darkness.

⟋⟍

Less than five minutes later, everyone was huddled outside underneath the carriage porch. Rain pattered on the glass overhead, but the humidity made our layers of clothing stick to our bodies anyway.

"It's probably not a fire," I said again, trying to raise my voice over the sound of the rain and the sirens from several blocks away.

Lula had tried to assure everyone that the fire alarm went off all the time, especially when it was humid out. Fire trucks were automatically dispatched, but all she had to do was call 911 and tell them it was likely a false alarm. Then the fire department would send out only one truck, without lights and sirens blaring. Mark Lester-Dean, however, insisted on "protecting the Beau's interests." So sirens it was.

"But what does the fire alarm have to do with the electricity being out?" Lindsey demanded, hands over her ears as the first truck approached.

"That's probably the storm," I shouted, gesturing at the weather. "The wind might have knocked down an electric line somewhere."

The sirens blipped off as a fire truck pulled up into the curved driveway.

"If Mr. Hoyt says something about this being the strangest carriage he's ever seen—" Jade whispered so only I could hear her.

"Goodness!" Mr. Hoyt exclaimed. "Where are the horses for that extremely large carriage?"

I stared at the asphalt to keep from laughing.

Four firefighters hopped off the truck. "Smoke or fire, Laura?" the captain called, jogging over in her firefighter turnout gear.

Lula tugged on her earlobe. "It's just the laundry room detector again, Kerry, but—"

Mr. Lester-Dean stepped forward. "I'm the artistic director, Mark Lester-Dean," he said. The captain nodded at him, but it was the sort of nod that said, *Cool. So?*

"I know I should have called to say it wasn't an emergency," Lula said, her voice brittle, "but—"

Mr. Lester-Dean's jaw tensed. "The *fire alarm* went off."

"In these old houses—" Lula, Maddie, and the captain began together.

Lula coughed, but it looked like she was doing it to cover a smile.

"Always happy to double-check," the captain said. She pushed a button on the radio on the front of her coat. "Ladder Eight finds nothing and can handle the situation. Other rigs can return to service."

Mr. Lester-Dean frowned.

"Let's go see the laundry room," the captain said.

Lula led the firefighters into the house with Mr. Lester-Dean and Maddie at their heels.

"So, that guy is the new artistic director," Jade began.

"Yeah."

"And we hate him, right?"

I laughed. "Well. He *does* want to sell the place."

Jade's eyes grew wide.

My knees buckled a little. "I'm—don't say anything. I—"

Jade put her hands on my shoulders. "Tell me. Or I'm just going to keep asking in louder and louder voices until you crack."

I clocked Nomi and my brothers talking to Martin Lord on the stairs. A neighbor was running through the rain in their direction. No one else seemed to be paying attention to us. I met Jade's eyes. "You have to promise not to tell anyone, okay?"

"I promise. Of course."

I took a deep breath and let it out. "Besides whatever money we make from the play going to fix the roof, we're doing this whole Victorian immersion thing so we can prove to Mr. Lester-Dean that the Jorgensen House could bring in real money. But the roof's more expensive than we thought it was going to be, and he's not convinced about the Victorian immersion. He's leaning toward selling the house."

Jade's hands dropped off my shoulders in shock.

Before I could decide whether or not to confess this was the real reason I wanted to find the necklace, Magnus cut in.

"Are you kidding me, Finn?"

I whipped around. Noah, Lindsey, Alexa, and Magnus stood in a loose circle, their faces aghast. My voice had projected more than I'd intended.

"That's why we're doing this? To save the house?" Noah asked.

"Um—" I shifted on my feet. Something in my stomach soured. "I—"

"Dude. I gotta get my sh—my *crap* together then," Magnus said. "I mean, you guys *live* here."

"And they have his whole life," Jade added.

"Man," Magnus moaned. "So that dude wants to sell your childhood!"

"Well—"

Alexa touched my forearm. "Mr. Hoyt said we were raising money to fix part of the house, but I didn't know you might lose the whole thing! I'm so sorry!"

I stared at her hand. The second my brain thought, *Hey! You could cover her hand with your hand!* she took hers back.

"I'm sorry for interrupting rehearsal so much," Lindsey said. She looked up at her brother. "I'll be good."

Noah put his arm around her shoulders. "Me too," he said, winking at me.

"Me three." Magnus held up both hands in surrender. "So good."

"I will be just as good as I always am," Jade said. But she was smiling.

I swallowed around the lump in my throat.

"We'll all help," Alexa promised. "What can we do?"

"Oh, uh . . . I don't know. I mean, I appreciate it, but I think we've got it under control—"

"No way, Finn," Jade interrupted. "We're helping." She turned to the others. "Flawless read-through when we go back inside. Don't break the Victorian rules." She eyed Magnus, who saluted her. "Try to work some of that Victorian vocabulary into conversation. Participate in the evening social events. Be on time. Don't give Laura any trouble."

"Does Maddie know?" Magnus asked. "About the house?"

"Oh. Most likely," I said. "She knows what's going on around here more than anyone, usually."

Magnus rubbed his face with his hands.

"The only reason I know is because I was eavesdropping on a conversation I wasn't supposed to overhear. My brothers don't even know yet—I still need to tell them." I wasn't sure why I hadn't. My shoulders felt positively light having this group of people on my side.

Nomi approached our circle. "Electricity is out in the whole neighborhood," she informed us. "But we're Victorians. We have candles!"

"What about the gas lighting?" Joan Dooley asked.

Nomi made a face. "Each fixture has to be lit separately, and it's just not very safe these days."

Andre and Kendrick joined us, too. "Are we going to be able to finish the read-through before it's time for lunch?" Andre asked.

I checked my watch. It was already eleven thirty. "As soon as the fire department gives the all clear, I should get started making it."

"But you're in Eleven B," Jade protested.

"But we're *hungry*," Kendrick said. "Plus, Finn's whole part is only, like, two lines. It's not like that'll be hard to cover."

In two sentences, Kendrick managed to entirely douse my newly found warmth and happiness. I knew he was crabby about missing his boyfriend, but he didn't have to take me down with him.

Maybe I didn't need to be in a huge rush to tell him about Mark Lester-Dean's plans after all.

"All clear, and the detector's reset," the captain called to the group as she returned. Lula, Maddie, and Mr. Lester-Dean followed close behind her. "You can all go back inside."

Standing on the carriage step, Lula held a hand up over her head to get our attention. "I was hoping to get through the whole show before lunch, but thanks to the electricity and the fire alarm, we're running long. Finn, can you get started on lunch—"

"Yup," I said in a clipped voice. I shot a dirty look at Kendrick, but he didn't notice.

"I'd help," Jade whispered, "but—"

"It's not your job. Plus, you have a lot to do line-wise," I said. "And so does everyone else. It's fine. I can do it."

"I'll try and lay some groundwork with Alexa," she promised. "Can you do a little necklace hunting in the kitchen and pantry?"

I softened. "Yeah. I can do that."

"Finn!" Kendrick called out. "Quit yapping with your girlfriend and get cooking!"

Mr. Hoyt's head snapped up.

Fury stopped up my esophagus and blurred my vision. I found just enough clarity to flip off my brother before marching toward the kitchen.

CHAPTER NINETEEN

My fancy footman shoes slipped on something wet on my way into the kitchen, and I swore. Who hadn't wiped up their spill? Did I seriously have to do *everything* around here? Or was this ceiling leaking, too?

I grabbed a towel off the rod by the door and threw it over the puddle, drying it up with my foot. It was so dark down here with the lights out, I could hardly see what I was doing. Add in the thunder, lightning, raging rain, and bars on the windows, and the kitchen felt like a prison.

I lit a few candles and clanged around, not totally sure why I was feeling so angry. Kendrick's remark about my small part was some of it. How I'd messed up in front of Mr. Hoyt and Mr. Lester-Dean so much—even with the script in my hand—was also in there. But there were other things, too. Things I had vague feelings about but couldn't name.

Soon, however, the rhythmic de-stemming of strawberries soothed my jangled nerves. Mr. Hoyt had been impressed by my tacos. I'd just impress him again with this lunch, and then keep the train going with a flawless, impressive performance this afternoon.

Unfortunately, I'd planned a simple lunch of cold meats and cheese and fruit for both the upstairs and downstairs crews so I wouldn't have to relight the stove and heat up the kitchen midday.

Still. Simple could impress.

Last week, my bucket muscles had come in handy beating heavy whipping cream into butter. It hadn't been complicated—it just took a while—but when my family tasted it, plus my strawberry jam all served on slices of bread I'd baked in the wood-burning stove, the volume of their collective appreciation drew Maddie in from another floor, demanding to be included.

Several more loaves of bread from another attempt a couple days ago were in cold storage. It wouldn't be hard to add that, plus the jam and butter I'd made, to this lunch.

A huge clap of thunder sounded, and the room darkened even more. But I smiled and moved the candle a little closer to my strawberry work.

The only thing that would have made lunch prep more enjoyable was an audiobook. I wasn't much of a reader until Nomi started narrating as a side hustle. Now I listened to audiobooks all the time—especially when I was cooking. But, of course, they didn't exist in 1891.

"Hi! It's Andre Turner."

I looked up. Andre's voice sounded like it was coming from the hallway. I opened my mouth to respond, but closed it when he spoke again.

"I just saw your text—"

Who was he talking to? And on what phone? I froze in place, listening for more. Just when I began to think Andre must have left, he spoke again.

"*Really?*... Oh my gosh. Thank you. That's—that's amazing. Um... Can I call you back?... Yes... Yes... Yes—absolutely. Yeah. No, seriously—thank you... okay. Bye!" Andre whooped and let out a series of celebratory curse words.

"Uh... Andre?" I called, my curiosity prickling.

Andre cursed again. Two seconds later, he appeared in the doorway, wincing. "I forgot anyone was down here."

"Who were you talking to?" I asked, a knife in one hand, a recently de-stemmed strawberry in the other. "And how? Our phones are in the office safe."

"You didn't put a decoy phone in there?"

I set my knife down. "A what?"

Andre took several more steps into the room. "Wait a minute, Finn. When teachers collect phones at school, you don't hand in your *real* phone, do you?"

"Uh, *yes.*"

Andre ran over and pulled my head into his chest, rubbing it like a good luck charm. "Little brother, we have *failed* you."

I pushed Andre away. "Well, excuse me if it doesn't occur to me to betray people!"

"Oh, Finnster, don't be so dramatic," Andre said, laughing.

I ignored the slight. "Who were you talking to?"

Andre plucked a few halved strawberries and popped them into his mouth. "No one."

I glared at him—both for the lie and for the strawberries.

Andre squinted at me. He seemed to be contemplating something. Then he sighed. "Car conversation?"

I dried my hands on the towel over my shoulder and raised my right like I was swearing in court. "Car conversation," I promised. It was our code for anything top secret.

"That was Ryan Thusing."

"Ryan Thusing . . . the Ryan Thusing who directed you in *Peter and the Starcatcher* at Park Square your senior year?"

Andre bit his lips. "Yeah. And he's directing it again at the Chicago Shakespeare Theatre."

I wasn't sure why that news deserved a personal phone call to Andre, but I smiled politely.

Andre laughed. "Well, his Peter just dropped out, and Ryan said he enjoyed directing me so much when *I* played Peter and—"

I gasped. "He wants you to reprise your role?"

Andre laughed again. "Yeah! Me! In a title role at Chicago Shakes!"

I leaped at him. "That's incredible!"

Andre couldn't stop laughing as he bear-hugged me.

"Your roommate's from Chicago!" I exclaimed as we stepped back. "You think his family would let you stay with them?"

"For sure." This time when he grabbed a handful of strawberries, I let it slide.

"So when do rehearsals start?" I asked.

Andre took his time chewing and swallowing.

I studied him—why did he look guilty?

Then, somehow, I knew. "The show's now, isn't it," I said.

"Tech starts in two days."

"*Andre . . .*"

"I know. But there's one way I can do it."

I shook my head, uncomprehending. How could Andre even *consider* taking the part? We needed him. "How?"

"Well, the cook gets here this afternoon, right?"

I strode back to the other side of the prep table, took up my knife, and continued de-stemming strawberries with a little more insistence than before. "So?"

"So you won't have to be down here anymore."

"Uh-huh."

"Well . . . what if *you* play James?"

Play James? "Me?" I squeaked. "But who would play Tobias?"

Andre's fingers drummed on the table. "Well . . . maybe your lines could be absorbed by other characters . . ."

This was essentially the same thing Kendrick had insinuated, but at least Andre was trying to be nice about it.

"Hold on, though," I said, my stomach twisting. "The show starts in three days. I can't be ready that quickly."

"Sure you can. You always have your stuff memorized at home, and the show's here! At home!"

I de-stemmed in silence, but for the first time let myself get a little hopeful. When I'd messed up today, it wasn't because I didn't know the lines—it was just distractions. And I *had* known my Acting Lab monologue inside and out in my bedroom. I glanced up at Andre. "You think the parents'll let you take it?"

"I . . . don't know," Andre said.

"But you *want* to take it."

"Yeah! It's Chicago Shakes, Finn. Another professional role."

"This time at a place that won a regional Tony."

"And a bunch of Olivier awards. And Ryan said it's a terrific cast."

I walked the strawberry stems over to the compost bucket by the sink. If I was going to tell Andre what I overheard Mark Lester-Dean say about wanting to sell the house, this was the moment. But I knew if Andre knew, he wouldn't take the part. And he was right—it was an amazing opportunity. And if I was being honest with myself, it was an amazing opportunity for me, too. "How do you think Kendrick'll react?" I asked.

Andre leaned his elbows on the prep table. "It helps that Peter plays the violin. Kendrick knows he's hopeless with instruments."

That was true. I saw another hole in this plan, however. "How are you going to explain the cell phone to Lula and Nomi?"

Andre rubbed his hands over his face. "I'm hoping they'll be so excited about the offer that they'll forget about the cell phone?"

The thing was, he probably wasn't wrong.

CHAPTER TWENTY

Hope flickered like the candle in front of me as I prepared the servant and family lunches. What was the actual likelihood of our parents agreeing to let Andre go to Chicago? And even if they agreed to that, would they really let me play his part?

After the servant and family lunches, I filled the sink in the butler's pantry to begin candlelit dishwashing with Lindsey, Noah, and Joan Dooley. But as I dropped a washcloth into the soapy water, Lula appeared in the doorway holding a candle of her own.

I fumbled with a knot in my apron strings, then handed it off to Noah. I wanted to ask Lula if this was about Andre, but as I had sworn to a car conversation, I wordlessly followed her to the second floor.

The Turner wing was home, but settling in next to Andre and Kendrick on our 1990s couch in 1890s garb felt very strange. Like we were different people intruding in on our old lives.

Setting her candleholder on top of a bookshelf, Lula sat next to Nomi on the wooden folding chairs facing the three of us.

"We think Andre's opportunity is too big to pass up," Nomi said. "We've decided he should go to Chicago, and Finn should take over his role here."

I took in a sharp, excited breath, and Andre shook my leg.

But before we could thank them, Kendrick coughed and flashed an *Are you kidding?* face into the middle distance.

Cheeks burning, I pressed my back against the couch so I didn't have to look at him. I mean, it shouldn't have been a surprise. He'd already ridiculed me today about my tiny part, and back when I'd failed to get into Acting Lab, he'd hardly said a word. Still—his reaction felt like a gut punch.

"But this puts a serious burden on you, Finn," Lula said. "Can you memorize James in three days?"

"Of course he can." Andre looped an arm over my shoulder. "I totally believe in him."

Kendrick rolled his eyes.

I glared at him. "It doesn't look like everyone does, though."

Kendrick waved a hand around. "It's—I mean, whatever, Finn. It's fine. You'll figure it out. It's more . . ."

"It's hard when one person gets offered a part and another doesn't?" Nomi suggested.

"No." Kendrick snorted. "Andre's played the part before, and I don't play the violin."

"Then what is it, honey?" Lula asked.

I studied him. If it wasn't that he didn't believe in me or feel jealous about Andre getting Peter, what else could it be?

Kendrick picked at the piping on the arm of the couch. "It's . . . If I knew taking other opportunities was on the table, I . . . well, wouldn't have picked *this* necessarily."

My eyes narrowed. He'd promised not to complain in front of Lula and Nomi. Didn't he know how much it would hurt them?

"I see. Okay," Lula said. She nodded many tiny nods. "Okay." Lula folded her hands in between her thighs and looked at no one.

"I'm sorry," Andre said, "I don't have to take the part—"

"*No,*" Nomi insisted. "Kendrick, what is it you wish you were doing instead?"

Kendrick re-twisted some of his hair. "Isaac's parents offered me an internship to work in their law firm, but I didn't take it because we were doing *this.*" He gestured at his cutaway suit. "Which was . . . whatever. But now *Andre—*"

"You don't want to be a lawyer," I said, frowning at him.

"But I *do* want to spend time with my boyfriend," Kendrick retorted.

I flopped back against the couch and inwardly rolled my eyes. He seriously wanted to throw away helping the family for one of his ten-minute relationships?

"Instead," Kendrick went on, "I have to make out with Maddie McGlynn a million times while the Neanderthal who wants to be her boyfriend cracks his knuckles and scowls at me."

"Neanderthals were actually pretty smart—" Andre began, but at Lula's and Nomi's looks, he stopped.

"Andre's opportunity is different," Nomi tried to explain.

"How?" Kendrick demanded. "Because it's theatre? Because that's the only thing that matters in this family?"

"No, but—"

"Well, excuse me," Kendrick went on, "if I'd rather be with Isaac than *here*, being threatened by a brute, doing a thousand shows in shoes that pinch, all to help save this stupid house."

I watched in shock as Lula covered her mouth with a shaking hand. "Who told you?"

He squinted. "Told me what?"

Lula and Nomi exchanged a glance.

My heart beat faster, and Andre leaned forward, his elbows on his knees. "What's going on?"

"Mark Lester-Dean wants to sell," I blurted to my brothers. "I'm sorry," I told my parents. "I overheard you talking to him on the phone yesterday."

"He wants to what?" Andre demanded.

Lula's eyes fluttered closed. "Sell the house. Fixing the roof is more expensive than we thought, and he's not in love with my plan to use the Jorgensen House to bring in money for the Beau."

"But you've been working on this project your entire adult life!"

Nomi squeezed Andre's knee. "That's why we're trying so hard to seal the deal."

Andre stood. "Well, I can't take this role now!"

"You have to." Lula tugged on his hand. "The opportunity is too important. I'd feel far too guilty if you stayed just for me."

"But Lula—"

I pulled Andre back down to the couch. "Take the part. You told me I had this, remember?"

Andre glanced at me, but even in that flash, I saw doubt in his eyes.

Another gut punch. So he only trusted me when the stakes weren't high? I studied the creases in my trousers.

Kendrick leaned forward. "I still don't see why Andre gets to go and I don't. Let Mark Lester-Dean sell the place if he wants to sell the place. Then we don't have to keep making sacrifices for a house some dead, rich white people owned that *we* never will!"

I recoiled. Kendrick's words felt like a slap.

"If you'll excuse me." Lula stumbled into her bedroom and closed the door, Nomi right on her heels.

It wasn't that Lula never cried. (*Was* she crying in there?) But she *never* ran away from a fight.

I sat in the silence and fumed at Kendrick. Why couldn't he just be happy for Andre? Do this thing for Lula? She had almost died this year. Was two weeks of hard work—that was also supposed to be fun, by the way—too much to ask?

"Laura," Nomi finally said, her voice muffled through the wall behind us.

All three of us leaned back in unison until Nomi's voice was clearer.

"Baby," she said, "you have got to stop apologizing for your dreams. Kendrick wants things. So do you. He is telling us what he wants. Now you tell him what you want."

"But he already knows . . ." Lula's voice was wobbly.

So was Nomi's. "Maybe he needs to hear it again."

Several long moments later, the bedroom door clicked open.

"Mom—" Andre began, but Lula interrupted him.

"You boys know some of this," she said, stilling a shaky hand on the back of her chair. "But I'm just going to say it all, okay?"

We nodded. Everyone was quiet for a long time.

Finally, Lula set her jaw and sat in her chair. Nomi sat next to her.

"My dad left when I was ten," Lula said, gripping her knees, "and I never saw him again. Then my mom and brother rejected me. Twice." Nomi leaned into Lula's shoulder, my brothers shifted on the couch, and I clenched my fists against Lula's whole damn family.

"But as long as I've lived *here*, with *you*," Lula said, taking Nomi's hand, "I've been home."

I blinked quickly.

"I know on some level, it's silly, what I've done here," Lula said. "I've been making a fantasy. And we only know about the Jorgensens because they had a lot of money."

"But they were more than that," Andre argued.

"Sure," Lula agreed. "They did some great things. Lillian married a governor and helped establish free school lunches in her state, Helen created a foundation to form women's shelters all over the country, and Alice was one of the first female doctors in Minnesota."

"And Millie hosted gatherings of the NAACP, women's rights groups, and meetings for the dissolution of Indian boarding schools right here in this house," Andre added.

"But they all could have done a lot more with their wealth," Lula insisted. "A house this size is unnecessary, other than to show off how much money you have. This house on the hill—on *Summit* Avenue—purposefully separated itself, and the people who lived in it, from folks like us. But that's why I'm doing what I'm doing. I want this house to be a place where people learn something. About who we've been, and more importantly, about who we're becoming. I don't see this house as aspirational—it's a warning of sorts. Is this what we want? So much for a few, at the expense of so many?" She met Kendrick's eyes. "You're not wrong, honey. People who look like you, like our family does, and who love like we do, would not have been welcome here in 1891. But we're welcome now. As long as I'm in charge, anyway. And that means something—about change, and progress, and hope. To me, anyway. Does that make sense?"

Kendrick pursed his lips. Then, after a moment, he nodded.

"I've been building toward this dream for twenty years," Lula said, eyes glistening as she leaned forward and took both of Kendrick's hands, "and right now it's make or break. You are an adult, and I love you, and you get to make your own choices. But I'm asking—and you know how much I hate asking—for your help."

Kendrick stared at their joined hands. "I just . . . I miss him. You know?"

Nomi's voice was soft. "What if you go to Madison for a week once this is over?"

"I'm supposed to take that landscaping job," Kendrick said.

"Can you start a week late?" Nomi asked.

Kendrick separated from Lula and sat up a little taller. "That . . . might be okay."

Kendrick'll last three days in Madison, tops. Then he'll break up with whoever he is and come home, I thought. I exchanged a look with Andre that told me he was thinking the same thing.

"Okay?" Lula asked.

"Okay," Kendrick said. "Look, I'm sorry. I didn't mean it, Lula."

She gave him a skeptical glance.

"I mean, I meant it. But I didn't mean to hurt your feelings so much . . . Your dreams get to be your dreams. Even if they're different from mine."

"Thank you, honey. I appreciate that."

Kendrick flicked a glance at me. "I can help you learn your lines if you want."

"Oh. Thanks," I mumbled.

"I can help you, too," Andre said. "Before I leave. But you're right, Finn—you can totally do this."

I couldn't look at him. But I nodded.

"Hey, everybody," Andre said. "I'm so sorry I threw a wrench in—"

"You get to ask for what you want, honey," Nomi said, tugging on his lapel. "We all do."

Andre offered up a half-smile.

"Now," Nomi said, standing, "I want a hug from each of you before we turn back into Victorians, then we need to motor. Except Andre, you'll stay here to call Ryan Thusing back. And your roommate."

"I'll give you my credit card so you can buy a plane ticket," Lula added. "Kendrick, when he's done, call Isaac and your boss at the landscaping company. The rest of us need to go to rehearsal—"

And then the most glorious music I had ever heard filled the house.

We immediately stopped talking and planning and floated out of our wing down the central staircase to the first floor and through the grand hall into the art gallery. The entire cast was drifting toward the organ, Magnus at the helm.

Other people had played our organ. But Magnus knew how to coax sounds from that instrument I had never heard before. His feet danced along the floor pedals, hands pulling stops and flying across both keyboards. It was less like he was playing a song and more like he was commanding the universe. Every hair on my body stood on end.

Too soon, it was over, and the notes reverberated in the air.

Magnus looked over his shoulder and grinned at us all. "Who's ready to boogie?"

CHAPTER TWENTY-ONE

We all burst into applause, and everyone within reach of the organ bench clapped Magnus on the back.

"That was wonderful, Magnus," Lula said from the doorway. "We'll block this scene during dance rehearsal later this afternoon. You have a couple of waltzes worked up?"

"You bet."

"Terrific. We're lucky to have such a talented musician on the project."

"Thank you." He cleared his throat and raised his voice. "I think *not* caring about this house is balderdash. I'm a body who cares a powerful lot." He searched the room until he found a stoic-faced Maddie. I exchanged a wide-eyed glance with Jade.

"Well. I certainly appreciate the caring," Lula said. "Say, before we walk through Scene Fifteen, everyone, I have an announcement to make."

My heartbeat thumped hard.

"Andre has been offered Peter in *Peter and the Starcatcher* at Chicago Shakespeare Theatre, so Finn will be taking over as James."

The cast members who hadn't seen me bomb my Acting Lab audition called out congratulations to both of us. But those who had stared at me.

My chest tightened as Mr. Hoyt sidled over to Lula and whispered something into her ear. But before I could figure out if they were talking about me, Noah reached out and shook my hand.

"Congratulations, man," he said. "Guess you and I will be fighting each other for the next two weeks."

"And kissing," Lindsey said.

Oh. I hadn't put two and two together. I'd never kissed anyone onstage before.

"And you'll be dancing with me," Alexa added.

"Right!" That was something to look forward to at least.

"Congratulations . . ." Jade said with faraway eyes like she was calculating something.

"Look, I hate to bring this up," Mr. Hoyt said in a low voice to Nomi, "but he can't make it through a monologue."

Now my heart was beating in my throat. "He" was definitely me.

"He'll be fine," Nomi insisted, her hand light on the brass railing.

I swallowed. I *would* be fine. My moms believed in me. And once I memorized James, Mr. Hoyt would believe in me, too.

"Hey," Jade said, and I could tell by the look on her face that she had overheard Mr. Hoyt. "You can do this, okay?" Then she tugged on my coat sleeve, her brown eyes setting the stage for some super nice thing to come out of her mouth.

And because I was still so worked up from our family conversation upstairs, and I knew even one borderline tender comment from her would flip on my waterworks, and I'd been vulnerable enough for one day, I lurched out of her grip. "Thanks. And hey—if you work your Alexa magic, maybe she'll be willing to help me learn those dashed lines full chisel." I splayed out jazz hands as punctuation.

Jade smirked. "You're as savage as a meat axe, Turner. I'll see what I can do."

Everyone was in the final scene in the dining room. It wrapped up all of the loose ends: who killed Cook, who stole the painting, and what was going to happen to the secrets. Nomi promised to revise the script that night, redistributing Tobias's lines to other characters just like Andre had suggested. In the meantime, Andre read them.

James had only four lines in the final scene, and I stared at the script with the focus of Mr. Hoyt. For now, I was going to have to press pause on the necklace and Alexa. Jade would understand.

After the final scene, Noah raised a hand to give me a high five, then, spotting Mr. Hoyt, dropped it and bowed slightly instead. "That was terrific, James. What jolly fun we'll have working together."

I bowed my own Victorian bow back. "Indeed, Henry. I believe our fight will particularly take the egg."

Noah winked and wandered off.

"I know you can appreciate how much is at stake here," Mr. Hoyt said.

I spun around. Now he was trying to convince Mr. Lester-Dean, too!

Mark Lester-Dean's face twisted with concern, but I couldn't hear what he said back. Then Mr. Lester-Dean addressed us all in a loud voice. "I'll be back in a couple days to check in. Break a leg!" He nodded at Lula. "Laura? Will you see me out?"

Was he going to tell Lula to find someone else to play James? Before I had a chance to take a deep dive down a worry wormhole, however, Jade stepped over to me.

"So this changes things," Jade said, and I automatically sought Mr. Hoyt's location—only a few feet away! "It's fine," she said out of the corner of her mouth, waving at him. He eyed us with suspicion but finally offered a curt nod in return. "See? Now that we're in the same social class, we can talk all we want." She tucked an escaping curl behind her ear.

I had a weird moment of wanting to tuck that curl for her.

Jade misinterpreted my facial expression. "We don't have to talk *all* the time." She stepped in a little closer. "But it's going to make communicating about the necklace easier. I have it all figured out."

I knew she'd been calculating earlier.

"We've lost access to the basement since you're not a servant anymore, so we'll each search the first and second floors," she said, "and then if we can't find anything there, we'll do a little middle-of-the-night espionage downstairs. No one's rooming there, are they?"

"Martin Lord is," I said. "But I'll think about how to get around that if we need to. Let's just hope the necklace is upstairs."

"Best-case scenario? It's in one of our bedrooms."

"Right! I forgot! After Andre leaves, I get a bedroom in the house! Then Noah can move into my old room in the gatehouse, and I can stop feeling guilty about him sleeping next to the front door."

Jade laughed, but when Lula stepped back into the dining room, my grin faltered. All of it was moot if Mark Lester-Dean wouldn't let me play the part.

"Okay," Lula said, clapping her hands. "Let's take five, then it's Victorian etiquette time." She curtsied, and everyone chuckled. As the cast split off, Lula called, "Finn? Can I talk to you?"

My stomach dropped, and another thunderclap sounded. This storm wasn't showing any signs of letting up.

CHAPTER TWENTY-TWO

I followed Lula to just outside the music room, ready to ask her what Mark Lester-Dean had said, but Maddie stepped in with a silver candleholder, shielding the flame with a curved hand. "I'll call Costume Rental to get some suits for Finn. Is the landline in reception still hooked up? And does it work when the electricity's out?"

"It is and does," Lula whispered. "After the call, can you make the fact that there's a phone in there a little less obvious? Hide it, maybe? I should have done that earlier." As Maddie scampered off, Lula called out, "Andre?"

He stuck his head out of the parlor. "Hi," he said, eyes twinkling in the candlelight.

Lula gestured for him to join us. "How about ditching Victorian etiquette to help Finn learn his lines?"

Lightness returned to my chest. She wouldn't be sending me off to work on lines if I wasn't playing James.

"Sure. If we do that while I pack," Andre said.

"Hello? Can anybody hear me?" a scratchy, unfamiliar voice called from what sounded like the front hall.

"That must be the cook," Lula said, her forehead a worry mountain range. "Packing? Lines? Can you guys make that work?" She fished the key to our wing out of her pocket and handed it to Andre.

"Yeah, totally," Andre promised as I insisted, "Don't give it a second thought."

Lula kissed us both on the cheek and strode toward the sound of the new cook's voice.

Something tugged at me to follow her and at least meet the new cook. Shouldn't I show her how I'd stacked the pots in the kitchen? Give her a tour of the pantry? But Andre had already plucked the candelabra off the hall table and was climbing the stairs. I scampered up behind him. The cook would figure it out.

<hr>

After Andre set the twisty brass candelabra on top of the dresser in his and Kendrick's bedroom in the Turner Wing, he pulled a suitcase out from under the bunk beds and set it on the floor between us. "Read through the scenes a few times. Then I'll quiz you, okay?"

Quiz me. I flipped the script open to the first scene and counted James's lines. Suddenly, I had a hard time drawing a full breath. There were more James lines in the first scene than Tobias had in the entire play.

My tailcoat felt like a straitjacket. I shrugged it off. Since we were in our wing, my instinct was to drop it on the floor like I usually did with my cast-off clothes. But years of directors and stage managers calling out, *Hang up your costumes!* were burned into my brain. Still, my eyes fell to the constellation of dried drops of blue, yellow, and cream oil paint on the hardwood floor.

Back in the day, Millie Jorgensen had used this bedroom as her painting studio. Whenever I noticed those drops of paint, I felt a zip of connection. Paint had dripped off her brush, and I was looking at the exact result of that moment, decades and decades later.

The whole house made me feel that way, really. The long-gone Jorgensens had touched these same doorknobs and flipped on the light switches and stormed up and down all the stairs. But the paint droplets in particular made the Jorgensens feel not so far away.

As hard as we'd tried to respect the house, there was accidental evidence of our lives here, too. The dent in the plaster made by the rocking chair from when we were babies. Scuffs on the servants' staircase from soccer cleats and tap shoes. Kendrick's and Andre's and my initials etched into the wall above the bathtub in the gatehouse.

The story of this house had been started by the Jorgensens, but we were characters in that story, too. We couldn't lose it. And unless Jade and I found the necklace, our only hope was putting on a perfect show.

But if I couldn't deliver a memorized monologue outside my bedroom, how on earth did I think I was going to be able to play James successfully?

What had I been thinking, agreeing to this?

Andre slid his phone out of his pocket, read it, and laughed.

"What?" I asked.

"The director posted this on Instagram." He held up the screen for me to see. The cast and crew of *Peter and the Starcatcher* were gathered around a handmade sign with Andre's headshot pasted on it that said, *Andre Turner is our hero!* "And you're my hero, Finn," he said, tucking the phone away.

"I don't know about that . . ." Wax sloshed over the side as I adjusted the candelabra on the dresser.

He laughed. "You *are*. I know you're worried, but there's no doubt in my mind—you can do this, Finn."

I hung up my tailcoat on the swirly brass doorknob. "I'm not worried," I said, trying to convince myself it was true.

"Good." Andre yanked open his chest of drawers and scooped up an armload of T-shirts. But then he smirked. "Not even about kissing Noah in front of our parents?"

I moaned. Kissing someone I wasn't into was one thing. But that was nothing compared to the fact that it was going to be in front of *our parents*. Visions flooded into my head of our moms giving me notes. *More tongue? No, less tongue. Gosh, honey. Why is your tongue so weird?*

Andre chuckled, dropping the shirts into his suitcase.

One of the T-shirts tumbled onto the floor. I picked it up and held it up against my chest. "Do you ever get used to kissing people in front of Nomi and Lula?"

He plucked the shirt out of my hands. "You know, I was just teasing you. You're going to be fine."

"*You're* the one who opened this can of worms. Out with it."

He sighed. "To be honest? I don't think about our parents while I'm acting. I just get in the head of my guy. I'm not really a murderous barber, or a crabby ogre, or a vengeful police officer. But when I'm Sweeney Todd or Shrek or Javert, I stand in their shoes, and I imagine wanting the things they want, and the rest of the world disappears. Even when I'm kissing someone."

"I mean. Sure. That's . . . No. You're right. Be an actor. Act."
I chewed on my lip. Would this be easier if I had more experience
kissing people in general?

Andre yanked open his underwear drawer and emptied it into
the suitcase. "You're doing that worried thing with your mouth."

I shifted on the bed. "Is it harder for you when the person you're
playing opposite is a girl?"

Andre leaned against the dresser. "Well, it's fun kissing people
when you're attracted to them. It's just part of blocking when you're
not. And I don't *mind* kissing girls. But I'm a lot more attracted
to guys. I mean, you kissed Noah at that theatre party. It wasn't
torture, right?"

"Right, but no one was watching. And now they will be—four
times a day. Six performances next Friday. Maybe on PB*S*? And I
have to kiss him like he's the love of my life."

Andre shrugged. "Acting."

Right. Acting. But . . . Alexa . . .

He peered at me. "You're going to chew a hole through your lip."

I scrubbed my face with my hands. "Do guys assume you're
straight when they see you play opposite a girl in a show?"

Andre examined his socks, sniffing a few different pairs. "Are we
actually talking about this because you're worried a certain girl in
particular will think you're not into girls if you kiss Noah in front
of her?"

I usually told my brothers everything. But in the run-up to getting the house ready for the show, I hadn't had a chance to tell them
about my crush on Alexa. It looked like Jade wasn't the only person
who'd guessed.

"Maybe . . ."

"Well, I really don't think it'll change how Jade feels about you."

"*Jade?*" I sat up straight. "No way—Alexa!"

Andre's face broke into a teasing smirk. "You're joking."

"Why would I be joking?"

"Because it's so obvious you and Jade are into each other!"

"We do *not* like each other that way," I promised, slicing a hand across my body. "Or at all, basically."

"Yeah, I mean, I know you've been at each other's throats for years, but it doesn't look like that now. Kendrick and I were talking about it this morning—"

"What?"

"And we think it's just a matter of time before one of you snaps and tugs the other one into a dark, empty room. There are plenty to choose from—"

"Andre!"

"I thought the linen closet"—I started chucking his suitcase clothes at him, and he grinned, batting them away—"but Kendrick said he remembers you hanging out in the schoolroom a lot. And you're very sentimental."—*Bat*—"Wherever it is, you're going make out super hard-core"—*Bat*—"and pledge your undying love to each other"—*Bat, bat*—"and then have a pile of theatre babies in ten to fifteen years. And they'll all have Shakespeare names like"—He punched a T-shirt into the air—"Banquo and Goneril."

"Shut *up*—"

Andre chucked a pair of his jeans back at my head, which I did *not* successfully bat away. "So when you kiss Noah, just close your eyes and pretend he's the mother of your future Shakesbabies."

I flung a pillow at him.

He laughed and put on a high-pitched voice, clutching the pillow to his chest. "Yorick! Hermia! Give Friar Laurence a turn on the swings!"

I covered my face with my hands so he couldn't see how hard I was laughing.

"Why Alexa? Why not Jade?" Andre asked, still smirking as he abandoned the clothes and pulled out a bin and started picking through his shoes. "Jade's totally cute. Supersmart. Seems to like you for some reason."

I snorted.

"Every time I turn around, you two are whispering."

"That's—" I stopped because I didn't want to tell Andre about the necklace. Both because Jade had asked me to keep it a secret and because it would add fuel to Andre's argument that we weren't enemies. *The two of you are hunting for treasure again? Oh, sweet little Finnster . . .*

"She talks a lot," I said instead, "and I just happen to be standing there most of the time."

"Sure." He set three pairs of sneakers in the suitcase and pushed the bin aside.

"Andre, trust me. We do *not* get along."

"Yeah, but *why*—"

I huffed. "It doesn't matter!" Now I stood up. "*Alexa*," I said, gathering Andre's clothes and dumping them back in the suitcase, "is beautiful and talented and nice to me."

Andre considered two different kinds of deodorant next to the candlelight, then chucked the winner in my direction, nearly knocking me in the head.

I glared at him and buried the deodorant between Andre's shirts.

"Well, chin up about making out with Noah, Finnster. With all that practice, you're going to get really good at kissing people. Think about it that way. Practice for making out with—"

This time, I knew it was coming, and said, "ALEXA" loudly over Andre's insistence of "JADE."

But he was right about practice. Practice was good.

And practicing would help me get this part on its feet, too.

CHAPTER TWENTY-THREE

Thanks to Andre, by the time I joined the cast in the grand hall two hours later, I felt halfway decent about the first few scenes.

"Hey," Jade whispered to me in the south alcove as she blew out her candle. Several candelabras had been set up to light the area for dancing. "I have an idea, but I need a hammer or a crowbar or something."

"Sounds destructive," I whispered back. "Am I taking the fall with Lula this time?"

She smiled. "I'll be careful. It's the bathrooms. They're all—"

"Waltz, everyone!" Nomi boomed from the stairs and clapped her hands. "Eyes up here."

Jade mouthed, "Later," and faced my mom along with the rest of the cast.

"The waltz is intimate," Nomi said. "In fact, when it was first introduced in the early 1800s, women had to have permission to dance it in public balls. All of that close standing and touching, you see."

There was a light chuckle as everyone digested the history lesson.

"At its core, the waltz is three steps. The emphasis is on the first beat: ONE, two, three, ONE, two, three—Say it with me."

Everyone chorused, "ONE, two, three," a few times.

"Good. Now the steps." She climbed up a few stairs so we could all see her feet and demonstrated the very simple ONE, two, three—DOWN, up, up, and without being asked, folks started copying her movement.

She turned and surveyed the bobbing crowd. "Excellent," she said. "Now, traditionally, there is a gentleman's part and a lady's part. Gentlemen, let's start with you. You'll be leading off with your left foot going forward—"

I watched Nomi, but I knew how to waltz, so I let my mind wander to how much fun it was going to be to wear a fancy cutaway suit. How I'd take off the coat and throw it over my arm. Alexa would float down the stairs, and I'd be dressed in a crisp white shirt and contrasting vest and say, *Why, Miss Margaret Jorgensen. Fancy seeing you here.*

"Uh, Mrs. Jorgensen?" Magnus asked. "May I ask a question?"

I startled, shaking off my daydream. Jade looked just as surprised as I felt. Magnus was using titles now? And asking permission to interrupt rehearsal? If this was what he'd meant by promising to "be good" during the fire alarm, it wasn't a bad start.

"C-certainly," Nomi stuttered.

"Will the servants be dancing?"

"Well, all except you. You'll be playing the organ, of course. The 'upstairs' people will be dancing in the hall, but the 'downstairs' people will also dance—just in the dining room or breakfast room, wherever they end up. This won't last for very long, as it's during the dance that the audience is guided back into the music room to discuss their theories. The organ will fill the entire time the audience deliberates, however."

"Oh, yeah—yes," Magnus said. "I recall that. Bully for us! Indubitably."

I choked on my laugh. Now everyone was staring at Magnus.

"All right then," Nomi said. "Can we get a slow waltz going?"

Magnus offered her an unnecessarily deep bow and slipped back into the art gallery.

Jade and Kendrick coupled up, as did Nomi and Mr. Hoyt. As far as the upstairs people went, it was just Alexa and me left. "Ready?" I asked. Holding my left hand out at eye level, I accepted hers and placed my right on her shoulder blade. Her tentative hand rested on my arm, and she looked down at me. Like, *down* at me. But she wasn't one of those girls who needed to be shorter than the guy she was with, right? That was stupid and old-fashioned.

Still, I tried to lengthen my spine and simultaneously flex my biceps without crushing her hand.

The music started. I nodded at Alexa, stepping forward with my left foot as she stepped back with her right. She was stiff in my arms at first, but I soon felt her relax as I led her in sure circles around the hall. Then I guided her into a spin, and an adorable laugh escaped her lips as I twirled her back into position without missing a step. The lights spluttered on, underlining the excellent way my day was turning around.

Alexa beamed at me for the rest of the dance.

"You're very good at this," she said, curtsying when it was over. "I mean, you were a good dancer in *Drowsy*, too, but—"

"Theatre parents." I bowed. "Comes with the territory."

She giggled, fanning herself a few times with her hands. "I didn't realize your dad was in theatre, too."

"Oh," I said. My brothers and I didn't really think of Aaron as our dad. Mostly, he just felt like a close friend of the family. But biologically he was our father. And he *was* an actor. Maybe filling Alexa in on my backstory was part of Jade talking me up to her. "Yeah. He's at Milwaukee Rep playing Herbie in *Gypsy* right now."

"Oh, wow!" she said.

"Well done, Margaret. James." Mr. Hoyt offered us a slight bow. I bowed back and Alexa curtsied.

When he was out of earshot, I said, "Maybe Lab-wise, things are looking up for us."

Alexa smiled. "Maybe they are."

CHAPTER TWENTY-FOUR

After dance rehearsal, I eagerly joined the upstairs folks around the table in the breakfast room for my first family dinner, covering my belly with my hands to muffle the growls. Nomi and Jade were giving me side-eye, but luckily, Alexa was down the table and didn't seem to notice.

When Magnus started dinner off by delivering a crock of black bean soup, he looked kind of shell-shocked, but once the onion and cumin filled my nostrils, my focus shifted to harnessing every fiber of my self-control to wait until Nomi began eating before diving in.

When the chicken came out, my eyes fluttered as I savored the flavors. The food I'd made was good, but this cook really knew what she was doing. The Victorians were into boiling meat, which didn't sound great, but somehow, she'd managed to make it into something I wanted seconds of.

Before we were finished, Magnus arrived with an egg-heavy dessert called Floating Island, leaving the door open that separated the breakfast room from the servants' stairwell. I cocked my head. Was someone yelling down there?

Nomi looked up, too. "Is everything all right, Jeremiah?" she asked Magnus.

Before he could answer, Lula rushed into the breakfast room from the grand hall. "So. Georgia Periolat from PBS just called and—"

"A call?" Mr. Hoyt asked with Victorian confusion.

Lula scrunched up her face. "I have created a breakfast room–sized, time-traveling portal. I need you in the present for, like, two minutes." She gripped the back of one of the chairs. "PBS has confirmed they'll be coming for our final Saturday performance. Which, according to Mark Lester-Dean, will indeed include a VIP dinner for twenty-two at a thousand dollars a plate."

"A *thousand*—" Magnus blurted.

Lula nodded. "If we sell out—which is likely, given PBS's involvement—and the donors are happy, and they write additional donation checks, we won't have to worry about—" She cut herself off with a sharp, panicked breath. "I mean—Everything's fine, but—"

"We all know, Mom," I said. All the teenagers did anyway. My eyes flicked over to Mr. Hoyt, but it was clear by his calm expression he'd been filled in, too. "It's okay. Everyone wants to help."

Lula's face wore the same expression it had when she found out Maddie dropped a class so she could manage rentals while Lula was recovering—astonished by the gesture. "Well then. Thank you, everybody. Again." She shook her head. "If everything goes well with the run, then especially with PBS and the final performance, the Jorgensen House as is just might survive. But it means the food has to be phenomenal." Lula put a hand on my shoulder. "How's dinner so far?"

"Oh, it—" I couldn't find words. I stabbed a few things together on a fork and offered it to her.

"Well," Lula said, chewing. "At least *that's* something." She handed back my fork and took a few steps toward the door leading to the servants' staircase. "So everything's going well downstairs?"

Magnus barked out a laugh as Maddie filled the doorway with her body. "It's fine. We're fine," she said, shooting Magnus a look.

The hair on the back of my neck stood up.

It must have on Lula's, too. "What's wrong?"

"Nothing," Maddie chirped as Magnus said, "She's the nicest cook ever."

"Maddie," Lula warned her.

My stomach turned.

"She's . . ." Maddie looked over her shoulder at the closed door but lowered her voice. "A little strict."

"Cooks can be like that," I said to reassure everyone (and myself). "Sort of like army generals."

"Okay, then." Maddie picked at a food stain on her apron. "She's . . . like an army general."

Lula tugged on her earlobe. "Do you want me to talk to her?"

"Yeah, would you?" Magnus began as Maddie said, "Nope!" She shot a death glare at Magnus. "We're *fine*. It's just a bit of an adjustment after Finn at the helm."

I opened my mouth to offer to help but closed it again. I knew how it would be: I'd disappear into the kitchen, there wouldn't be enough time to learn my part, and then the show would be ruined, and we'd lose the house—not to mention I could kiss Acting Lab goodbye.

"Hey," Kendrick said. "Maybe Finn could be the cook and—"

I kicked him under the table. Kendrick fired off his own death glare.

I smoothed the white linen napkin in my lap as Lula chattered about the rest of the PBS arrangements.

They'd be okay in the kitchen. Maddie was down there. It would be fine.

It had to be.

CHAPTER TWENTY-FIVE

After dinner, the upstairs cast gathered in the library to play blindman's bluff. I was so distracted by warring kitchen/James worries, I didn't notice that Andre was patting himself down and checking his pockets until Mr. Hoyt asked, "What's wrong, Mr. Turner?"

"I think I left the blindfold upstairs," Andre said. "I'll be right back."

The circle broke up, and Kendrick flumped onto the couch. Even Nomi looked weary.

"Mr. Turner?" Mr. Hoyt called.

"Yeah? I mean, yes?" Andre jogged back into the library.

"Perhaps instead of a parlor game," Mr. Hoyt suggested, "everyone would prefer a quiet night. There are plenty of books." He eyed me. "And scripts."

I gulped.

The group agreed and split off. My parents disappeared somewhere together, my brothers climbed the stairs to pack up Andre's character's room, and Mr. Hoyt and Alexa selected novels and settled into the wingback chairs flanking the fireplace.

I hovered in the doorway. With all the rain today, I needed to go up to the attic and empty the buckets, but maybe first I could hang out in the library and go over my lines with Mr. Hoyt watching. Plus, Alexa was there.

"Hey," Jade hissed. She was tucked behind one of the ferns at the bottom of the central staircase.

With a parting glance at Alexa, I slipped down the hall into the south alcove.

"Seven thirty, remember?" Jade whispered. "Right there?" She thumbed at the door to the coat closet under the stairs. "Think you can find me a hammer and crowbar by then?"

"Oh. Right. Um. I'm really sorry, Jade, but I'm just not going to have time tonight. I'm working on my lines in the library, and then I've got to go check on the buckets in the attic. Can we put this off until—"

"What buckets?" she asked.

I lowered my voice. "The ones I set up to catch all the rainwater leaking through the roof."

"Right! I suppose!" She put her hands on her hips. "How many buckets are we talking about?"

I looked around. No one was in the grand hall or climbing the stairs. "A lot."

"Like ten a lot?"

"More like thirty-one a lot. And counting. Please keep it to yourself."

She pursed her lips. "New plan," she said. "Kendrick's helping Andre right now, so go search Kendrick's room. Then write out your lines for forty-five minutes *away* from the library so you don't get distracted by Alexa, then meet me in the attic. We'll talk treasure while I help with the buckets."

I eyed her dress. "That corset is going to make lifting difficult."

"Actually, it gives me great back support."

I squinted at her. Her plan wasn't terrible.

"I really think I'm on to something with the bathrooms," Jade said. "They're all built up a step."

"That's where the plumbing is."

"It's also a great place to hide something." Her eyes glowed.

It was an idea I hadn't considered before.

"Fine," I agreed. "But meet me in the schoolroom instead of the attic. The toolbox is still in the closet there. Then we'll head upstairs."

<hr>

The guest room Kendrick was occupying was just a short walk across the hall at the top of the stairs. But first, I pressed my ear to the door of the room where Andre was staying. Once I confirmed both of their voices through the door, I dashed across the hall and slipped into the cheerful yellow room Kendrick was staying in as Simon.

I squatted in front of the fireplace and poked at the pale yellow subway tile. Nothing seemed loose. I ran my hands over the ceramic floral surround and tugged at the wooden mantel. All solid.

Standing up, I peered at myself in the mirror over the fireplace. My eyes were dull, and my skin felt heavy. Between the read-through mistakes, the meals, the fire alarm, Andre's phone call, and the dancing, it had been a long day.

Rubbing my forehead, I glanced around the rest of the room. There was no way the necklace was in here. That disgruntled maid didn't want it to be found, and who poked around in places they shouldn't more than guests?

But I'd promised Jade I'd look.

My eyes flicked to the bathroom door and the step up it took to get there. Jade was right—the false floor was a great potential hiding place . . . I'd look for a loose board. Then I'd go.

The first thing I saw in Kendrick's bathroom was something tucked into the mirror of the medicine cabinet above the sink, and without thinking, I plucked it up.

It was a greeting card. A narwhal with a rainbow horn proclaimed, "You are a magical homosexuwhale!"

I flicked it open.

Kendrick—

Three things:

One: Thank you for my birthday gift. How did you find time to think *of, much less* make *me an electron filling shell coloring book? It's amazing. You're amazing.*

Two: It's so strange to think that we've seen each other basically every day since March 17th, and now, suddenly, we won't. But last night when you confessed you were worried I'll find some hot Lands' End model in Madison? I still can't believe you'd think that. Please solve $e^{i\pi} + 1$ for the likelihood of me meeting anyone I like more than you.

Three: You say you can't stop thinking about me, but I don't ever want you to. You aren't in my thoughts, you are my thoughts.

Love,

Isaac

P.S. Okay, the answer to the equation is 0. I'm just going to give it to you because I don't want you to worry.

P.P.S. $e^{i\pi} + 1 = 0$ is "Euler's Identity" and is sometimes called "mathematics' most beautiful equation." That's the other reason it made me think of you.

Like it was on fire in my hands, I dropped the card into the sink. Kendrick famously wasn't a gift guy. I had enough birthday present IOUs to cash in for a used car. But he'd *made* Isaac an electron filling shell *coloring* book? I swore and tucked the card back into the cabinet while a wave of regret washed over me. Regret for snooping and for reading Kendrick's private things, but mostly for doubting my brother's commitment to his boyfriend. How was I supposed to expect everyone to give me a chance to be different if I wasn't willing to let other people change, too?

CHAPTER TWENTY-SIX

Sitting at the big desk in the schoolroom on the third floor, I printed out my cues and watched the evening sun struggle to shine through the post-rain clouds. I should have been able to move on to quizzing myself, but I kept staring out the window, thinking about Kendrick's boyfriend and the things he'd written in that card.

"The tools are in here?" Jade asked by way of greeting.

I looked up. Jade had changed out of her dress. Now she was wearing a white cotton nightgown that enclosed her from her throat to her wrists to her ankles and a buttery yellow dressing gown knotted at her waist. She was entirely covered, but it was still pajamas. It felt so intimate, I couldn't speak. So I just nodded.

"Great. I'll grab them on my way back downstairs."

Was she wearing a corset? Some Victorian women slept in theirs. I couldn't imagine Jade would want to do that, though. It couldn't be comfortable. If she wasn't wearing a corset, what *was* she—

"Anything in Kendrick's room?" she asked, flipping through the pile of paper I'd written my lines on.

My combined thoughts about Jade's undergarments and the greeting card were too much for me. I blushed.

She sat on the corner of the desk and tucked the copies of my lines into my script. "What is it?"

"Nothing." I wasn't going to tell her I'd been wondering about whether or not she was wearing a corset, of course, but I couldn't even distract her with the news about the card in Kendrick's bathroom. Kendrick wouldn't want her to know. He wouldn't want me to know, either, but that ship had sailed.

"You found nothing? Or you don't want to talk about what you found?" she asked.

"Neither. Both. It's fine. There's nothing there. Plus," I barreled on, "why would she have hidden the necklace in a guest room? Much less control than other, more private spaces."

"True," Jade allowed. Then her eyes lit up. "Maybe the attic, then. That's a private space I bet Anna Jorgensen never went to."

"Sure," I said. I tripped over my feet getting out of the chair. *Calm down, Finn.* "Let's go."

We began to retreat into the hall, but then I thought I heard someone talking. I threw out my arm to stop Jade, and she ran into it with her . . . top half.

Why couldn't I even think the word "breasts" when it came to her? Big deal. She had . . . breasts. So did billions of other people. The impact hers had made with my arm told me she happened to not be wearing a corset right now, but whatever. That was just a fact and maybe hers were objectively nice and also who cared and was she sweating, too, or was it just this stupid tailcoat?

Jade stepped back from my arm wall. "Why did we stop walking?" she whispered.

My tongue was too big for my mouth. I swallowed. "I thought I heard something." The only sound, though, was my heart pounding in my ears. "I guess I was wrong."

Maybe it was safer for Jade to lead the way.

Out in the hall, we stood at the top of the flower stairs and listened for foot traffic.

Nothing.

Then we crept toward the door to the servants' wing where Maddie, Joan Dooley, Lindsey, and the cook were staying. Jade breathed the door open.

"She's just so mean!" Lindsey was crying from a room down the hall.

"Transitions are hard," Joan Dooley said in a calming version of her tiny voice.

Jade and I exchanged a confused look. Who were they talking about?

"Look." Maddie's voice now. "There just aren't that many people who can cook Victorian-era food, much less on a wood-burning stove. Much *much* less who are willing to come to St. Paul and stay here for two weeks and cook six meals a day and throw a huge fundraising Victorian dinner on said ancient, ridiculous wood-burning stove."

I stepped back. They were talking about the new cook. But the wood-burning stove wasn't ridiculous. Once you learned that sticking your hand in the oven and counting to three would tell you it was ready to bake, it was pretty straightforward.

"I want Finn back," Lindsey sniffled.

My eyes widened. It had to be really bad with that cook if Lindsey wanted *me*.

"We all want Finn back," Joan Dooley chirped. "But this is the way things are. Come on, sweetie. She could be up here any minute. It's your turn to think of an answer for Twenty Questions."

"Yeah," Maddie agreed. "Let's try and shake it off."

I was feeling so guilty about Lindsey crying, I forgot to tell Jade about the squeaky step fourth from the bottom until it was too late.

"Mrs.—" Joan Dooley called out. She darted to the staircase. "Oh! You're not Cook. What's going on?"

"Uh, Jade's helping me with the, uh—" I swallowed and started over. "We're going to empty the buckets. Just one or two. Because of the rain." I pointed upstairs. "Leaky roof."

"We'll help," Joan Dooley offered as Maddie and Lindsey appeared beside her.

"That's okay," I said, waving them off. "It's really just a one-person job, but Jade insisted."

"Because you want to make out?" Lindsey asked.

"Now, Lindsey," Joan reprimanded her. "But . . . in terms of the Victorian rules, the two of you really shouldn't be upstairs unchaperoned."

"I'll go with them," Maddie offered.

"It's dirty work," I said to discourage her, or anyone's, help but then blushed immediately to the tips of my ears.

"But somebody's gotta do it," Jade said, and skirts in one hand, she dashed up the stairs.

I managed to fire off an awkward wave at the others before following her, Maddie pounding up the steps right behind me.

Strangely, I could have sworn I heard Lindsey and Joan Dooley giggle to each other.

CHAPTER TWENTY-SEVEN

"Whoa," Jade said as we passed through the door into the attic. "*That's* the stage?"

"Uh, yeah," I said, exchanging a look with Maddie as Jade wove around the buckets and pails toward the far end of the room.

"Haven't you been up here before?" Maddie asked her. "Like at a cast party or something?"

"No," she said. She climbed three short steps and stood center stage, gazing at the rigging overhead. "Finn was always like, 'Come upstairs and look at the stage, everybody,' but I thought he was exaggerating."

I knew neither Jade nor I wanted to explain sixth grade and how we were too busy scouring the third floor for treasure to be bothered with the attic. "The Jorgensen girls loved to put on plays for their parents," I said instead. "But *my* parents definitely leveled it up."

"The curtains are gorgeous," Jade said.

"Cut down from an old set from the Beau," I replied as Jade slipped into the wings.

"Oh my god!" she exclaimed.

The lights onstage flipped on, then dimmed up and down. She'd found the light board. "Finn," she said, sticking her head out of the wings. "This is outstanding. It might be my favorite part of the house."

"It sure is mine," I admitted.

"So we'd better save it, then," Maddie said. "I'll start with this bucket." She lifted the red sand pail by its handle. "It's going to take me a long time to go down and empty it. I might get confused and nearly come all the way back before I go downstairs again. See you in maybe, I don't know, a half hour?"

"Maddie," I whined, embarrassed by the implication of what Jade and I would need a half hour by ourselves for, but Jade had disappeared backstage again and just called out, "See you then!"

Maddie grinned and slipped out the door with the pail.

"Jade," I complained as I wove through the rain receptacles. "Maddie thinks we're—" But Jade stepped back onstage and cut me off.

"Who cares?"

"But—"

Jade crossed her arms. "Let's empty the buckets so we can find the necklace."

Huffing, I shrugged off my tailcoat and laid it on the stage. Then I showed Jade where the Home Depot buckets were and how I transferred the smaller pans and pails into them.

When we filled the first one, she lifted it. "Jesus," she said.

"Miss Elizabeth," I admonished her. "Your father wouldn't want you using such language."

She mock-glared at me, but then her look grew skeptical. "Why don't you just pour them into the sink in the bathroom?"

I knew I was starting to blush again, so I fixed my attention on a can that had once held yellow paint. "The flowers under the eaves of the house don't get rained on. This is a good way to water them." I transferred the paint can's contents into the second Home Depot bucket.

Jade was quiet for a few seconds. "But you started doing this in March. There aren't any flowers in March."

I replaced the can in its precise, spike-taped boundaries.

"You didn't even *think* to pour the buckets into the sink, did you?"

If only I were across the room, I could have pretended I didn't hear her.

"Oh, Turner," she teased me, half-laughing. "It's these kinds of inefficiencies that happen when I'm not around. How often do you have to carry these downstairs?"

"Pretty much every time it rains for more than an hour," I said.

"It's been a wet spring."

"Yeah."

"So, like, three times a week?"

"Sometimes four."

"By yourself."

I snorted a little. "Why are you so surprised?"

"I guess I didn't realize you were that strong."

"I wasn't, really. Until the buckets."

She lifted the Home Depot bucket again and grunted, thunking it back down. "I know your brothers were gone. But why didn't your moms help? They definitely would have told you to pour the water down the sink."

My throat seized up. I reached for a six-quart pot on the edge of the stage. As my fingers closed around its handles, I felt a whisper of a touch on my elbow and froze.

"Why couldn't your moms help?" Jade asked, her voice careful.

"It's—no reason," I stammered, adding approximately four quarts of water to the bucket. "They were—busy." Not a lie, technically.

"Turner." She sat on the edge of the stage and took the empty pot from my hands. "Tell me."

I reached for Kendrick's old goldfish bowl and emptied it as well to avoid her eyes. The cancer was gone now. What reason did I have not to tell Jade? Other than the fact that we weren't that kind of friends. Of course, I wasn't really that kind of friends with anyone. I set the goldfish bowl back in its spike-taped boundary and opened my mouth to say, *It's nothing*, but "I'm not quite ready to talk about it yet" came out instead.

She set the six-quart pot in its place and smoothed the spike tape with her finger. "Well . . . I'm here when you are." She didn't seem angry or irritated at me, which is what I'd expected. She'd reacted like she had back when we were the two shortest kids in our class.

She pushed up her sleeves. "You know what? If you don't mind, I'm going to poke around up here while you finish transferring to that second bucket. Is that okay?"

"S-sure."

She lifted her nightgown to climb the steps onto the stage, and I caught a glimpse of her bare calf.

I dropped my eyes.

What was happening to me? It's not like I'd never seen her calves before—I'd even seen her thighs when she wore shorts.

This onset of modesty had to be a side effect of living like a Victorian.

"When are your parents using your comp tickets?" I asked as I emptied a Tupperware bowl. Not the most riveting of conversations, but I'd talk about anything to stop thinking about Jade's body.

"They're not coming."

"Really?" Jade's parents were linguistics professors who worked a lot but always came to see her shows.

"They're at a conference."

"For ten days?"

"They're staying long because the head of some International Phonetic Alphabet think tank is going to be there and they're invited to have drinks with him like three days later and 'It's the opportunity of a lifetime, Jade!' And 'Anyway, you're not even the lead in this play.' Blah, blah, blah." She was rummaging backstage, hidden from my sight by a curtain leg. "It's fine. They didn't come to *Drowsy*, either. Since I was 'just' stage managing."

I stopped repositioning the Tupperware bowl. "They didn't? Jade. That sucks."

The rummaging stopped. "Yeah. And I'm not quite ready to talk about *that*."

"Well . . . *I'm* here when *you* are."

The attic was silent for a moment. I wondered if she was as stunned as I was that we'd just had another friend-like conversation.

A few seconds later, sounds of her rummaging began again. "What's up with this blue couch?"

"The settee? Lula weeded it out of Beauregard stock and gave it to us to use in our plays. It's not original to the house. So the necklace won't be in between the cushions or anything." I took a few steps and picked up the purple sand pail with the missing handle.

"It's really pretty." A muffled squeak pinched the air as she flopped onto it. "I can't get over this place, Finn. It's amazing."

Jade thought something I'd help build was amazing. And she'd had a hard time this spring, too. And we were being nice to each other. Suddenly, I really wanted her to know about Lula.

Staring at the pail, I tried out the words, "Lula had cancer." But I said them at the same time Jade said, "My parents may have told me that if I took Acting Lab instead of Calc II, they wouldn't come see anything I was in until I 'reset my priorities.'"

I fumbled to regain my grip on the purple pail. "Wait, what?"

The rummaging began again backstage. "And I told them if they felt that way, they never needed to come see a show ever again."

"*Whoa.*"

"Then Mr. Hoyt called about this whole thing, and I knew they didn't want me to take it, but they said I should do whatever I wanted since that's what I was going to do anyway, so here we are."

I abandoned the pail and sat with one leg bent on the edge of the stage. I wanted to reach out—to hug her, to say *something*, but I didn't know what.

She stepped out of the wings with a floral tin box. "I can't get this lid off."

"It's safety pins."

She withdrew into the wings again.

As far as I knew, Jade and her parents hadn't fought like this before. She often alluded to the fact that they never talked about anything "real," which I took to mean anything with feelings attached.

They were smart, accomplished people, her parents, but not particularly warm.

"That sounds really hard," I called.

I wished she'd come out of the wings. It was difficult to have a serious conversation when I couldn't see her eyes.

Jade stepped out holding a cardboard box I knew to be broken castoffs from the prop shelves in the basement. It was super unlikely the necklace was in any of the boxes backstage, but I didn't want to break the spell of our conversation.

"They've been cool with you being in theatre up until now, right?" I asked.

Setting the box on the floor of the stage, she kneeled behind it. "Not like your family is." She selected an ivory-handled mirror, the glass missing. "You know how hard it is to have family who's different than you. I mean, race for sure. But in this case it's more about—" Her wrist wilted, and the mirror went slack in her hand.

I looked into her face. Oh, god—those were *tears*. "Hey, hey, it's okay." I scrambled over and pushed the box aside and put an arm around her shoulder. "Just, uh—let it out." That was what my parents always told me when I cried.

She leaned into me, and it felt so normal—like we did this all the time. Not the crying part, but the sitting together part. The comfort part.

"I'm fine," she insisted, but I kept my arm around her shoulder. "It's just . . ." She glanced at me, and I nodded to encourage her to keep talking. She rubbed her forehead with the heel of her hand. "What if they're right? What if I *should* take Calc II instead of Acting Lab because it's the difference between getting into an Ivy and not? But . . . what if I don't actually want to go to an Ivy? Or what if I decide I do, and I don't get in? Will they . . ." She glanced at me, then stared down at her twisted hands.

"Will they what?" I whispered.

She was so quiet I almost couldn't hear her. "Will they still be proud of me?"

I hooked Jade's elbow, pulled us both to standing, and wrapped my arms around her. She laid her head on my shoulder. Her tears pooled on my shirt, and her pain leeched into my chest. "Of course they will, Jade," I murmured, my voice rumbling. "Of course they will."

She started to sob. I couldn't hold her close enough.

"Your parents are always proud of you," I promised after a while. "I know they are. They love you . . . They *love* you."

Finally, she let out a shuddery breath and lifted her head. "But we want such different things."

I pressed my open palms against her back. "Maybe they don't understand you. But how could they stop being proud of you?" I asked. "You're the perfect daughter. You care so much about . . . everything. You're a terrific actor. And you're never in trouble. You have perfect attendance and perfect grades and you're ahead of me by at least a hundred-and-fifty points in that insane-balls system you dreamed up last year because getting perfect grades wasn't hard enough for you—"

She laughed through her tears. Then she stepped back, and that was good because it meant she wasn't feeling quite so terrible anymore, but I had to admit, I missed holding her.

"And yeah," I said, tucking my thumbs into my pockets. "Family's hard sometimes."

She took a handkerchief out of her robe pocket and blew her nose.

"But no matter what choices you make, they're never going to stop loving you."

She sighed. "I mean, I know they *love* me. But . . . you didn't hear the disdain in their voices, Finn. It's like they've been storing it up. Hoping theatre was a phase or something." She blew her nose again.

It physically hurt me seeing Jade like this. Jade was supposed to be impermeable. She was supposed to be a brick wall. I handed her my handkerchief as backup. "I mean, you're majoring in theatre in college, right?"

She took it and ran her thumb over the white stitching. "Maybe. To spite them."

I smiled. Jade's eyes were red, and her nose was swollen, and I hated seeing her so hurt, but I also hadn't felt this close to her in so long. All of Jade's bravado and sarcasm and walls were gone. All that was left was . . . her. Twinges of emotion welled up in my chest.

"Look," I said, clearing my throat. "I know you know this, but if you want some adults to talk to about . . . talking to adults . . . you can talk to my parents. They really like you . . . for some reason."

Jade choked on a laugh and wiped her eyes on my handkerchief. "Thank you. They're great, your parents. So are your brothers. I mean, the five of you . . . sometimes it hurts to look at it from the outside—it's like staring into the sun."

I didn't know what to say.

"You're lucky to have them."

I nodded and nodded. Then I blurted, "Lula had cancer."

"*Had* or *has*?" Jade grabbed my wrist.

"*Had.* This winter and spring."

"What kind?"

"Kidney. So she's down a kidney. But it's okay, since we have two." I smiled a little so I didn't cry. "She's okay."

Jade was still holding my wrist. "I'm sorry, Finn. That sucks. I wish I'd known."

I shrugged. "I didn't tell anyone."

"Why not?"

"I . . . I don't know."

Our eyes locked. My heart started racing. So I flexed my muscles. "Now you know why I've got biceps for days," I joked.

She cough-laughed again and pushed me. "That's ridiculous." Then she took a step closer and pulled my shirt taut over my arm, peering at it like it was an alien life-form. "Good god, Turner. You're ripped. Next thing you're going to tell me is you've got a six-pack, too."

I thumped a fist against my stomach. "It's at least a four-pack. Wanna see?" I started pulling at my shirt.

"No—I . . . believe you," she said, staring at the floor.

I chuckled and tucked my shirt back in. Apparently, I wasn't the only one afflicted with Victorian modesty.

When my clothes were back together, she met my eyes. "I wish you would have told me," she said.

"About my muscles?"

She glared at me. "About your *mom*."

One side of my mouth tugged up. "Yeah?"

"Yeah."

"I could have, I guess."

"*Should* have."

God, I liked this Jade so much.

But what would happen to her after we left the attic?

If I kept talking, at the very least, this version of us could go on for a little longer.

I tugged on her yellow bathrobe sleeve. "I hope you and your parents can talk for real when they come back."

"Thanks," she said, but she didn't look terribly hopeful. "I'm so sorry about the kidney cancer."

"Thanks." She *was* sorry—I could tell.

"But I'm not sorry about those muscles." She eyed my biceps. "You're definitely going to have to be careful fighting Noah."

I laughed, but petered off.

"What?"

I took a deep breath and swallowed. She wouldn't make fun of me, would she? Her eyes were still a little red from crying, but they were open. Earnest. "I'm . . . nervous about the kissing."

"Because you've never kissed a guy?"

"No," I said, relieved she was taking me seriously. "I kissed Noah at a party two summers ago."

"You did?" she asked, eyes wide.

"Yeah. I mean, it was a *theatre* party."

"Sure, but I didn't think—"

My hackles rose. "You didn't think what?" That anyone would want to kiss me?

"Settle down, Turner. I didn't think you were questioning."

"Oh. Well, I was."

"And?"

I scratched the back of my neck. "I'm pretty sure it's just girls for me."

"So if you've kissed him before, why are you nervous?"

"Because it's in front of my *parents*. But Andre said—"

Her laughter filled the attic. I pushed her, and she pushed me back. "I'm sure Andre told you blocking that sort of thing out is what acting is, but whatever. Kissing in front of your parents is totally embarrassing."

Somehow that made me feel a little better.

"I thought you were going to say it would be hard to make out with someone who was just a friend," she said. "Because yowza. One of you in a fit of passion shoves the other against a column or something at one point."

My face must have lost all its color because she started to laugh. "Oh, no! I'm sorry. No, come back here, Turner." She grabbed my arm as I tried to pull away. "I'm sorry!" I let myself get wrapped up in her embrace. She smelled like lavender. "It'll be fine," she said into my hair. "Probably."

Chuckling, I closed my eyes, glad for an excuse to wrap my arms around her again. "I've never kissed anyone with *passion* before," I admitted. "It's just been . . . friends at parties."

She leaned back from our hug, but we were still holding on to each other. "Well, we're just friends. Kiss me."

Suddenly every nerve ending came alive in my body. "What?"

"We're just friends," she clarified. "Pretend to kiss me like you mean it. Then it won't be so awkward with Noah."

"But—"

"Look, you don't have to. But it might make it easier if you've practiced with someone when no one's watching."

It was a fair point. "Are you sure?"

"Yeah. It's just acting, Finn. It'll be fine."

I searched her eyes for teasing, but it wasn't there. Could we really do this? We were already holding each other. That didn't feel weird. And there was no way kissing her would lead to either of us developing feelings for the other—there was too much baggage and history between us. "Okay," I said.

She closed her eyes, so I had a few seconds to study her face. Her lashes laying on her cheeks. That tiny nose mole. Her quirked smile. But how did someone start this sort of thing? My hands were getting sweaty.

"If you need a visual," she said, opening one eye. "Just pretend I'm Maddie, and you're Magnus."

"No way," I said, laughing.

"Okay, then," she said, laughing, too. "Pretend *you're* Maddie, and *I'm*—"

"*Jade!*"

She scrunched up her nose into an accordion, and then I was kissing her. And she was kissing me back. And it was slow and soft and every part of me felt warm.

This was . . . magical. She was *good* at this. Who knew it would feel like this with *Jade*?

I smiled through our kiss, and she pulled away.

"What?" she asked, smiling, too.

"Nothing," I said.

She squeezed one of my biceps. "Dammit, Turner. This is so dense, you could use it to hammer in a nail. It would be an awkward angle, though, so maybe, like, an overhead nail."

I laughed again. Then my breath hitched. Her hand had dipped down and was tracing my stomach muscles, lighting my insides on fire. At the sound of my breath, she met my gaze.

She started to say, "These are . . . also—" at the same time I said, "Should we—" and then we were kissing again. I pulled her closer.

The side of her nose stroked mine, and now her fingers were in my hair and I ached to slide my hands inside her robe but anchored them to her back instead, and if there was any doubt I preferred girls, that doubt was so gone, and then her *tongue*—

A step squeaked. "Hold on a second!" Maddie called up from the stairwell.

We leaped apart and stared in the direction of the door, our breaths shallow and quick.

"I should dump the bucket out *down*stairs, not bring it back filled, right?" Maddie pondered, still on the steps. "Yes. That seems right. Silly me. Here I go!"

When Maddie was safely out of earshot, my mind began to race. How was Jade feeling about what we'd just done? Because somewhere in there, it had stopped feeling like acting to me.

She coughed and straightened her dressing gown, all business. "Okay. I guess that's that."

That's that? "Right. Thanks for the . . . practice," I said, turning my body away from her so she couldn't see that not all of me had gotten the message we were just acting. "I'll finish the buckets."

"Great. I'll look for the necklace."

"Great," I said. But I couldn't meet her eyes.

CHAPTER TWENTY-EIGHT

The next morning at breakfast, I tore apart a roll and repeated the mantra I'd developed last night as I'd struggled to fall asleep: *That was your body, not your brain.*

In the light of day—literally, when Jade and Alexa walked into the breakfast room, the sunshine streaming in through the lace curtains—I knew I'd been right. Jade teased me about stealing all the rolls, and I laughed. Then Alexa smiled at me, and my heart started thumping.

See? Jade and I were friends, and my crush was on Alexa. That thing last night with Jade wasn't real—it was just chemical reactions. She'd touched my stomach, for the love of god. Some things didn't involve a logical trip through the brain.

After breakfast, the cast gathered in the music room to begin rehearsal. I couldn't help but notice that all the downstairs people seemed to be suffering. Lindsey was sniffling, and Noah had his arm around her. Magnus was feverishly whispering to Maddie, who kept shooting concerned glances at Lula. Butler Mr. Lord and House-keeper Mrs. Dooley looked exhausted.

It might have been the demanding early mornings stacking up, but it also could have been the demanding cook. I glanced at Kendrick, who met my gaze. Kendrick's raised eyebrows could have meant anything, though I was pretty sure they were telling me I should help in the kitchen. But I couldn't. I needed to focus on this role.

"Places for the top!" Lula called out. As we arranged ourselves for the first scene in the art gallery, Mr. Hoyt passed me and said, "Break a leg."

"Thanks." I gripped the brass railing.

I managed the entire first scene without looking at my script once. Kendrick muttered, "Not bad," after it was done, and Mr. Hoyt nodded. He hadn't seemed *overly* impressed but also hadn't looked *not* impressed.

My two lines in Scene Two went well, and I only looked at my script during Scene Three A twice.

When we reached Six A, however, which was right before my big scene with Noah, my heart started thudding uncomfortably.

"We won't do the fighting or the kissing right now," Lula said, studying the script. I didn't want to hurt Noah's feelings by looking too relieved, but after the thing with Jade, I didn't mind a break from making out with my friends.

"This afternoon, Jade will work with the boys to choreograph the fight, and then Naomi is going to take the two couples from etiquette rehearsal and choreograph the intimacy."

My heartbeat ramped up again. So not a *very* long break, then.

During a five-minute breather, Jade slid over next to me in the north alcove, and her eyes lit up. "You are going to be so excited!"

"Really?" I asked, resting my elbow on the potted fern. "Did you talk to Alexa?"

I knew immediately it was the wrong thing to say.

The joy on her face was replaced by—I wasn't sure. Disappointment, maybe?

Wait a minute. Had our kiss meant something to Jade after all? That couldn't be it. Jade had said a very perfunctory *That's that* the night before, like it was a business arrangement.

Now her face was calm. Polite. "No. I haven't talked to Alexa yet," she said. "I'll do it today."

"Okay. Thanks," I said.

"You're welcome." She pivoted away, but I caught her elbow.

"Did I say something wrong?" I asked.

"No." But she shook off my touch.

"Are you—" I tried to sweep dirt off the rim of the pot back into the fern, but a bunch tumbled onto the rug. "I mean—" I wiped my hand off on my trousers. "That kiss was acting . . . right?"

She glared at me. "What are you suggesting?"

I blushed. "Well—your whole face changed after I asked about Alexa, and I thought—"

She pressed her lips together. "My face changed because I'm annoyed that you keep pestering me about it. I'll do it. Quit double-checking my work."

"I'm sorry, I—then what was it you wanted to tell me?"

"Later. Rehearsal's starting soon."

This time when she spun away, I didn't stop her.

The rest of rehearsal went smoothly. I consulted the script more and more as the play went on, but I assured myself that made sense—I'd studied the earlier lines more than the later ones.

I'd work on them again after the intimacy rehearsal. And during the break before dinner. And instead of the evening activity, whatever that was today. Maybe Jade would talk me up to Alexa during the afternoon break. Maybe Alexa would even be willing to help me with my lines.

"Andre's plane landed," Lula said in a low voice to Nomi as we were breaking for lunch.

I gave her side-eye.

"*I'm* not living as a Victorian," she whispered. "Relax." She ruffled my hair, and Nomi squeezed my arm as she followed Lula. It sucked for Jade, not having her parents' approval. I was grateful I had mine.

Lunch was nothing short of magnificent: lamb chops and bacon, mashed potatoes, beet salad, and artichokes with hollandaise sauce. As I savored my last taste of hollandaise, I pushed away the worry that this elaborate meal wasn't what my lunch plan had been. All of this food was parts of two different dinners, in fact, and was a lot of the budget to spend all at once.

I raised a forkful of light, buttery mashed potatoes to my mouth. *Relax,* I told myself. *Maybe she's showing off a little.* If I focused on the flavors, I decided, I could stop worrying and just enjoy the food. That is, if I could also ignore the banging sounds coming from the basement.

When Magnus slammed open the door into the breakfast room,

fire in his eyes, I knew the cook issues weren't going to smooth themselves out.

"She's *awful*," Magnus spat. "If Mrs. Turner doesn't fire her, the play might become real life." He drew his finger across his throat.

Nomi wiped her mouth and stood. "Let's not worry Laura about this. I'm sure we can find a solution."

"Yeah, I've got one. It's me or her," Magnus insisted.

"And me," Noah said, cracking open the door. "And Lindsey."

Lindsey pushed her brother aside. "I don't *cry*, usually, so I'm telling you, she's—" She wiped her nose with the back of her hand. "The *worst.*"

"What's so terrible about her?" Lula asked, appearing in the doorway.

"Nothing, Laura, uh—Mrs. Turner," Mr. Hoyt said. "We have this under control."

Laura? Mr. Hoyt must be feeling something pretty big to make a mistake like that.

"I'm sorry, Mrs. Turner, " Magnus said. "We wanted to do this for you. Save your house and all that. But that cook. At first it was just that she was really yell-y at us as we were trying to help with the food. But—" He lowered his voice. "But then it got personal."

"She called Lindsey the b-word," Noah said.

"What?" Lula started forward in alarm, and Nomi's arms hung heavy at her sides.

"And Noah the f-word," Lindsey added.

"Both kinds," Noah said. I could tell it was killing Noah to complain.

Magnus's face twisted. "And Maddie ran out after she called her a—"

Laura held up her hands. "Stop. I'm sorry." She closed her eyes. "I'll just—"

Joan Dooley and Martin Lord excused themselves through the traffic jam at the doorway. "Laura," Mrs. Dooley said, "the way that woman is treating these children is—"

"She threw an actual tantrum! The floor is a lake of stew now and—"

"Clearly, there's something very unbalanced about her, and she needs help, but—"

Lula cleared her throat. "I should have intervened last night. I'm sorry. I'll ask her to leave."

Maddie stormed in from the grand hall shaking a stapled stack of papers. "We contracted her for two weeks. Even if we could find another person willing and able to cook here for the rest of the run, we can't afford to pay someone else."

Everyone looked to me. "I . . . I'm James. I c-can't."

"We could find someone else to play James," Kendrick said.

I shot eye daggers at him.

"What?" Kendrick protested. "There are a million actors in town. There aren't a million Victorian cooks."

"But—"

Lula waved our argument away. "No, it's fine, Finn. I know how important this part is to you."

I stared at the linen tablecloth. Was I being selfish?

"I'll be the cook," Lula decided. "The show will be on its feet soon, and then all I'll be needed for is house managing. I can do it. If you can read, you can cook. Right, Finn?"

I nodded slowly. That was usually true. But . . . Nomi and Kendrick and I exchanged a worried glance. Worry for overworking

Lula, still regaining her stamina, but also worry for her cooking: It was the pits.

Kendrick liked to joke (only behind her back) that if anyone could burn water, it was Lula. No one outside the family knew that, however. The downstairs cast exclaimed their thanks, and Lula set her features. "Maddie, can you get the cook's things from her room? I'll escort her off the premises."

"Will do!" Maddie exclaimed. Without being invited, Magnus followed her.

"We'll give you fifteen minutes to clear her out, Mrs. Turner," Mr. Hoyt said. "Then we can help with the dishes and the kitchen floor."

I blinked.

"We are a family in crisis," Mr. Hoyt explained. "And families stick together."

I smiled at him. There was one place we were on the same page.

CHAPTER TWENTY-NINE

I fumbled with the mashed potato serving bowl, nearly dropping it onto the breakfast room floor. I was having an increasingly difficult time believing the cook disaster wasn't all my fault. I turned to bring the bowl into the butler's pantry when Jade stepped in front of me, used silverware clutched in her fists. "So you *really* like her?" she whisper-accused me.

But before I could respond, Mr. Lord appeared with a tray, and Jade dumped the silverware onto it, offering him a forced smile of thanks. When he stepped away, she raised her eyebrows at me and jerked her head toward the grand hall.

Huffing a little, I set the bowl back on the sideboard and followed her. Maddie was coming downstairs with the cook's belongings, so I jerked *my* head toward the door to the coat closet under the stairs. When we stepped inside, I squinted at the sun shining through the stained glass. I closed the door behind Jade and faced her.

"What are you talking about?" I asked.

"Alexa," Jade said with precision, rubbing her thumb over a spot on one of the tarnished brass coat hooks. "You really like Alexa?"

"Oh. Yeah." I'd made that abundantly clear, hadn't I?

Jade pursed her lips, still rubbing the hook. "Well, I just overheard her comment to Magnus what a small world it was that Naomi and Laura's last names are both Turner."

"Small world?"

She dropped her hand and met my eyes. "Alexa doesn't know that Naomi is your mom."

Oh. That would explain why she'd asked about my dad being in theatre, too. "Well . . . she won't have a problem with me having two moms, will she?"

"The opposite. When she finds out Naomi Turner is your mother, she'll be really into you."

"Then lead with that fact, please."

"She'll be really into you," Jade repeated slowly, "because Alexa has big theatre dreams. You won't get a chance to see if she likes you for you. She's *going* to like you, and it's *going* to be for the connection to Naomi."

"But we've been flirting for months."

"Are you sure she wasn't just being friendly?"

I choked and changed the subject. "Why didn't you bring this up in the first place if you were so concerned about it?" I glanced over Jade's shoulder at the stained glass door. Shadows of people walking back and forth made my feet feel itchy. They needed our help.

"Because I thought Alexa already knew! And haven't you noticed how she's always agreeing with Naomi and following her around?

Alexa's going to lose her mind when I tell her. I'm just trying to warn you."

"I really don't think it's going to be that big of a deal," I said. "What could Naomi possibly do for her that's bigger than knowing Mr. Hoyt?"

Jade banged the back of her head against the wall. "You're serious?"

I shrugged.

She held up a hand and ticked a list off on her fingers. "Mr. Hoyt's BFA is from the University of Minnesota-Duluth. Your mom's is from the Yale School of Drama. Mr. Hoyt toured one anti-bullying play to six schools in the metro in, like, 2004. Your mom has toured in a half-dozen Broadway productions. Mr. Hoyt was once the voice of a parrot in a national commercial. Your mom has done countless commercials and narrated a billion audiobooks. Mr. Hoyt gets a lot of stage work, but theatres build *seasons* around your mom. Do you seriously not know how special she is?"

I scoffed. "Of course, but—"

"When I tell Alexa about you, and she finds out you're Naomi Turner's *son*, I'd bet an entire safe full of Victorian necklaces that suddenly your height isn't going to matter anymore."

My body went cold. "My height?"

She blinked. "Never mind."

"*Jade*—"

She pressed her lips together, eyes full of regret. I knew that look. That was her pity look. I steeled myself against it. "A few months ago," she began in a forced gentle voice, "Alexa told me she couldn't see herself dating someone shorter than her—"

I exploded. "And you *knew* that and still used her as a bargaining chip?"

"Finn—"

But I wasn't done. "You *knew* Alexa wouldn't go out with me. But you wanted your thing so badly—"

"No! Height difference is a stupid reason not to date someone! With a little work, I was sure I could help her see that—"

Jade was unbelievable. I folded my arms over my chest. "So you've come to tell me I'm too short for Alexa, but that won't matter once she learns about my mom. Feeling awesome. Thanks, Jade."

"Look, I'm just being honest about Naomi. I don't want to see you get hurt." She pushed my shoulder. "And I'm sorry for not telling you about what Alexa said. But I've been subtly dropping hints about all the famous couples where the woman is taller than the man—a *pile* of supermodels to start—"

I snorted.

"But for the record, Turner—who cares how tall or not tall you are? *I* certainly don't."

The coat closet suddenly felt very close. *Body, not brain*, I reminded myself, tightening my arms. My body might want to forgive Jade, but my brain—who was in charge—was furious with her.

I didn't respond.

"Whatever. We should go." She flung open the door and left me standing all alone.

⌒

After everyone helped restore the kitchen, we split off: Lula to wrap her head around dinner that evening, the downstairs folks to continue working on food service etiquette, a number of upstairs folks to run lines, and Jade, Noah, and me to the library to choreograph the fight.

On my way to the library, I saw Alexa leaning against the table in the dining room. She'd complimented my dancing. She'd laughed at my jokes. And I was playing James now. All of that was more important than whatever poison Jade had just tried to pour into my ear. I'd felt confident enough about Alexa's feelings for me that I had been planning on asking her out well before Jade offered to "help."

So I stepped inside.

"Hey," I said, determined to prove Jade wrong, but then also wishing I'd taken three more seconds to make sure my breath smelled okay. "Um, listen, stepping out of character here, but do you think, after all this is over, you'd ever want to, like, go get coffee or something? Just the two of us?"

Alexa stopped flipping through her script. She didn't meet my eyes. "Oh. I . . . I'm not really into coffee?"

"Oh. Well." I scratched the back of my neck. "It doesn't have to be *coffee*. It can be . . . anything, really."

"That's nice of you," she said, clutching the script to her chest. "But . . . I thought we were just . . . It's . . . I'm not really . . ."

Not really what? Into short guys?

"It's okay," I said, my face burning. "It's whatever."

"Okay," she said.

"Yeah . . . Thanks." *Thanks? What did I say thanks for? Why had I said anything?* Jade had *told* me she would talk me up—and now I'd blown it. But I'd blown it because Jade was in my head. She was always in my head!

"There you are," Jade said as I entered the library. I could hardly look at her. Not only because I was furious with her, but because she'd changed out of her day dress into a loose pair of white bloomers, a close-fitting white blouse over her white corset, and a blue sash around her waist. By Victorian standards, she was practically naked.

"Why are you wearing that?" I demanded.

She looked down at her ensemble. "This is standard Victorian woman calisthenics wear," she insisted. "It allows for full range of motion in the arms and legs." She demonstrated with some arm circles. "Now, Turner has combat experience," she said, returning to her agenda, "but what about you, Noah? Any stage fighting?"

"Nope!"

"No problem," Jade said. "The basic thing we have to remember is the victim—the person getting punched or strangled or whatever—is the person in control. Stage combat is stage magic. We err on the side of safety over realism every time. Turner, will you help me out? Let's start with a few basic moves."

Reluctantly, I showed Noah how to receive a stomach punch (taking your attacker's fist in your hands, bending over, your vocal reaction selling the hit), a few kinds of face slaps (clapping the victim's hand next to their own face being my favorite—the trick being the reaction again, and the sound of the victim), and getting kicked in the stomach (similar to the punch, the victim's hand thumping the floor, helping out the sound).

"Let's start with James leaping over the couch to tackle Henry," Jade suggested.

"I'm not sure that's the best place to start," I said.

"It's the first thing that happens." Jade's voice was tight.

"Sure, but—"

"Turner?"

"Yeah?"

"My rehearsal."

I seethed.

After we choreographed the tackle and ran through it a few times, Jade picked up the script. "Let's take it at half speed with the lines. I'll read Mrs. Jorgensen, Margaret, and me." She affected a Mrs. Jorgensen voice. "That's lovely, dear. Why will it be a challenge, Henry?"

I marked leaping over the couch and caught Noah-as-Henry around the waist. We slowly tumbled to the ground and counted through our wrestling moves as Jade read the lines of the women.

"Sorry, madam! Sorry!" I called out as James.

Then Noah pinned me facedown on the ground. "Permission to slug him, madam?"

"You know what?" Jade said. "Now that I see it with the lines, I think it might be more interesting if you're facing each other."

Noah hopped off of me, and I stood up. "What do you mean?"

"Here," Jade said. She took Noah's place. "Take it from the last One, Finn. If we go One, Two, Three," she said as she and I marked out the last bit of wrestling before I ended up on my stomach, "but then, instead of Four being you facedown, Finn, try Four faceup."

I lay on the ground on my back.

"I'm going to climb on top of you now," Jade said. "Cool?"

"S-sure," I said, even though I wasn't quite sure I *was* cool. After all, the last time she'd touched my stomach . . .

"So then, Noah, you'll pin him like *this*." Jade sat on me and leaned over, trapping my arms above my head, the heat from her body propelling me into flashbacks from last night. *Body, not brain, body, not brain*, I reminded myself. But then her brown eyes trapped mine, and I was lost. "You're so angry with him," she said, "but"—she smiled a little and lowered her face close to mine—"you also really want to kiss him—"

197

My chin tilted. Our breath tangled, and my heart lurched—*this was happening again.* I closed my eyes—

"But you remember just in time: He's an asshat."

Noah barked out a laugh. I blinked, blushing fire as she finished instructing Noah and shifted off of me. I couldn't believe my body had fallen for her acting. Again.

CHAPTER THIRTY

A few minutes later, I led Noah upstairs. How was I going to make it through a sure-to-be embarrassing intimacy rehearsal when I was still blushing from the combat one?

At the main staircase landing under the bank of stained glass windows, I opened a narrow door for Noah to let him outside. The sun warmed our faces, and as we climbed the steps to bring us even with the second floor, Noah gasped. "This balcony is huge! Look at that view!"

I smiled but only half-listened as Noah marveled at the white-and-tan mosaic floor tile and the backsides of the stained glass windows behind us. *Let the combat rehearsal go, Finn*, I told myself. *Who cares about Jade?*

"I'm glad you like it up here! I thought we could use some fresh air," Nomi said, clasping her hands at her waist as the circle widened to accept us. "Now. Just like theatre has fight choreographers, we also have intimacy choreographers. And as we create fights that are safe, where everyone feels as comfortable as possible, we insist on those same tenets where intimacy is concerned."

Maddie's jaw was set. Noah's hands were in his trouser pockets. Kendrick looked bored. I pressed my hands against my cheeks to cool them down.

Nomi spread her arms wide. "Let's start by splitting off to opposite sides of the balcony. I'm going to call out some questions designed to give you space to get to know each other even better than you do."

"Should we answer them as ourselves or as our characters?" Maddie asked.

"Good question," Nomi said. "As yourselves. We'll get to characters in a few minutes. First, share something with your partner that they don't know about you."

I led Noah to a corner way on the other end of the balcony and sat on the short sandstone railing. Noah stopped several feet away.

"I'll start." Noah's voice was strangled. "I'm not a big fan of being so close to—" He flicked a few fingers toward me. "A strong breeze could just, *whoop*—and you'd be—"

I coughed out a laugh and stood up. "You don't like heights," I said, striding toward him. He led me a little closer to the house. "Roger that. Let's see . . . Something you don't know about me . . ." I scanned the backyard, my gaze landing on the garage. "Did I ever tell you I didn't learn how to ride a bike until I was nine?"

"Nine? Who finally taught you?" Noah asked.

"Who *didn't* teach me is more like it. My whole family tried. Then one day Kendrick locked me in the garage with my bike and said I couldn't come out until I could ride. I'm not sure where everyone else was, but I got hungry, so . . . I figured it out."

I expected Noah to laugh, but he smiled sadly instead.

"Now," Nomi called out, "if you're ready, hold hands and share a secret—big or small."

"You start this time," Noah said.

"Big secret or small secret?"

"You have big secrets?"

I laughed a little. "Doesn't everyone?"

He shrugged. "If I have big secrets, they never last long. I always feel better when I say them out loud."

I'd told Jade my biggest secrets in the attic, and I *had* felt better.

Noah offered me his hand, and I took it. It was warm and strong and . . . comforting. My god. When was the last time I'd held the hand of a friend who wasn't a girl?

"Okay, then," I said. "Here's a big secret . . ." Haltingly, I told him about Lula's cancer and why I learned to cook and Geoffrey Thatcher dying and missing my brothers and finally the extent of the leaking roof and what I'd done to keep the water from ruining the rest of the house.

Noah tugged on my hand to invite me to sit on the tile. We arranged ourselves cross-legged, knee to knee. "That's, like, five big secrets," he marveled. "Is your mom okay now?"

I nodded.

"Good . . . Thanks for trusting me, Finn."

"Yeah."

"Feel a little better?"

"A little . . . yeah."

He smiled.

"But now it's your turn," I said. "*Huge* secret."

He laughed. "I'm not sure I have one."

"Well . . . what sad thing were you thinking about after my apparently not hilarious bike-riding story?"

One side of Noah's mouth drew up. He looked over the edge of the balcony, and his forehead tensed. I pulled at him, and we scooted even farther from the drop.

"I'm not sure it's really a secret," Noah said, "but your story made me think about how I wish I were friends with Lindsey."

"*Why?*" I blurted before I could stop myself.

Noah laughed, but there was pain in the squint of his eyes. "My best friend used to live next door. She's two years older than me, and she graduated and moved away, and she has this whole new life. Last year without her was . . . lonely. I'm kinda jealous of you and your brothers—permanent friends. I learned I don't have that with Kelly, and I definitely don't have it with Lindsey . . . Yet, anyway."

Permanent friends. That's exactly what I had with Andre and Kendrick. Even when we fought, I knew it was temporary because the three of us were bound together by our experiences and our parents and even by this house. No wonder their absence pulled at me so hard. And now Noah's attempts at mollifying his sister made more sense.

"Geez, how stupid were you and I this year?" I joked. "Your best friend gone, my brothers gone—we should have been better friends."

"Well, we can be better friends now." He squeezed my hand, and I squeezed his back. "You think Jade'll mind?"

"*Jade?*"

"It kind of seems like she's your person now."

What was wrong with everyone? "She's *not* my person."

Nomi interrupted us. "Now let's talk about nonverbal communication."

I had never been so glad to stop talking and pay attention to my mom.

CHAPTER THIRTY-ONE

Nomi circled up with the four of us on the balcony again and spread her hands. "Consent is as simple as 'Is this okay?'"

I tugged at my collar.

"Intimacy has the potential to be awkward," Nomi continued. "As we choreograph, nerves are okay. Feeling unsafe is not. I will ask you, and you will ask each other, 'Is this okay?' Got it?"

Talking to Noah had been fine—good, even. Holding his hand was nice. But the kissing was soon, and the person determining where my hands and lips would go was my *mother*.

"I'm going to start with Kendrick and Maddie. Finn and Noah, why don't you pop down a level to the first-floor terrace and run your scene up until the kissing. I'll call down for you when we're ready to switch."

Relieved we didn't have to go first, I flew with Noah toward the metal stairwell.

"So, hey," he said as we clattered down the steps to the terrace, "I was thinking we might sell the James/Henry romance more if we pick some stand-ins."

"Stand-ins?" I repeated.

"Yeah. Like, someone to imagine when you're pretending to be in love with me."

"Oh!" I jumped down the last few steps. "Good idea!" Why hadn't Andre suggested that?

"Any idea who you might pick?" he asked, leaning against the railing.

"Yeah." Here went another secret. "I've got it pretty bad for Alexa."

Noah pushed off the railing. "Really? I didn't know you liked Alexa."

"I did. Do. Shouldn't."

"Shouldn't?"

I rubbed my eyebrow. "I asked her out today, and she pretty much said she's not into short guys."

He pushed my shoulder. "She didn't!"

"She did."

"But Finn! You're such a good guy! Who cares how tall you are?"

I laughed.

"Oh my god. You're taking it a lot better than I would be."

"I didn't at first." I shrugged. "But your reaction's helping."

"Well, while you're busy being the most forgiving guy in America, if it's okay with you, maybe I'll pretend you're Jade."

My body did not like that one bit.

"Or someone else," Noah said, giving me side-eye.

"No, it's fine. You can totally pretend you're making out with Jade. What do I care?"

"You sure?"

"Absolutely." I reached for my script on the steps. *No.* I knew this scene. I set it down. *But what if*—I picked up the script again. *Finn*—

"So . . . the memorizing," Noah said, studying me. "It's . . . hard for you?"

The secrets just kept coming. I was starting to wonder why I'd kept so many. "It's not the memorizing itself. I mean, memorizing takes time, but I can totally do it. It's . . ."

"Stage fright?"

"Not really. Well . . . I don't know. I'm not afraid to dance onstage, or sing in a group. But when I have lines, there's something that happens between the memorizing and the actual delivery that feels . . . out of my hands."

"Then . . . how are you going to do this part?"

I laughed a little. "That is an excellent question. But it's got to be done."

"Why?"

I squinted at him. "Because my family is counting on me. Theatre is our thing. It's who we are."

"Do you like it?"

"I love it. I'm no good at it—"

"That's not true. You're great with the script in your hand."

I rubbed the back of my neck. "Thanks. I'm hoping this show being at my house will . . . destroy some demons or something."

"I bet it will." Noah offered me my script. "We can read the scene out loud one more time if that helps."

I took it from him. "It would. Thanks."

━━

We ran the scene four times, with me completely off book during the last two.

Noah high-fived me. "See? Demons destroyed!"

I shadowboxed the demons, and he laughed.

"Run it again?" Noah asked.

We got as far as James's line, "I came here under the *auspices* of courting a Jorgensen girl. But I actually came here . . . for you," when Nomi called down, "Let's switch!"

⌐•--

I was both more and less nervous kissing Noah this time than I'd been at that party after freshman year. Less because we were better friends now. But more because Nomi was there saying mortifying things like, "Just so we're clear, stage kisses rarely involve tongue," and "Your hips make that decision, honey, not your brain," and "The kiss is tentative at first, Finn—it asks a question. Wait until Noah's lips and hands answer. Then *really* go for it. But again—not with your tongue."

⌐•--

After several million years, Nomi pronounced us "well choreographed."

We bowed politely.

"Now let's move on to Twelve C," she said.

Wait. We were doing that one right now, too?

"The kiss in the art gallery is a quick exchange, gentlemen, but handsy."

At "handsy," I couldn't take it anymore. "You know what?" I asked. "Why don't you call Kendrick and Maddie back and do their second scene? Like you said, ours is quick. Noah and I will go down to the art gallery and figure it out ourselves. We'll talk it out first. It'll be super consent-y."

"It's fine with me," Noah said.

207

Nomi paused, consulting the clock face on a ribbon around her neck. "Okay. But I want to see it after you're done."

One minute later, we were striding down the grand hall toward the art gallery.

"I don't know how you did that," Noah said.

"What? Kiss you and make it look real?"

"No. Kiss *anyone* in front of your mom."

We were laughing as we stepped into the art gallery and found Alexa and Jade, scripts in hand.

Alexa cocked her head. "I thought Naomi was running the intimacy rehearsal."

"She was. Is," I said.

"But," Alexa continued, "didn't Noah just say you had to kiss him in front of your mom?"

I glanced at Jade. But Alexa had already turned me down. Jade was wrong. This wasn't going to change anything. "Naomi *is* my mom. Laura and Naomi both are."

Alexa gasped. "Naomi Turner is your *mom*? Laura and Naomi are *married*?"

"Yeah," I said.

"So Kendrick and Andre are—"

"My brothers. Yup."

Alexa blinked a few times. Then she said, "Oh, wow. Sorry—boy, that's a lot of embarrassing assumptions on my part all coming up at once."

"It happens," I said.

"Naomi Turner's your mom . . ."

Jade was boring holes into my skull with her eyes, but I refused to look her way.

"We've got to choreograph the kiss in Twelve C," Noah said. "Do you two mind—"

Jade waved a hand. "We're just running lines. Go ahead."

"No," I said. "Can you please go somewhere else?"

Jade raised an eyebrow. "We got here first."

"But you're just running lines. You can do that anywhere. We need *this* space."

"It's fine," Noah said, touching my arm.

"See?" Jade picked up her script.

I looked up at Noah to protest, but he leaned in. "I have an idea that might help things with Alexa. Trust me?"

Help things with Alexa? "Uh, sure."

With his full voice, Noah said, "Let's take the lines and blocking from—" He pointed at the script, partway through our scene. "Here? On book?"

"Sure."

The girls sounded like they were running their parlor scene. I tried to ignore them as Noah and I took our places: me facing the brass railing in front of that painting of a large ship, Noah a few feet behind me.

"Jamie—" Noah as Henry pleaded.

I ran my fingers through my hair. "Dammit, Henry."

Even though I couldn't see him, I knew Noah was approaching me. "What?"

"I'm already wrecked, Hen. But when you call me Jamie . . . I'm undone."

209

Noah touched my back, and as James, I flinched. "Listen," Noah as Henry said. "If you'd stop talking for one minute, I'd be able to explain."

I laughed mirthlessly. "Explain why you're staying here with the horses?"

"No. Explain why I'm going . . . and why I want you to come with me."

Still facing the railing, I repeated, "Come with you."

"Yes."

I turned around. "Yes."

Noah as Henry laughed. "But I haven't even told you—"

"Yes."

"Jamie, let me finish."

"Keep calling me Jamie, and I will do whatever you want."

Noah laughed a little. "If you hate law school—"

"And I do."

"Then . . . I have a little money saved up."

"Which we will use toward . . ."

"Running a posting inn in California? Together?"

"A posting inn?"

Noah smiled for the first time in the scene. "Your business acumen, my knowledge of horses, if we can—"

I gestured to the door. "Let's leave. Right now."

Noah as Henry laughed. "I don't have enough money to buy a posting inn in California *yet*."

"But you want to. You want me."

"*Yes.* Cook was murdered, and it made me realize life can be so fleeting. I want to spend whatever time I've got with you. If you'll have me . . . Jamie."

"Oh," I breathed as James. "I'll have you."

Noah had one more line, and then he was supposed to press me up against the column by the organ and kiss me. But it hadn't been choreographed yet. I was all ready to break character, but Noah held my eyes. "Stay in it," he whispered so only I could hear him. "I'm going to push your shoulder and walk you backward. Keep your head forward so it doesn't smack into the column. I'll say the line, then I'm going to cup your head and kiss you. Okay?" He took my script and dropped it on the organ bench.

"Okay." It was fine with me, but why weren't we just stopping?

"Forgive me," Noah said as Henry, his voice back at full volume, "but I—"

He did just as he said he would: pushed my shoulder so I took several quick steps backward, and thudded me up against the column. Then Noah as Henry gathered my head in his hands. I closed my eyes and gripped his wrists as he kissed me like I was the only person he'd ever wanted. Like I was water in the desert. Like kissing me would save his life. After breaking the kiss, he winked at me as Noah and strode out of the room as Henry.

When he was gone, I had a perfect view of Alexa and Jade, who had stopped rehearsing. And who were both staring. At me.

CHAPTER THIRTY-TWO

I stepped away from the column, and Noah popped his head back into the art gallery. "Did that work for you?"

"I'm not sure I made any decisions from my hips," I joked, "but it worked."

"What did you think?" Noah asked the girls. "Was it believable?"

Jade and Alexa seemed to be in some sort of daze. Finally, Jade said, "It . . . looked . . . good. To me. Lex?"

Alexa jerked her head in Jade's direction, then back to Noah and me. "Yeah . . . good."

"Great," Noah said. "Then we'll see you later."

"You don't—" Jade stuttered. "Don't you—Shouldn't you run it again?"

"Naw, we've got it," Noah said. "Ready to show your mom?" he asked me.

Noah was up to something, but I wasn't sure what. "Sure."

A few steps into the parlor, I started to ask, "What—" but he shook his head and whispered, "Outside."

Then Noah opened the door onto the terrace. "This might be terrible of me," he said, "but when you said Alexa didn't want to go out with you, I thought, 'What if I brought the heat?' She might imagine herself as me. Or short of that, she might think us kissing was hot. And that might work in your favor, too . . . Is that bad of me?"

"I mean, I originally thought seeing me kissing a guy would make her unable to picture me kissing girls. But if the reverse is true . . . I guess I'll take it."

"Well," Noah said, "the opportunity presented itself and . . . we're friends."

"Yeah." I clapped a hand on his back. "We're friends."

<hr>

After Noah and my choreography was approved by Nomi (with minimal embarrassing comments this time), Noah trotted down the stairs calling, "See you later, James. Have fun working on lines in your *new room*!"

"Ha! Thanks!" I took the stairs two at a time up to the second floor. But the smile fell off my face when I swung open James's bedroom door and found an unexpected guest sitting on my window seat.

I yanked the door closed behind me. "Jade, what are you doing here?" I hissed.

"I'm—"

"Victorian rules."

"The—"

"And Mr. Hoyt's bedroom is literally down the hall."

"I know, but—"

"I thought you were—"

"*Will you just listen to me?*" she demanded. "You have two days left to learn your lines, and then it's opening night. That scene with

213

Noah looked great, but you're not off book for the rest of it yet. Are you?"

"Mostly—"

She stood up from the window seat and smoothed her skirts. "Well, until you're one hundred percent ready, you're useless to me hunting for the necklace. And you're not going to have time to make any headway with Alexa, either."

I stuck my hands in my pockets and leaned against the fireplace mantel. "It doesn't matter anyway. I asked her out already, and she said no." I studied Jade's face for her reaction, but she didn't even blink.

"There's still the necklace to find," she said. "And to even have a *chance* of getting into Lab, you have to prove you can do this part first." She pointed at the desk between the windows. "Sit."

<hr />

We started with Scene Seven A. First, we read the lines out loud. Then I wrote them over and over at the desk for fifteen minutes. Then we read them out loud one more time. Finally, I set down the script.

"Ready?" Jade asked.

"Yeah. I did this scene earlier with Noah, and it went okay."

"Great. Then it should be a cakewalk. Let's do it." Jade cleared her throat and stood at the foot of my bed. "Good god, have you been running for sport?" she asked in a monotone voice.

"Sometimes," I said, standing at the desk, also in monotone. "To clear my head."

"Well?" she asked.

"Well what?"

"Why'd you attack me?"

I paused, fishing for the line in my brain.

But it was gone.

I tried to visualize the words on the page. But Lula's and Nomi's disappointed faces flashed like a strobe light instead. Then jerking images of Kendrick's smirk alternated with Andre's devasted frown. None of them looked surprised.

I faced the window and clenched my jaw.

"Maybe we try it with blocking." Jade's voice sounded like it was coming from far away.

Everyone was counting on me.

I couldn't let them down again.

I had to keep it together.

I *would* keep it together.

But then Jade touched my shoulder. "Finn." Her voice was gentle but firm as she led my shaking body to the bed. "You can do this."

"No, I can't." Panic roiled in my stomach. She tugged me to sit down next to her, and I pressed my palms into my thighs.

"Why not?"

"It'll happen again."

"What will happen?"

I shook my head.

She scooped one of my hands into her lap and held it tight. "Talk to me, Finn. What will happen again?"

I did not want to go back there, but I ground out, "The one-act competition."

Her voice changed from sympathetic to curious. "Which year?"

"Sophomore. I forgot my lines at State and we lost."

Her voice returned to sympathetic again. "Oh, Finn—"

But I didn't want her sympathy. "Nationals was at the Kennedy Center and it was Kendrick and Andre's senior year, and Jade, the looks on their faces—"

She tugged on my hand. "You are not the reason we lost."

"Sure I am. I couldn't remember my line and it was like crickets for*ever*."

"People forget lines! It happens! No one saved you—do you blame the rest of the cast?"

"No. It was *my*—"

"Finn—"

"Jade, I let everyone down."

She hauled me to my feet and gripped my arms, her eyes locked on mine. "Listen to me. You did not let everyone down. And even if you did—which you didn't—it doesn't mean you're going to do it again. The past doesn't have to dictate the future."

I chewed on my lips.

"I didn't even know you still *thought* about that day. No one else does."

I wasn't convinced that was true. Mr. Hoyt didn't cast me in the one-act play last year, after all.

"But now I get why you write your lines on your props."

"Like I said . . . insurance."

She dropped my arms. "Well, this is good news, actually."

"*How?*"

"Now we know what your deal with lines is: It's a mental block."

I blinked at her. "A mental block."

"Yeah. Baseball players get the yips. Gymnasts get the twisties. Actors get mental blocks. But we can work through it. We'll get you so memorized and so confident, you'll be able to do James's lines in your sleep. Then, on the heels of that success, you'll feel invincible again and you'll get into Acting Lab, and then you'll be such a cocky, memorized-line-delivery superstar, you'll be like, 'Watch me recite

"The Jabberwocky"! Here are twelve Italian sonnets I learned this morning! Who wants to hear *Beowulf* in Old English?'"

A laugh escaped my throat.

"Look," she said, scrunching her accordion nose at me. "Your parents are supersmart."

"I never said they were—"

"So you can do this," she said. "Because your supersmart parents believe you can." She tugged on the lapels of my jacket and swept imaginary dust off my shoulders. "I believe you can, too." My heart started thudding in my chest. "And no one has to remind you how smart I am."

I smiled.

"Can we meet somewhere tonight?" she asked. "To work on your lines?"

"Don't we already have our nightly meeting in the coat closet?"

"Oh . . . right."

I covered my mouth with a theatrical hand. "Jade Montgomery, did you forget about the necklace for a quarter of one whole second?"

The sound of her laughter felt like a reward. I was still grinning when her face flashed concern. "Finn . . ."

Jade and I were standing so close to each other now. I wasn't sure when or how that had happened. Her breath smelled like ginger. Would she taste like ginger if I kissed her again?

I blushed. *Calm down, body.*

I took a step back and crossed my arms over my chest. "What is it?"

She blinked twice. "We should go. We've got dance rehearsal soon."

Then someone knocked at the door. We both froze.

"Bathroom," we whispered in unison.

"Wait," I hissed, "me or you?"

She looked at me like I had just asked her how many heads I had. "Me," she whispered. "This is *your* room."

I threw her a disgusted look to cover my embarrassment and crossed the hardwood floor to the bathroom door in five steps. We reached for the doorknob at the same time and glared at each other. Then we both reached for it again. She threw her hands back in a mock *Go ahead!*

Someone knocked harder.

I yanked open the bathroom door and bowed at the waist as she scoffed at me, hurrying inside.

Another knock.

After running back across the room and double-checking Jade was hidden, I forced myself to take a slow, deep breath, then opened the door into the hall.

"Good afternoon, James," Mr. Hoyt said. "I thought I heard your voice and wanted to make sure you weren't late for dance rehearsal. Running lines in there?"

"Oh! Yes, sir."

He grunted. "I've been looking for Elizabeth. Have you seen her recently?"

I knew I was blushing. "I—I'm sure she's around," I said. "She was rehearsing with Miss Jorgensen in the art gallery earlier." *And then she was in my bedroom*, but I definitely wasn't going to tell him that part.

"How are your lines coming along?" Mr. Hoyt asked as we approached the central stairs.

"Terrific," I said. *Mostly*, I thought.

"Plenty of focused practice plus hard work is the recipe for success," Mr. Hoyt said.

I wanted to defend myself. But what was worse—a Mr. Hoyt who believed if I worked harder I could be like my brothers and moms, or a Mr. Hoyt who knew I worked hard but believed something was broken in my brain?

I stuffed it all down. "Yes, Mr. Jorgensen. Focused practice and hard work for sure, sir."

CHAPTER THIRTY-THREE

The cast was milling around the grand hall when Mr. Hoyt and I reached the bottom of the staircase.

"Where are Elizabeth and Margaret?" Nomi asked me.

I tried to fix an innocent look on my face as I crossed over to her. "I know they agreed to make up a story to go along with the slides for the magic lantern show," I said. *Technically true.*

Alexa hurried down the steps, smiling at Nomi, but Nomi's attention was drawn away by the sound of Jade's voice.

"Sorry I'm late!" she called, flying down the stairs two at a time. Jade was never late. But she'd had to wait until Mr. Hoyt and I were out of sight, and then, apparently, Alexa, too.

"Decorum, Elizabeth," Mr. Hoyt scolded her. "How many times must I remind you that you are a young woman and not a racehorse?"

Jade slowed down. When she reached me, I tried to catch her eye to commiserate, but she blew past me and crossed right over to Kendrick, her dance partner.

Something twinged in my chest. But I knew the reason Jade wouldn't look at me was because Mr. Hoyt had just reprimanded her—she needed to stay in character. Still.

But then Nomi said, "Laura is . . . busy in the kitchen," and my heart lurched. "So I'm going to run dance rehearsal. Couples, please pair up. Jeremiah, are you ready on the organ?"

"Mom," I whispered, "should I check on her?"

Nomi shook her head. "Lula seems determined to do everything herself. Her exact words were, 'If I beat cancer, I can cook a damned chicken.'"

I laughed. Nomi wiggled her eyebrows at me. "Go dance."

Grinning, I let Alexa pull me into the south alcove beside the stairs, away from the other dancers.

The walls reverberated with the opening notes of Magnus's waltz, and I led Alexa in neat circles.

"I really like dancing with you," she said.

"Oh. Thanks!" I replied.

"You're so confident," Alexa said. "Very . . . masculine."

I looked up at her. "Is that a surprise?"

"A surprise?"

"That there's something masculine about me?"

"No! I was just . . . paying you a compliment."

I waltzed us out of the alcove into the grand hall near the others.

"Listen, Finn," she said, "I've been feeling badly about earlier when you asked me to go out for coffee. You caught me off guard."

"Off guard?"

"Yeah. And I just wanted to say that I hope you're not mad at me. Because the thing is, I've been thinking about it, and if the offer's still on the table, I'd like to get that coffee. Or, whatever the Victorian equivalent is while we're still here at the house."

I stared at her. Alexa saying yes to going out with me was what I wanted. So why did it feel so wrong?

"You *are* mad."

I pressed my lips together. "I'm not. Confused, maybe."

"Confused?"

What was there to lose? "Sure. I mean, look at it from my perspective: You turned me down, found out Naomi Turner was my mom, and now you're suddenly like, 'Hey! Maybe you're not so bad and short after all, Finn!'"

She stopped dancing. "That's an awful thing to say."

I dropped my arms. "That's what it looks like."

"I don't *care* that you're shorter than me."

"Okay."

"I *don't*. It . . . maybe it used to be true, but that was before I got to know you. And the thing about Naomi is a coincidence." She held up her hands again in dancing position. "I promise."

I didn't really believe her, but I stepped in, and we resumed waltzing.

Nomi had been circulating, adjusting arms and slowing the steps down for folks who needed it. Now she approached the two of us. "This is beautiful. You look very sweet together."

Alexa flashed a smile at Nomi. When my mom was out of earshot, Alexa leaned down and whispered, "See? We look very sweet together . . . You're a nice guy, Finn. I'd like a chance to get to know you better. Isn't that what you were hoping for with me?"

"I mean, s-sure." *But—*

"Those who want me to go over the steps again," Nomi called, "come over here. Everyone else, take five."

Kendrick and Jade walked arm in arm toward Alexa and me and my shoulders relaxed. Jade would save me from this spiraling awkwardness.

"Did you know that Finn got the high score in our class on the final in calculus this spring?" she asked the group.

I stared at her. What was she doing?

"Really?" Alexa and Kendrick asked. But Alexa's "really" was one of shock, and Kendrick's was one of boredom.

"Yeah," I said. "But it was only because of Jade's study group."

"His foods teacher also said he should have tried out for Teen Chef Cook-off this winter."

"Why didn't you do it?" Alexa asked.

"Probably because our mom had can—" Kendrick began, but I interrupted him loudly. "We were busy with the house."

He shot me a look. "Well, speaking of things Finn has done, he was still wetting the bed in third grade."

I blushed and shot fire out of my eyes. I wanted to retort back, but my brain was busy envisioning all the ways I could murder him.

"Um," Alexa said, slipping her hand into Jade's arm, "maybe we should go check with Maddie on how her 'conversation' went." Alexa winked at me, then she and Jade curtsied and left the group.

"What the hell are you doing?" I said through clenched teeth.

"I'm just teasing you," Kendrick said. "Who cares? Or do you actually have a thing for Jade again?"

"*No.*"

"Alexa then? But she's, like, a *lot* taller than you."

My body vibrated with anger. At the same time, something else vibrated in Kendrick's pocket. He slid his hand inside to silence it.

"You too?" I bit out.

"I have a very hot boyfriend, Finn. Look, if it helps, I can let it drop in future conversations with Alexa that you haven't wet the bed in years." Kendrick smirked. "Excuse me." He bowed slightly and disappeared into the library.

He was lucky I wasn't the cook. Even though he was my brother, I wasn't above spitting in his food.

CHAPTER THIRTY-FOUR

Waiting for dinner to be served a half hour later in the breakfast room, I slumped in my hardback chair and stared at the silverware. There was nowhere else to look. Mr. Hoyt made me feel inadequate, Kendrick made me feel angry, Alexa made me feel weird, and with Mr. Hoyt around, Jade was still being super in character and wouldn't look at me. That left Nomi, but she wasn't at the table yet.

The silverware was pretty interesting, though. It was actual silver. The polished handle featured a loopy *J* for Jorgensen. A lot of the furniture and paintings had been taken by Millie Jorgensen's nieces and nephews when she died, but somehow the silver had been missed.

So here I was, more than one hundred years later, using the same Victorian fork that had fed the actual Victorian Jorgensens.

Jade would love to know that. When my eyes tried catching hers across the table from me, however, they were focused on her lap. No matter how hard I stared at her, she didn't look up. Mr. Hoyt's reprimand really must have rattled her. I gazed over her shoulder and studied the sea-foam textured wall covering.

My stomach rumbled. Where was the food? And where was Nomi?

"Do you think you should go down there and see what's going on?" Alexa asked.

"Me?" I asked, my eyes flicking down the table to gauge Mr. Hoyt's reaction to Alexa's out-of-character query. "That seems highly improper, doesn't it? A houseguest going downstairs to check on—"

"Your parents need you, Finn," Mr. Hoyt said.

My lips twitched. Why did Mr. Hoyt get to be the one who decided when we were all in character and when we weren't? I forced my face into a neutral expression. "As you wish."

I crossed the room and opened the door that led to the servants' staircase. As I descended the narrow steps, the atmosphere felt increasingly eerie. There was a clatter of pots and dishes but no voices.

In the servants' dining hall, Joan Dooley, Martin Lord, Noah, Lindsey, Magnus, Maddie, and Nomi were all facing the closed kitchen door, their bodies alert but silent.

"What's going on?" I whispered.

Nomi put an arm around my shoulders. "There's a problem with the chicken. It's burned on the outside and raw on the inside."

"Oh. She must have tried to roast it. The oven was just too hot," I said. "We can cut up the raw part and sauté it in a pan."

Nomi smoothed my hair and kissed my head. "Yes, well, Lula is not exactly . . . open . . . to suggestions right now."

"Ah," I said.

"Why not?" Magnus asked.

I licked my lips. "Sometimes she gets . . ."

"Willful?" Nomi finished for me. "She feels terrible about how the cook treated you all, so now she's insisting on doing everything herself."

We heard a string of curse words, feet running across the hardwood floor, and a squeak as the spigot turned on and water rushed out of it.

"Sounds like she burned herself." I grimaced. Nomi took a step toward the kitchen, but I grabbed her hand.

"Jeremiah!" Lula demanded. "Mr. Lord! The food is ready!"

"Coming!" they called.

Joan Dooley swept over to Nomi and me. "Better get upstairs, loves," she chirped.

Nomi and I climbed the steps in silence. This whole cook/kitchen thing was eating at me. I'd been spilling everything else lately; why not confess my guilt, too? "Mom?" I asked, just before she opened the door back into the breakfast room.

"What's up, Finnster?"

I smiled a little at the endearment. "Should I have taken the cook job? Am I being selfish playing James?"

To Nomi's credit, she paused and thought about the questions. "Would it have made our lives easier for the immediate future?" she asked. "Sure. But if James opens doors for you that so far have remained closed, you get to fight for that."

"But . . . what if we lose the house?"

For the second time that night she smoothed my hair. "You held us together this year with your buckets and the cooking and no one to help you." She wrapped her arms around me. "I'm sorry we needed you like that. But your moms have got this, honey. You just focus on your part."

I returned her hug, breathing in roses. "Thanks." There was still a weight on my shoulders, but it felt a little lighter.

"Say," she said, "is there something going on between you and—"

Feet thundered up the stairs.

"Later," she whispered, opening the door into the breakfast room. Nomi and I took our seats. I was grateful dinner was on its way, but I also kind of wished I knew who Nomi was going to ask me about.

"Is everything—" Mr. Hoyt began, but Magnus flew through the door carrying a platter. Martin Lord and a soup tureen followed several sure steps behind him.

"Mrs. Turner *says* the chicken is fine," Magnus hissed. "And I don't know how to say this in Victorian, but it's *not* fine. It's hella raw. Don't. Eat. The chicken."

"The cold soup appears edible," Martin muttered, setting the tureen on the table, "if you enjoy cold soup."

We sat stunned for a moment. Then, in unison, everyone's heads swiveled my way.

"Can you think of anything we have downstairs to . . . augment this meal?" Nomi asked me.

The contents of cold storage materialized in my mind. "Taking into account what we've eaten so far . . . there should still be bread, butter, and a couple blocks of cheese."

Nomi nodded at Martin and Magnus. "Can you two sneak that up?"

"Certainly," Mr. Lord said. "Jeremiah, can you create a diversion?"

Magnus grinned. "Does the Pope have a dope-ass hat?"

Mr. Hoyt coughed.

Magnus's face grew serious. "I mean, does the Pope have a Catholic-ass hat?"

Jade and I snorted, then caught each other's eye. My heart leaped. But then she looked away and went back to being Miss Elizabeth Jorgensen. I chewed on my lip.

"Let's go, Lordy," Magnus said, and swept Martin down the stairs.

"In the meantime, what are we supposed to do with this raw"— Alexa poked a fork at the pink meat on the plate—"and also burned in places chicken?"

"Raw chicken is a salmonella disaster waiting to happen," I said. "Be careful not to touch it or eat anything that has touched it. Like, don't eat anything with that fork now, Alexa."

Whoops. I waited for Mr. Hoyt to correct me that she was Miss Jorgensen, but he remained silent.

"We could sneak it into the neighbor's garbage," Jade suggested.

"I don't know," Nomi said.

I leaned forward and plucked the flowers out of the enormous vase in the middle of the table. "In here. I'll take care of it after dinner."

We each took a piece of chicken, moved it around on our plate with utensils to make it look like we'd eaten, then stood and scraped it into the vase.

"Let's make a pile of these plates and the silverware that touched the chicken," I suggested. "Then we can deliver them into the butler's pantry and wash our hands."

A few minutes later, raw chicken in the vase, dishes in the pantry, and hands freshly scrubbed, we sat back at the table facing our second challenge of this meal.

"It's strawberry rhubarb soup," I said as Nomi lifted the lid from the ceramic tureen, "a Norwegian recipe. It *is* supposed to be served cold, actually. But it's also supposed to be for dessert."

"*I* certainly don't mind dessert first," Jade said. She ladled soup into her bowl.

"Neither do I," Alexa agreed, and shared one of her crooked smiles with me.

I dropped my eyes to avoid responding to it, and my gaze landed on the red soup with green flecks—that were now on their way to Jade's mouth. "Stop!"

She jerked, and the soup spilled off her spoon onto the linen tablecloth.

Stumbling out of my chair, I crossed to the tureen and ladled through it. Diced up bits of foliage floated among the berries. "Oh, no. She used must have used rhubarb leaves instead of the stalk, which is the part we eat. The leaves are poisonous."

"Poisonous?" Alexa echoed.

"Did you get any in your mouth? Are you okay?" I asked Jade, scanning her face.

"I'm fine, Finn," she said.

"Into the vase?" Mr. Hoyt asked.

I pulled my attention away from Jade. "Yeah. Yes."

For the second time, we dirtied our dishes, then stood and dumped our food.

My stomach grumbled again.

"This is dumb," Kendrick muttered. I hated to admit it, but he wasn't wrong.

Panting, Martin Lord stumbled through the door and unceremoniously dumped two loaves of bread and a paper bag onto the table. "I'm ever so sorry. It's a bit of a . . . cock-up down there."

Everyone stared at the meager meal. Finally, I reached over and tore off a hunk of the bread and passed it to Jade. Then I shook the bag. "These walnuts have been toasted, and the bread is sourdough," I said. "Let's dig in."

After a few moments of silent chewing, Kendrick admitted, "The walnuts are really good."

"Thanks." I glanced at him, surprised.

"I didn't know they could taste this good," Kendrick went on. "Where did you learn how to make them like this?"

This was out of character talk for sure. But Mr. Hoyt seemed interested.

"Foods class? And YouTube. And *The Great British Baking Show*."

"The bread's delicious," Alexa added.

"How old is your sourdough starter?" Mr. Hoyt asked.

As I answered Mr. Hoyt, Alexa kicked me under the table and smiled a tiny smile at me.

I smiled a tiny smile back. But when attention shifted to Mr. Hoyt as he told us a story about some member of his family bringing a sourdough starter over on the Mayflower, my eyes kept flicking over to Jade. She still wouldn't look back.

Still. In an hour, we'd meet under the stairs to go over my lines. Then I could tell her how impressed I was by her in-character concentration. And about Kendrick's contraband cell phone. And going downstairs to check on Lula and what Nomi had said about it being okay that I was playing James and not being the cook and—well— there'd be time to tell her everything.

CHAPTER THIRTY-FIVE

I was early meeting Jade.

Grinning, I opened the stained glass door under the stairs, script in hand, but the long, narrow closet stood empty.

Evening June light shone bright through the red glass, coloring the floorboards. I clicked the door closed behind me and wrapped a finger over one of the coat hooks. Where was she? The soup hadn't managed to make her sick after all, had it?

The stairs creaked above me—there she was. I couldn't wait to see her.

I shook my head to clear the thought. But it came right back. *I couldn't wait to see her.* I couldn't wait to see her? That suspiciously sounded like my brain talking to me.

I wiped my sweaty palms on my trousers and shook my head again. Impossible. Jade was body not brain. Never the twain shall meet.

But then the thought rose up again: *I couldn't wait to see her.* My stupid heart started thudding.

I stared at the hook on the wall. If anyone else had been making my brain and body go through this circus, I'd swear I had a crush on them. But this was Jade we were talking about. *Jade.* Who drove me crazy and was always right and who knew my biggest secrets and made me laugh the hardest and who I wanted to talk to about everything and needed to kiss again as soon as possible and—

Oh my god.

Oh my *god.* I covered my mouth to muffle a laugh. My brain had betrayed me and we were going to have to have a serious talk later, but I kind of didn't care right now because Jade was about to open the door and *I couldn't wait to see her.*

But a few seconds later, I had to act my brains out to keep the grin on my face.

"Fancy seeing you here," Alexa said. She closed the door behind her. "This is cozy."

No words. Just heavy body. Just thick throat. Why was she here? Where was Jade?

Alexa played with a ribbon on her dress. "Jade sent me."

Jade had *sent* her? "I—" I managed to sputter, torn between dismay at Jade's replacement and relief I hadn't blubbered all over the place to her when she clearly didn't feel the same way.

"I'm here to help you with your lines."

I blushed. How had I been so off base? "S-sure. Let's go to the library. It's a lot more comfortable in there."

"But here we don't have to stay in character."

"True, but—"

She held out her hand. "Just give me your script."

I hesitated for a moment, then handed it over.

Then, for the next half hour, we sat on the floor and ran lines.

"Okay. Scene Fourteen!" she exclaimed after a while. "You're doing really well, Finn!"

I wasn't, though. There were so many holes in so many scenes. And not being able to stop thinking about Jade sure wasn't helping.

She held out her hand. "Time for a break. Let's dance."

"Wh-what?"

"Come *on*." She hauled me to my feet. "Scene Fourteen is dancing, and you're such a good dancer. Dance with me. It'll clear your brain."

"It's too small to waltz in here."

"Then just sway." She put her hands on my shoulders. When I didn't respond immediately, she placed my hands on her waist. "Sway, Finn," she insisted.

So I swayed, and our shoes scuffed on the floor. "I know my lines are rough," I said. "You don't have to pretend I'm doing well."

"They're a little rough. But of course they are—you just got your part yesterday."

"Right." *Right!* I let myself relax a little, and she stepped in closer, linking her hands behind my neck.

I knew what I was supposed to feel, Alexa's body inches from mine. And it wasn't unpleasant, but I couldn't stop wishing she was—

"Finn?"

"Yeah?"

"Listen, I saw your Lab audition. And I noticed your cues on your props during *Drowsy*."

I stiffened. And not in the good way.

"So I want you to know that I'm a good improviser. If you forget your lines in our scenes together, don't worry. I've got your back."

I met her eyes. "That's . . . that's really nice of you, Alexa."

"Well, we Acting Lab rejects have to stick together."

I laughed a little. "Listen, I know why Mr. Hoyt didn't put me in there, but why didn't you get in? Did you kill his dog or something?"

She laughed, too. "No, but I think I figured it out."

"Yeah?"

"Yeah." She led me in a circle. "Now that I see how intense he is acting in this show, I'm wondering if the reason I didn't get into Lab was because I asked him if anyone ever did sports and theatre at the same time."

My eyes widened. "You asked him that?"

She made a face. "I swam at my old school. Swimming's in the fall. I think he thinks I'm not totally serious about being an actor."

"Well, are you?"

Now she stiffened. "Totally. This is one hundred percent what I want to do. More than anything." She shrugged. "But work/life balance, man. I like swimming, too."

Did people ever do sports and theatre? What kind of question was that to ask Mr. Hoyt? It was definitely why she hadn't gotten in. "I'll try to put in a good word for you with him about how dedicated you are."

Her eyes softened. "Thanks, Finn. You really are one of the good ones."

"Oh. Well. Thanks. But, you're also looking out for me, Alexa. That makes you one of the good ones, too."

She chuckled and dropped her eyes. Then she met mine again. "You want to make out?"

CHAPTER THIRTY-SIX

Twenty minutes later, I stumbled back upstairs, struggling to figure out how I felt about what had just happened.

Because I'd kissed Alexa. Kissed her. Kissed *Alexa*. And it had been . . . ?

Halfway to James's room, I remembered I hadn't moved out of the gatehouse yet, so I jogged back down the steps, through the first floor, out the main entrance, and across the driveway.

When I yanked open the door to the gatehouse, Noah was reading on the bed under the window.

"Hey," Noah said, marking his place in the book. He sat up. "How you doing?"

I glanced up the stairs. "Is Magnus here?"

"No. He's off somewhere with Maddie."

"Is that . . . working out?"

He leaned against the window. "If you want to know the status of the jumbo box of condoms, I think at this point it's still factory sealed. But Magnus seems into it. So. Did Alexa pounce after our rehearsal or what?"

"Um . . ." I flopped onto the foot of his bed. "Yes, actually."

"*Seriously?*"

"Yup. We met under the staircase after dinner. Worked on my lines. Danced a little. Then she asked me if I wanted to make out, and—"

"Nice!" Noah offered me a high five.

I slapped his palm, but he cocked his head. "You don't seem very excited."

"It was . . ."

"Oh, no. Worse than kissing me?"

I laughed. "I mean, this thing with Alexa should have been amazing. But . . ."

"You just weren't feeling it?"

I shifted on the bed and tucked up a knee so I was facing him. "No. But then, to make matters worse, she found a step stool in the corner and backed me up onto it."

"She *didn't*."

I dropped my head in my hands.

"Oh, Finn . . . Well, at least now you know."

I lifted my head. "Know?"

"That it isn't Alexa. Maybe it's Jade after all."

I blushed and lurched off the bed. "Jade doesn't like me."

"Uh, Finn—"

"Trust me. She and I were supposed to meet tonight, and she sent Alexa instead. So. It's not even . . . a discussion."

"But—"

I backed up toward the stairs. "I'm going to go and pack my stuff so you can have my room." I smacked my heel against the bottom step and fell back on my butt.

"Are you okay?"

I pulled myself up before Noah could stand. "I'm fine." Spinning around, I took the steps two at a time. Why was this so hard? For the past five years, Jade hadn't made a secret of disliking me. Did I really think one session of fake kissing in the attic and a couple deep conversations could change that?

From how stupid my body felt, I guessed I had.

"Hey," Noah called from the first floor. "Do you want me to tell you why I think Jade likes you?"

I hesitated on the landing, something fluttering in my stomach. I covered it with my hands. "I mean . . . if you want to. For the record," I said. "Even though she doesn't."

"Sure. Purely for the record."

As I descended the stairs, Noah smiled up at me and dropped his book onto the bed. "Reason one: She always knows where you are in a room. It's like you're a . . . lighthouse, and she's a ship, and the only way she wants to navigate the harbor is with you in sight."

I shook my head. "I mean, that's really beautiful, but—"

"Two, she talks about you constantly when you're not around."

"To complain about me?"

He laughed. "Sometimes. But only once she's realized she's told too many stories in a row that paint you in a good light."

"Okay, well, I—okay." I sunk back onto the bed.

"Three, she touches you every chance she gets."

"We're theatre people—"

"Finn. She tagged me out to *crawl on top of you* during stage-combat rehearsal." He kicked me a little. "You think she would have done that with Magnus? Or one of your brothers?"

"I don't know! Maybe!"

"Well, none of it matters, anyway. Because you don't like her back. Right?"

Moaning, I slipped off the bed and flumped flat on the floor like a sea star.

He peered over the bed at me, a half-smile on his face. "You want advice or commiseration?"

"Oh, god, advice."

"Tell her how you feel."

I banged my head against the floor. "I was going to do that tonight under the stairs. But then she sent Alexa. If she likes me so much, why did she do that?"

"Because she doesn't have anyone to translate Finn actions into sense for her. Alexa's her closest friend here, and Jade's operating instructions have been to hook her up with you."

I guessed . . . that made sense. I squinted at Noah. "You really think—"

"I *really* do. Everyone does. It's all the servant staff talks about."

I pushed myself up on an elbow. "Really?"

"Joan Dooley in particular is shipping you two *hard*."

I laughed out loud. But then I groaned, thumping back onto the floor. "I just realized that if I tell Jade how I feel about her, I have to tell her I kissed Alexa. *Why did I kiss Alexa?*"

Noah shrugged. "We're all fools in love. Isn't that Shakespeare or something?"

"It's Jane Austen. Jade loves Jane Austen."

"Does she now."

I ignored the jibe. "What am I going to do?"

"About Jade and Alexa?"

I sat up and crossed my legs. "Just add it to the list. Playing James. Apparently I have a mental block. My mom. She's a disaster in the kitchen and too concerned about being a burden to ask for help. Alexa thinks we're . . . something, even though I don't want to be. But she said she'd have my back during our scenes, and I definitely need that. So I have to tiptoe around letting her down gently. And if Jade really—"

"Likes you? She does."

Hope knocked a dent out of my chest. "So if . . . that's ever going to be a thing, I have to get to her before Alexa does. Because Alexa is definitely going to tell her—"

"Then go!" Noah exclaimed. He held out a hand and pulled me to standing. "I'll pack up your stuff and drop it in your room. That's within the bounds of my job . . . well, *a* job."

I laughed. "You really think I should? Like, really really?"

"I really really do."

"And you're positive she likes me back?"

"Finn, I wouldn't knowingly send you into a den of lions. Or a pit of vipers. Or . . . to her, which is basically the same thing. I promise. She likes you back."

"Okay. Okay. Hey, Noah?"

"Yeah?"

"I'm lucky you're my friend."

"That you are. But trust me—I'm lucky, too."

To avoid Mr. Hoyt on my way to the third floor, I took the servants' staircase. Pausing for a moment at the door into the hall, I caught my breath and rehearsed my speech. *Jade, I have something to tell you. A bad thing. But it leads to a good thing. At least I hope you think it's a good thing. Which one of those things do you want first?* I ran a hand through my hair. It wasn't a very good speech. But time was of the essence.

I pushed the door open a crack and peered into the servants' wing. Voices were coming from the bedrooms, but as long as I stuck to the carpet, the brick and steel floors would keep those voices from realizing I was there.

I looked at my watch. Nine p.m. Curfew was soon. It was now or never.

I slipped through the servants' wing and tiptoed down the hall that led to Jade's bedroom. Taking a deep breath, I knocked as quietly as I could.

The door cracked open.

"Jade?" I asked.

"Come in," she said, swinging the door wider.

I stepped into her room and put a hand on the fireplace mantel, ready to launch into my speech, but movement caught my eye. I swallowed a groan: Alexa was sitting cross-legged on Jade's bed.

"Hi!" Alexa chirped.

"Hey." I found Jade's face, but she wouldn't look at me. She knew I'd kissed Alexa. Of course Alexa would have told her immediately.

"Sounds like you had a nice time under the stairs," Jade said. She tightened her dressing gown belt and perched next to Alexa on the bed. Then she smiled at her.

"Yeah." *Keep talking, Finn.* "Uh . . . some good line rehearsing."

Jade paused long enough to let me know she knew I was omitting a very important under-the-staircase activity. "Glad to hear it."

"Same time tomorrow?" Alexa asked.

"Oh, uh . . ." The last time I felt this dead inside was when I'd bombed my Acting Lab audition. "Actually, Jade and I were going to talk about—" How did I say *hunting for the necklace* without actually saying *hunting for the necklace*? "Jade said she'd help me run lines tomorrow."

"If Alexa's willing, that's fine by me," Jade said, smoothing her nightgown over her legs.

"Great!" Alexa beamed at me. "Same time, same place?"

What circle of hell was this?

"Uh . . . I'll have to double-check my . . . Hey—what time does rehearsal start tomorrow?" I asked, to talk about anything else.

Jade looked out the window. "Eight. Like it has the past two mornings."

"Right."

"Weren't you the person who typed up the schedule?"

"I just . . . proofread it." I had to leave. I had to leave before things got worse. Before I said something ridiculous that I couldn't take back. "I should go."

"Yeah. Curfew's at nine fifteen," Jade said.

I backed toward the door. "Right. Okay then."

Alexa scrambled off Jade's bed. "I'll make sure no one's in the hall."

I tried to tell Jade with my eyes that there was nothing between Alexa and me. That kissing her hadn't mattered. But Jade was back to being a brick wall.

242

"Coast is clear," Alexa whispered.

As I slid past her, she grabbed my hand and pulled me to a stop. "Tonight was fun," she whispered, then kissed my cheek, her lips lingering longer than strictly necessary.

Please let Jade not be watching this. "Okay," I said, pulling away. "See you tomorrow."

I had sweat so much in this shirt today, it was probably ruined.

CHAPTER THIRTY-SEVEN

At five in the morning, our last day of rehearsal, I woke to a rough pounding on my bedroom door. When I cracked it open, Mr. Lord and Joan Dooley stood side by side, grave looks on their faces.

"The vase wasn't emptied of raw chicken," Mr. Lord said at the same time Mrs. Dooley pointed up the stairs. "Part of the ceiling collapsed."

I swore. Then again. "The ceiling in the west servants' bedroom?"

They nodded.

More swearing. "Sorry," I said. "Okay, I'll clean it up. Both. Um. Did all of the ceiling fall onto the tarp?"

"Not quite."

I winced. "Does Laura know about the chicken?"

"She asked what was smelling so terribly."

"I'll put on some clothes."

"How can we help?"

I rubbed my eyes. "Put the chicken vase back behind the garage. Tell Laura the butler's pantry garbage didn't get emptied—that's what smells so bad. Clip some lavender from the potted herbs under the eaves on the south side and tuck it in with the flowers in the breakfast room and any other room that stinks. I'll take care of the ceiling first—who knows about it?"

"Besides the three of us, just Lindsey, Maddie, and Noah," Mrs. Dooley said.

"Let's keep it that way."

When I first noticed the water discoloration on the ceiling of the west servants' bedroom months ago, I'd laid the largest tarp we had on the floor, anticipating that the ceiling plaster might collapse one day. But when I surveyed the actual damage, I realized that the tarp had been as effective at containing the wet plaster and brown water as newspaper had been when my brothers and I carved pumpkins on the kitchen as kids: a nice thought, but a severe underestimation.

I needed help fast, because directly below the west servants' bedroom was the ceiling to the art gallery. And if water leaked through the ceiling, it could damage our priceless pipe organ.

Noah and Lindsey helped me mop up the water and scoop the plaster onto the tarp. It took most of the day in fits and starts, because we had to work around rehearsal. And during our short breaks and odd, tasteless meals, to make matters worse, Alexa was in my face, and Jade was perfectly friendly. Like she was totally happy for Alexa and me.

Jade didn't like me back after all. I'd definitely misread the situation.

I made excuses to get out of meeting Alexa, and finally, around nine p.m., Noah and Lindsey and I decided we'd contained the damage. Then Noah and I sneaked outside and took turns writing my cues and lines onto a prop newspaper and burying the chicken and poisonous rhubarb soup deep underground.

⟋⟍

The next morning, the day of opening night, my brain started revving the second it hit that liminal space between sleep and fully awake.

Jade wouldn't look at you the night you kissed Alexa, my liminal brain told me. *Because it bothered her. Yesterday's cheerfulness was an act. She might like you back after all . . .*

I sat up. Liminal brain was right. I just had to find a way to get Jade alone long enough to talk to her.

⟋⟍

Failed Attempt at Talking to Jade Number 1: Breakfast in the breakfast room.

I got there early—even earlier than Mr. Hoyt. And then, gods be praised, Jade was next, now wearing a light blue day dress. She looked so beautiful, I couldn't speak right away. I managed to say, "Jade. Can we please talk?" before Mr. Hoyt and Kendrick swept in. Then our efforts turned to attempting to find the edible parts of Lula's breakfast buffet. (Sliced cheese. Berries. My last loaf of practice bread.)

⟋⟍

Failed Attempt at Talking to Jade Number 2: Opening night. Hubbub in the grand hall outside the music room two minutes before places.

Alexa was hovering a few steps away from Nomi by the stairs, and Mr. Hoyt was talking to Lula in the north alcove. I tugged Jade into the library.

"Jade—"

"Miss Jorgensen," she corrected me.

I narrowed my eyes. "Since when are we doing that?"

She blinked. "Doing what, Mr. Pendercast?"

"Places, everyone!" Lula stage-whispered. "It's a small but enthusiastic audience. Break a leg!"

<hr>

Failed Attempt at Talking to Jade Number 3: Scene Seven, split between the dining room and the art gallery.

In the dining room, I was busy as James confessing my continuing love for Noah's Henry. There was only one audience member in there with us, and he was mostly asleep on a chair. Everyone else was in the art gallery on the other side of the open pocket door. Including Jade as Elizabeth, right in the doorway.

My back was to her, but I knew which line of mine was coming up. And that Lula wasn't watching our scene. I changed the blocking. My back to the doorway, I said, "I came here under the auspices of courting a Jorgensen girl." Then I turned, searching for Jade's eyes. "But I actually came here . . . for you." I successfully caught her attention, but only because my accompanying gesture knocked over a plant that fell on Alexa.

<hr>

Failed Attempt Number 4: Impatiently waiting outside the bathroom on the second floor, where Jade was helping to discreetly bandage Alexa's head.

My next scene started before they emerged.

<hr>

Failure Number 5: Scene Nine in the art gallery.

Lindsey was this audience's clear favorite, so all fifteen of them followed her into the dining room for her scene with Maddie. With no one in the art gallery besides the rest of the cast, I scooted over to the side of the organ. "Jade, what happened with Alexa—" I hissed.

"Is just what you wanted to happen. So I did my part. Now do yours and search for the necklace."

"Jade—"

Two docents from the historic Ramsey House who had helped me learn how to use the wood-burning stove appeared in the doorway, and I spun away.

—

Failure 6: Scene Ten. The den.

The den was small, so even though we were accompanied by only half a dozen audience members, the room was thick with people.

Jade, I scribbled on a spare page of script, grateful to have just one line, and not until the end of the scene.

Please let me explain that night under the stairs. I'm begging you. —Asshat

I gave the note to Noah to pass to Jade since his blocking passed right by her, but Nomi intercepted it and put it in her pocket. I slipped the note out during Jade's emotional query, *"He doesn't have a left arm?"* and chucked it toward her lap on my exit line, "I'll go tell the organist to keep it down."

Unfortunately, there was a reason I was in theatre and not basketball. The note missed its mark and slipped between Jade's and Alexa's chairs. My heart lurched into my throat as Alexa plucked it off the floor.

"Oh!" I panic-improvised. Everyone stared at me. "If he doesn't have a left arm, this note can't be his! It was written by a lefty!" I snatched it and fled.

—

Failure Number 7: Scene Twelve. The art gallery.

Internal spiral, much self-flagellation. So much so that when I missed a line, I couldn't begin to find it on the prop newspaper. Noah saved me by improvising until I caught the thread again.

⌣·⌣

Big Stupid Failure Number 8: Scene Fourteen. The grand hall.

Magnus started playing a waltz. "This was amazing!" Alexa murmured as I twirled her in the north alcove and Lula corralled the audience back into the music room to solve the crimes. "I can't believe we pulled it off!"

I smiled with my mouth, but my eyes were searching for Jade. There she was. South alcove.

"Wasn't it so great to have an audience? This whole thing just exploded to life!"

"Totally," I agreed. It had been awesome. Everything felt heightened, more important. It was just that it would have been so much better if I'd been able to talk to—

"Oh, god," Alexa murmured.

"What is it?" I whispered.

"Is my bandage leaking? I think I got blood on my dress."

"Oh, no. I'm so sorry." I inspected the spot. To be polite. Since I knocked over the plant that caused her injury in the first place.

But as Jade and Kendrick appeared, I realized my face was basically buried in Alexa's cleavage.

⌣·⌣

And scene.

CHAPTER THIRTY-EIGHT

PIONEER PRESS

Tickets are going fast for the Beauregard's interactive play meets murder mystery meets escape room!

JUNE 19

... Beloved local actor Naomi Turner penned and stars in the production. "Due to the outside assistance we received casting the teen actors, I have to confess that it wasn't a conscious choice to cast all white actors as servant staff and mostly actors of color as members of the upper class," Turner said. "But I like how it asks audiences to consider their unconscious biases, as well as the role race has played in our country's history. On the other hand, the queer representation was written into the script ..."

... With its limited two-week run, the Beauregard Theatre's world premiere of *A Midsummer Night's Art Heist Garden Party Escape Room Murder* is already nearly sold out. Artistic Director Mark Lester-Dean says VIP tickets are still available for the final performance . . .

RACKET

SERIOUSLY WEIRD, SERIOUSLY FUN

June 20

I wasn't sure what to expect from the outrageously titled *A Midsummer Night's Art Heist Garden Party Escape Room Murder,* but my god was it a trip. The characters are fantastic, the romances swoony. The audience is instructed to follow who interests them, but I had a hard time deciding—I wanted to be everywhere! The group I was with was organized and determined, as someone had already attended with an audience that didn't solve the murder . . .

June 20

@thebeautheatre

Don't miss the limited run of Naomi Turner's A Midsummer Night's Art Heist Garden Party Escape Room Murder at the historic Jorgensen House June 20–29th!

@Bbressler

I'VE NEVER FELT SO SEEN! #gorightnow #trustme #unmissable

June 21

@KCWest

My daughter's friend is in this, and it has ruined me for every other play! Also, can I just live in that house? (Pro tip: Lots of walking. Make sure you wear #sensiblefootwear.)

@Mnmagpie

We saw it yesterday. It's an interesting experiment, but the races and sexual orientations of the different characters in unexpected places took me out of the story sometimes.

@KCWest

What do you mean by "took [you] out of the story"?

@Mnmagpie

I just kept being surprised, and then I remembered I
was watching a play and it wasn't real.

@KCWest

I'd love to have a longer conversation. Not
sure Twitter is the place for it. Chat at drop-off
tomorrow?

@Mnmagpie
If you want.

June 22

@KSTaff

I was the only one in the art gallery for a whole scene.
Took my breath away. (Don't understand why James
carries around a newspaper the whole time though?
Is it symbolic???)

June 23

@AnnieHarding55

The cast is really great, but Jade Montgomery
(Elizabeth Jorgensen) steals the show. She goes to
my school!

@ImprovLance

I didn't even recognize Mr. Hoyt at first! Did you know that the scullery maid is Noah's little sister? And yeah Jade is so amazing I want to die. But I hate not seeing all the scenes!

@Minnesnowtah4eva

Jade's cool, but that organ player guy is superhot. I call dibs.

@AnnieHarding55

You can't call dibs on Twitter about a guy you don't know in real life, Jordan.

@ImprovLance

Does anyone want to go again tonight? I want to see different parts. I'll check for tix.

@Minnesnowtah4eva

DIBS, Annie. And yeah, Lance. I'll go.

@AnnieHarding55

Yes to tonight! Should we meet at Cosetta's first? And seriously, Jordan! Respect the rules of dibs!

@Minnesnowtah4eva

ANNIE. DUDE CAN PLAY THE ORGAN. DIBS. (I'm getting the mostaccioli.)

JORDAN. YOU ARE RIDICULOUS. (Again?)

June 26

@VueandVang

Full review on our website. TL;DR: We found that the
racial optics make for both a sobering and electrifying
experience. Definitely check it out.

June 29

@BebeWatts

I am so here for the #queervictorianrep! BUT
THIS IS ONLY RUNNING FOR ONE MORE DAY?
AND IT'S $1,000 A PLATE???? WHAT THE HELL,
BEAUREGARD? *Shakes fist*

CHAPTER THIRTY-NINE

I slammed the door behind me and dropped facedown onto my bed. We had just completed our nineteenth performance in nine days, but I still had to meet Lula in the kitchen in fifteen minutes to talk her through the VIP/PBS closing night dinner tomorrow. Had I ever been this exhausted?

Knock-knock.

"Who is it?" I called, my voice muffled by the bedspread.

Someone banged open my door. I flipped over. "What do you need, Kendrick?"

"Hoyt just caught me texting with Isaac," he said, voice full of venom. "He confiscated my phone."

"There's one day left," I said, forcing myself to sit up. "I'm sure you'll survive."

Kendrick snapped, "You know, for a guy who says his family's so important to him . . ."

I sat up straight now. "What's that supposed to mean?"

"I don't know. That maybe if I was Andre or our parents, you'd actually care."

"What do you want me to do?" I snapped back. "You weren't even supposed to have your phone in the first place."

"Forget it," Kendrick said, and stormed out.

Was he seriously complaining about not having a phone for twenty-four hours? I hadn't touched mine in nearly two weeks.

I flopped back onto the bed.

My leg started to jiggle.

No way was I going to be able to relax with Kendrick's accusation hanging over my head.

"Kendrick," I called, hauling myself to my feet. I opened the door.

Alexa had a hand raised, ready to knock. "You're late," she said. "Come on."

Our meetings under the stairs had taken a sharp turn after the first one. After the opening night performance, she'd kissed me hello on the cheek, then spent fifteen minutes asking questions about Nomi's career. The night after that, and all the nights since, it was just Nomi talk: Where had she gone to school? What shows were her favorites? Did she teach voice lessons?

I was definitely feeling used by Alexa, but she kept saving me by whispering my next line when I couldn't manage to be carrying a newspaper around. I wanted to stop meeting but couldn't risk that line help going away.

I closed my eyes briefly. "I'm—I can't tonight. I have to talk to Kendrick."

"We can meet after." She smoothed my lapels. "And you know, we can keep hanging out like this, even after the play is over."

My stomach dropped. The one thing getting me through was figuring it would be over as soon as the play was. I forced myself not to step back from her ministrations. "I—Oh. Yeah. Um. We'll have to do that."

"Can we meet after you talk to Kendrick?"

"I have to help my mom."

"Which mom?" Alexa asked, her eyes wide with anticipation.

"Laura."

"Oh." Her whole demeanor dimmed. "With the food. Yeah. I guess you better."

Under Lula's reign, the food had continued to suffer. One night, Magnus had sneaked out and brought back six pizzas to the gatehouse. He'd invited everyone who he figured wouldn't rat him out, and we devoured the pizzas in minutes. But Magnus had used up all his contraband cash that night, and everyone else's wallets were in the office safe.

The rest of the meals were boring and repetitive, but at least they weren't potentially poisonous anymore. My new meal plan had seen to that. It was a lot of cheese and nuts and fruit and beef (because beef wouldn't poison us if it was undercooked).

A few days ago, after Mrs. Dooley, Mr. Lord, and Maddie had all reported Lula kicking them out of the kitchen, I had tried to go down early to help her, but she had refused.

"Go practice your lines, Finn," she'd said, pushing me through the door. "I'm not letting you take care of me." It was raining, and she'd looked gray in the apathetic light coming through the basement windows.

I'd wanted to argue that it wasn't really *her* I was trying to take care of—it was everyone else's digestive systems. But I knew arguing would only hurt her feelings.

The food had to be good for the VIP dinner, though, and even Lula knew she needed assistance for that. I was going to help her with prep tonight. There was only the final show the next day at four in the afternoon, so even though the PBS people were showing up early to film interviews and some B-roll footage, I would still have time to duck out and help her sauté vegetables. I hoped. There was approximately a forty percent chance this would all go off without a hitch.

Then I remembered the tough beef in the flavorless stew from the night before.

Maybe closer to thirty-five.

Alexa traced a finger down the buttons of my shirt. "Do you know what monologue Naomi auditioned with when she—"

"*No,*" I said, more irritated than I'd intended.

"Fine." She dropped her hand. "I'm sorry I'm so *exhausting* to you." She gathered her skirts and stomped up the flower staircase to the third floor.

Now I had *two* people accusing me of things that weren't true.

Well, mostly weren't true. Alexa's fangirling over my mom *was* exhausting. But would I really have been more empathetic if Andre had come complaining about his phone being confiscated rather than Kendrick?

I stood outside my door, trying to decide where to go: upstairs or down? Alexa or Kendrick?

Taking a deep breath, I crossed the hall and jogged down the stairs. Family first.

The grand hall was empty of people. Everyone had probably escaped to their rooms, just as exhausted as I was.

"Kendrick?" I called, not even caring if Mr. Hoyt was hiding somewhere to reprimand me for not calling out for Simon instead.

Something thumped from the direction of the library and I followed the sound.

"Kendrick?" I asked as I pushed the thick brocade curtain aside and crossed the threshold.

"Haven't seen him," Jade said, picking up a stack of books off the floor. "But I heard some people say they wanted to have a faro tournament tonight. Maybe he's with them."

"Oh. Okay." I stared at her. Things were at an all-time low with us. This, in fact, was our longest conversation since the day I'd failed a million times to talk to her. I'd worried she suspected how I felt and was pushing me away because she didn't want to have to come out and tell me she didn't like me. Not even "like that"—not at all. So I'd stopped trying. I searched all the male bedrooms and bathrooms, just like she'd asked, but every time I attempted to tell her about it, she said we'd talk later.

Maybe now was later.

"Hey," I said. "About the necklace—"

"It's silly, Turner." She set the books back on the shelf one at a time. "You can stop looking."

"It's not silly," I insisted. "Like you said, it's documented in that disgruntled maid's letter home. And Mr. and Mrs. Jorgensen both wrote about Anna's lost treasure."

"A million things are called treasure that aren't really treasure. The treasure of a sunrise. Of family. Friendship. The maid was likely bragging. And who knows—maybe Mrs. Jorgensen donated that necklace a long time ago. Or sold it. We're probably searching for nothing." She dusted off her hands on her skirt.

"If you think something's worth searching for, then it's worth—"

"But I don't." She met my eyes now. "It was a silly childhood game, and it's over now. I'll still help you with your audition for Acting Lab, though." She forced a smile, and as she strode away from me, her bustle knocked over a framed photo on the table.

I righted the photo—taken of the building crew, partway through the house's construction. I stared at their faces. All of them were long gone by now. But the thing they'd built together was still standing.

Theatre wasn't like that. By its very nature, it was something that existed only in the moments it was being performed. You could film a play, or read the script, but it wasn't the same. Plays were living, breathing things. You were part of something singular and fleeting. Plays were like people that way.

"Joan? Martin? Kendrick? Someone! Finn?" Nomi's panicked voice called from the hall.

I dashed through the library's door. "What's wrong, Mom?"

Nomi spun toward me, tears streaming down her face. "Call 911. It's Lula. She passed out in the kitchen, and I can't wake her up."

CHAPTER FORTY

I raced down the hall, and heaved open the pocket door into the reception room. Throwing myself at the L-shaped desk, I searched the shelves, cursing, my hands shaking. Where had Maddie hidden the phone?

I got the brilliant idea to find the jack in the wall and trace the cord to wherever the phone was hidden, but the phone jack sat empty. I swore again, louder this time.

"Language, Finn." Maddie appeared and dumped over a display of books, jerking away the fabric they were sitting on to reveal a box. She tipped it over and pulled out the phone.

"*Maddie McGlynn, what the hell?*" I demanded.

She knelt on the floor behind the desk, plugged the phone into the jack, and dialed. "We need an ambulance at number four Summit Avenue for an unresponsive woman in her mid-forties with a possible head injury."

I clutched the desk. *Possible head injury?* I had to see her. But Maddie tugged at my wrist. "Stay here, Finn. We need to show the first responders where to go."

"But—"

"We're going to stand outside and wait," she said, meeting my eyes. "Naomi and Kendrick are with her."

Wordlessly, I let Maddie lead me out the front door.

Lula wasn't waking up. She might have a head injury. And it was all because of me and my selfishness. Kendrick was right—there were a million actors. Why hadn't I just agreed to be the cook? If I had, Lula wouldn't be in this situation. If I had, I wouldn't have been hanging out with the wrong girl.

I shook my head to get rid of that last thought. Not important right now.

We stood on the carriage step in front of the house. Maddie touched my elbow. "Breathe, Finn. Laura's a fighter."

All I could do was nod.

<hr />

What felt like three hours later, but was probably only minutes, Lula was awake but groggy and strapped to a gurney in the back of the ambulance with Nomi by her side. The sight of Lula as the paramedics took her out—so gray, so tiny—made me flash back to all those days last winter. Had her cancer come back?

Now, everyone was outside, breathing in unison, staring at the place where the ambulance had disappeared down Summit Avenue.

"They took my Geoffrey away in one of those, and he never came home again," Martin Lord breathed to Joan Dooley.

"I'm so sorry, Martin." Joan caught my eye. "But Laura's going to be fine."

I took three halting steps toward him. "I'm sorry, too," I said. "Lula was so sick—" My voice cracked on the word. I coughed to recover. "And we—I—didn't really get to tell you how sad I was that Geoffrey died. We loved him so much."

Two tears, one right after the other, spilled out of Martin Lord's eyes and down his papery cheeks. "Thank you, Finn. Being in this house, this place Geoffrey loved, has been . . . difficult. And also wonderful. I feel close to him here."

Another reason to save the house. I offered Martin a small smile.

"We need a plan," Maddie said softly. "For if Laura—"

"She's not dying tonight, Maddie," Kendrick bit out, and I flinched at the word.

"That's right," Maddie said in that same soft voice. "But she still might be in the hospital tomorrow."

"Oh, no. PBS," Magnus moaned.

"I say we cancel it," Kendrick said. "We can't do it without her. We need her." He tapped his pocket like he was reaching for his phone. But it was in the safe. His face tightened.

I stepped over to my brother and lowered my voice. "Does Isaac have a car?"

Kendrick looked at me like it really was 1891. But then he said, "Yeah."

"Call him." I tried pouring I'm-sorry-for-not-taking-your-relationship-with-Isaac-seriously and I-want-to-be-a-better-brother-to-you into my voice. "Use the phone in the reception room. Tell him what happened. Ask him to come."

"But—"

"Even if it takes a little while to convince his parents and throw some clothes and a toothbrush in a bag, he'll get here by three in the morning at the latest."

"I—"

"Call him," I repeated. "You need him. Our parents aren't here, and this is scary, and . . . he's your person. He'll want to help."

Kendrick's jaw clenched like he was trying to hold back tears. Then he nodded and strode inside the house.

I faced the group. "I think the best thing we can do for my moms right now is to keep this thing going. Agreed?"

Everyone nodded.

"Because the show must go on," Lindsey said. "That's a thing, right?" She looked up into Noah's face.

Noah tugged her close. "Totally a thing."

"Good," I said. "Then we have to write Mrs. Jorgensen out of the script."

"I'll do it," Jade offered.

I looked into her earnest face, at curls tumbling from her careful updo after such a long day. I never wanted to stop looking at her. Kissing her. Talking and laughing and holding her. But it was too late. Why hadn't I fought harder for our friendship back in middle school? Why hadn't I fought for it a thousand times since?

"Magnus and I will clean up the kitchen," Maddie announced.

"What's wrong with the kitchen?" I asked.

Maddie and Joan Dooley exchanged a look.

"There's dinner dishes," Mrs. Dooley said at the same time Maddie admitted, "There's a lot of blood."

I took in a sharp breath.

"Heads bleed like crazy," Jade said. "Remember? IB Bio?" She held my gaze.

I wanted to believe her.

"I'll help clean up, too," Lindsey said.

"And me," Joan Dooley volunteered.

"We can all help." Mr. Hoyt's voice was thick.

The tortured expression on his face—out of fear for his friend?—was too much. I needed to keep it together. I found Jade's steady eyes for a moment instead. Then I nodded at everyone else. "Thank you. I'll step back in and organize the meal-making. Tonight, as soon as you can, please go to bed. We all need our beauty rest to be on TV." I pressed a brave smile onto my face.

Jade held up a hand. "Let's have a pickup rehearsal tomorrow with the script changes. What time is PBS showing up?"

"I'll check the schedule in Laura's office," Maddie offered.

"Seriously, everyone—thank you," I said.

The cast started to move back into the house, but I blurted out, "Alexa?" This had not been the time or place I'd envisioned this conversation happening, but now with Lula . . . life was so . . . delicate. I couldn't keep living this ruse with Alexa for one second longer.

"Yeah? What can I do to help?" Alexa asked.

I led her a few steps away from the carriage porch near a patch of leafy green hostas. "We can't keep . . . meeting," I said.

She frowned. "Your mom's in the hospital. You've got a show and a house to save. You think I'm a monster? It's fine, Finn."

"No, I . . ." I sighed. "I don't *want* to keep meeting."

Alexa quirked an eyebrow.

"I should have said something earlier. I just didn't want things to get weird for the run of the show. I'm *really* sorry."

She let her eyes flutter closed for a second. "It's fine, Finn. We don't have to—if you aren't—"

I felt guilty for a second but pressed on. "You aren't . . . either, though. Are you. All we do is talk."

Her face hardened. "Were you hoping for more of an exchange of goods and services? I make out with you, then you'll talk to me?"

"Oh, *god*, no. But you said—"

"I *said* I wanted to get to know you better, but making out wasn't very fun, was it?"

"Well, no . . ."

"But talking together is. Or I thought it was. I liked that time together under the stairs. It felt special."

I was sweating everywhere, feeling like the worst human being ever, but I had to get it all out. "It's just—I felt like you weren't interested in who I was at all—except the part of me that could help you mine the success story that is Naomi Turner."

Her face was granite rock. "Look, Finn. Your mom is in the hospital, so I'm going to keep this civil. But this thing I want? A career in theatre? Your mom has somehow cracked it. Of course I want to know all about her and how she did it."

"Then talk to *her*."

"But she's . . . *Naomi Turner*."

Jade had been right. Again and again and again.

"Well, I'm Finn Turner. So if you want to be friends with me, then great. But I'm done being the live version of my mom's Wikipedia page."

"Whatever, Finn." Alexa stomped off toward the front door.

I stood by the hostas until my hands stopped shaking.

CHAPTER FORTY-ONE

The door into the reception room muffled Kendrick's voice. "Drive so safely. Promise me."

I hung back in the front hall, trying not to eavesdrop on his phone call as I waited for it to end. When I heard the receiver clatter into its cradle, I opened the door and stepped into the reception room. Kendrick was sitting on the L-shaped desk.

"Hey. Is he on his way?" I asked.

"Yeah." Kendrick pulled a bowl of paper clips into his lap. "Said he wouldn't miss it."

"That's nice."

I watched Kendrick straighten three paper clips nearly flat as I tried to figure out what to say next. Then three quick tears dropped into the bowl.

"Hey!" After darting around the short end of the desk, I hopped up and slung an arm around him, but Kendrick's shoulders remained tense.

"How did you do this last year?" Kendrick demanded.

"Do what?" I asked.

"Watch her in ambulances! See how frail she looked." Kendrick's eyes were wet and furious. "Why didn't Andre and I come home?"

"She wanted you to stay focused on school. She said there was nothing you could have done here except worry, and so—"

Kendrick shook off my arm. "We could have helped!" His voice was sharp. "Why didn't you tell us we should be here?"

I stared at my rejected arm. Shook my head.

"It was your job to tell us. We should have been here, Finn. Don't you get how that makes me feel?"

How many times had I stood in the attic amid my buckets and sobbed all by myself, needing my brothers there beside me? I wanted to tell Kendrick that, but emotion clogged my throat, and the words wouldn't form.

"Just because you *could* handle it doesn't mean—" He swore. Then he swore again and pounded the table. "You should have called," he insisted, his voice wavering. "We would have come."

"I know," I fought to whisper, my shoulders hunched against my impending tears. "I wish I would have called. I really missed you."

Kendrick started to cry.

And so did I.

He slung his arm around my shoulder, and I pulled him to me, and we held on to each other for a long while.

When we pulled apart and blew our noses, he pointed at me. "No more toughing it out on your own."

"Okay. I promise."

"You don't have to be—oh my god." His face looked like something had just dawned on him. "You learned to cook to take care of them, didn't you?"

I bit my lip. Nodded.

He closed his eyes.

"But I like cooking," I said. "If that helps."

He wrapped me up in another long hug.

"So," he said after we pulled apart again. "Are we still doing the show?"

I nodded. "For Lula and Nomi. We can't give up now. You okay with that?"

"Yeah. For sure. Yeah."

I squeezed his arm. "I should go pop into the kitchen. See how things are."

"Right. I'll stay here by the phone in case Nomi calls."

"Or Isaac," I said, smiling.

"Or Isaac," he agreed.

<hr />

Unexpected library light shone into the grand hall. Stepping into the room to turn it off, I found light spilling out of the den as well. I reached around the corner and pushed the off button.

"Hey!" a voice protested.

Startled, I pushed it back on and stepped inside. "Jade! Sorry, I—"

"It's fine."

"Sorry," I said again. "I didn't know you were working in here. I'll leave you alone."

"Finn?" Her voice stopped my retreating footsteps. "What did you and Alexa talk about when you pulled her aside after the ambulance left?"

I turned around. "I said . . . we shouldn't meet anymore."

"Why not?"

"It's just not . . . working."

"Oh," she said neutrally. I fought to keep my own face neutral, too. "Will you look at the first few scenes I've doctored?" Jade handed me her script, and I smiled despite myself, reading the notes she'd written in the margins about her own performance.

What do I want here?
Margaret's ruining my plan!
Perch—don't relax into couch.

I wanted to trace each notation with my fingers.

She reached over me to flip ahead in the script. "Okay. Here." She pointed. "It's already established the other daughters are at the lake with the nanny and nurse, so I figured it made sense that Mrs. Jorgensen could be away with them, too. Then I switched it so Margaret tells Henry—well, just read it."

I tried but couldn't concentrate. Jade was all politeness. The tension that used to crackle between us was gone.

"Does that make sense?" she asked after the time it should have taken me to read the pages.

I closed the script and handed it to her. "Yeah, it looks great." Two weeks ago, I would have teased her about double-checking her work. But it was too late for inside jokes now, too.

"Good. Any word from the hospital?"

The hospital. My stomach churned. "Kendrick's waiting by the phone."

She sat back down at the desk and opened the script. She didn't look at me, but her voice softened the tiniest bit. "Hang in there."

As I stepped out of the library, I heard Kendrick's voice, so I sprinted down the grand hall.

"Any news?" I asked as I barreled into the reception room.

"Just that Isaac's officially on the road." Kendrick laid the phone in its cradle. "You should go to bed, Finnster. You look—"

I touched the doorjamb. "But what if Lula—"

"No what-ifs." Kendrick hopped off the desk and planted a hand on my shoulder. "Worrying's a waste of a perfectly good imagination, remember?"

I cracked a small smile. It was one of Lula's favorite aphorisms.

"Go to bed," Kendrick repeated. "I'm wide awake. I'll come get you as soon as Nomi calls."

Kendrick and I might be permanent friends, but that didn't mean our relationship didn't need attention. In his way, he'd been trying to tell me that for weeks. So I asked, "Can I wait here with you?"

Kendrick's mouth drew up in a soft half-smile. "You bet."

I climbed up onto the L-shaped desk and picked up a paper clip. "Tell me something about Isaac."

He chuckled, watching me unbend it. "What do you want to know?"

"Everything. Start from the beginning."

He told me how they met (at a party), what Isaac first thought of Kendrick (that he was a snob), and when they started flirting (after Kendrick asked Isaac to tutor him in chemistry).

"But you're really good at chemistry," I said.

Kendrick laughed at me until I put it together.

"The first thing I'm going to do when I meet him is show him your AP Chem score," I joked.

"Oh, he figured out pretty quickly I knew what I was talking about. Thanks for pushing me to call him tonight."

"Of course. It's clear how much he means to you."

He smiled to himself. Then he sat up straight. "Hey. Did I see you sneaking into the coat closet with Alexa a few nights ago? What about you and Jade? I thought you two were—"

I moaned. "It's a long story. But the end of it is Alexa and I are over. It was nothing to begin with, turned out. And Jade—" I made a sound of frustration. "I didn't see what was there until it was too late."

"No way," Kendrick said, studying my face. "You two come alive when you're together."

I blushed and tried to redirect the conversation. "Does Isaac make you feel like you come alive?"

Kendrick glanced at the phone. "He's . . . Yeah. I mean, he's smart. He makes me *think*. And he's funny." He laughed. I laughed, too. It was nice to see Kendrick so happy. "And I know that blue eyes are just the absence of melanin in the iris, and so we're really seeing a refraction of light, but it's an *incredible* refraction—"

Maddie appeared in the doorway. "I found an email that says PBS will be here at eight a.m. They've scheduled interviews with the cast and *Laura* in the morning, and then they'll get some B-roll of the show and the dinner and *the kitchen* in the afternoon." She folded her arms. "So that's problematic as we have no Laura and no head cook. Any word from the hospital?"

Kendrick and I shook our heads.

"What are we going to—"

The phone rang. Kendrick snatched up the receiver. "Jorgensen House—Mom!"

I leaped over and pressed my head against Kendrick's to hear the phone. "How's Lula?"

Kendrick tilted the receiver so we could both listen.

"She's having a CT scan right now," Nomi reported. "I'm not allowed in. They said it'll be about half an hour."

A question swirled in my head. I didn't want to scare anyone, but I had to know. "Nomi . . . Do they think the . . . cancer is back?"

Kendrick inhaled sharply.

"Oh, honey! Oh, no no no," Nomi said, her voice an octave higher than usual. "They think it's a concussion. She fainted from exhaustion and hit her head on the stove. It's nothing to do with cancer except she should have been resting more."

My relief was soon overtaken by guilt. "I should have—" I began.

"Finn," Nomi's no-nonsense voice cut in. "It's not your fault."

"But if I'd—"

"Honey, you are not responsible for Lula's actions. If she'd asked, would you have helped her?"

"Of course!"

"You can't force someone to accept assistance. Lula should have asked for help cooking, or at least accepted when we offered to help. She also should have been sleeping a lot more than she has been, especially after still being in recovery from her surgery. But she wouldn't listen to me about that, either. I'm the one who convinced her this whole mess was a good idea. Do you blame *me* that she collapsed?"

"Of course not!"

"Then don't blame yourself."

I looked at Kendrick. Somehow I needed his forgiveness, too.

He nodded, and my heart rate slowed. Then Kendrick asked, "How long will Lula be in the hospital?"

"Not sure. But—" Nomi took a deep breath. "Boys, I can't leave her, so—"

"Jade's writing you out of the show," I interrupted, "and I'm supervising the kitchen."

"And if Lula's still in the hospital tomorrow," Kendrick added, "we'll send over modern clothes for you. Can you borrow scrubs for tonight?"

Nomi was quiet.

Kendrick and I looked at each other. "Is . . . is that okay?" I asked.

"Yep," Nomi said, and I could hear she was trying very hard not to cry. "More than okay."

<hr>

"Go to bed," Kendrick insisted after we hung up the phone. "After all, you've got a lot of cooking to do on top of your part, and we've just learned how important sleep is for staying upright in the kitchen."

I breathed out a laugh. "What about you?"

"I'm going to call Andre. Let him know what happened. Then I'll curl up in here."

"In case Isaac calls?"

Kendrick's lips twitched. "Yeah."

I hugged him. "I'm sorry."

"For what?" Kendrick asked, hugging me back.

"For not asking you to come home when Lula was sick. For not asking for help. For not believing you were serious about Isaac."

Kendrick squeezed me harder. "It's okay. I'm sorry, too."

"Why?"

He released me from our hug. "Dude, I don't know. I've been angry about this house for a long time, I think. And you love it. And it made me angry at you. And then not seeing Isaac. And those freaking kissing scenes?" He snorted. "I've been an asshat."

My face fell. Two weeks ago, I'd asked Jade not to call me that. Now I wished she would. This cold politeness was worse.

"What?" Kendrick asked.

I opened my mouth to say, *It's nothing*, but after tonight, that felt like a step in the wrong direction. "Jade used to call me asshat," I said instead.

Kendrick nodded. He seemed to understand.

CHAPTER FORTY-TWO

I woke up the next morning at five without an alarm. I skipped the long underwear and threw on my trousers, a long-sleeved shirt, and suspenders. After slipping into my socks and shoes, I jogged down half a flight of stairs from the second floor and opened the landing door to the balcony where Nomi had held the intimacy rehearsal last week. I wanted a calming moment to myself before the day truly began.

My shoe splashed down into a shallow puddle on the tile, and I cursed. *Just what we need. More rain.* Shaking off the thought, I climbed the last few steps up to the balcony and scanned the sweeping view of St. Paul. One day left. Then, with any luck, even with the collapsed ceiling and without the necklace, the house would be saved.

After taking in a final deep breath of the ozone-y post-rain smell, I retreated into the house deciding, *Kitchen first. Then buckets.*

When I crossed the threshold into the kitchen, I smiled. The bars on the windows had felt like prison before, but now, as I tied on an apron, they made me feel protected.

I was still smiling as I fed lengths of oak into the stove's firebox when Joan Dooley and Lindsey appeared.

"Any word from your parents?" Mrs. Dooley asked.

Swinging the door closed to the firebox, I explained about the exhaustion and probable concussion.

"Oof," Joan Dooley commiserated, tying an apron behind her back. "My granddaughter got a concussion playing hockey. They are no fun to come back from." She patted my cheek. "But Laura's come back from worse."

Lindsey glared at me. "Never leave this kitchen again, Finn."

"Well, I have to do my part in the play," I said, striding over to the sink with the kettle to fill it up for tea. "But I'll be around a lot. Plus, today's the last day!" I twisted the spigot open and let the water tumble into the kettle.

Lindsey and Joan Dooley were frowning when I returned to the stove with it.

"Why the long faces? *Today's* the last *day*!" I repeated. "Aren't you excited to use the Internet? Drive in a car? Wear your own clothes?"

Mrs. Dooley made a sound of uncertainty. "It's been hard work with all those performances. And I won't miss this corset. But . . ." She looked to Lindsey for an answer.

"I like it here," Lindsey said, shrugging. "The mean cook left, and everyone else is really nice to me. And yeah, it's hard work, but Laura wouldn't let us help a lot in the kitchen, so Mrs. Dooley and Mr. Lord taught me how to play cribbage. And sometimes I read to them at night after we we're done with the sweeping and dusting upstairs. And the play is fun." Lindsey tucked her arm into Joan's. "And Mrs. Dooley promised I can come over after this is all over, and we'll make gingersnaps and watch *Murder, She Wrote* together. She's been telling me the plots of her favorite episodes when we do the dishes. Finn. It sounds *so good*."

I pressed down a chuckle.

"Now, you'll see Laura before I do, Finn," Mrs. Dooley said, "so will you please tell her how wonderful this experience has been? I know I urged her toward historical restoration, but living here has made me see this 'experiencing history' way might also have some value." She squeezed Lindsey's hand. "Even though it will eventually ruin the floors."

I had to turn away so she didn't see me smile. "I promise I'll tell her. Well. Shall we?" I ran my finger down the elaborate plan I'd written out step-by-step for Lula. "I'm thinking of switching out the dessert," I said. "I want something more showstop-y."

"Is there time?" Joan asked.

"If you two can keep following this list, I'll pop upstairs and look in *Mrs. Beeton's* in the library."

"*Mrs. Beeton's?*" Lindsey asked as I took off my apron.

"It was *the* British guide to household work," Joan Dooley explained. "It includes hundreds of recipes."

"Aren't there recipes from this house? Back when the Jorgensens lived here?"

"Yeah," I said, "but they were lost a long time ago."

"What about American recipes, then?" Lindsey asked.

"Oh, well. Did you know . . ." Mrs. Dooley began. Chuckling to myself, I jogged out of the kitchen.

⌁

I greeted Martin, Magnus, and Noah on the servants' stairs as they headed down to the kitchen to help Lindsey and Joan.

When I opened the door into the grand hall, Maddie stopped me, clipboard in hand. "How are things downstairs?" she asked.

"Great!" I said. "Surprisingly great. There's a step-by-step plan, everyone's helping, and I'm going to see if I can get a fancier recipe for dessert."

She made a notation on her clipboard. "Mr. Hoyt is stepping in for Laura for the long PBS interview. It looks like they'll have short conversations with everyone else. I thought we'd set them up on the second floor in Mrs. Jorgensen's room so they'll be out of the way."

I nodded. "Are Kendrick and Isaac awake?"

"There's a car in the back with Wisconsin plates, so I assume that's him. But no, I have not seen them yet. I slid a note under Kendrick's door to come find me as soon as they wake up." She made another notation. "Grab yourself a copy of the new script in the music room. If you see anyone, we're going to run the changes at two o'clock. That will give folks time to memorize their new lines this morning and for the PBS people to conduct their interviews. If all goes to plan, everything should be set well before the VIPs come at five thirty." She peered over her clipboard at me. "Is *everything* set for dinner?"

"Yeah. I think so. I hope so." It was going to be tight, prepping for the seven-course meal I'd devised and also memorizing new lines. *New lines*. Nausea roiled around in my stomach.

"Have you seen Noah? He said he'd polish the silver."

"He's in the kitchen." I gave her a little smile. "So is Magnus." Maddie blushed and shook her head.

"How's that all—"

"Thank you for your help, Finn," she said in a loud voice and continued writing on her clipboard as she strode away toward the servants' staircase.

Laughing, I jogged down the grand hall toward the music room. Unbelievably, we might actually pull this off.

CHAPTER FORTY-THREE

After grabbing a new script from the stack in the music room, I climbed two flights of stairs to the third floor and took a right down the hall, passing through the door into the servants' wing. Buckets first, I'd decided. Best to save the fun thing—picking out a new dessert—for last.

I took another right and stuck my head into the west servants' bedroom, home of the epic ceiling collapse. Luckily, the rain from last night had dripped into an old crisper drawer I'd pulled out of a 1950s prop fridge in the basement. After taking a quick left and climbing the attic steps, leaping over the squeaky one, I threw open the door and stepped inside. A voice called out, "Stop!"

Out of habit, I slammed the door shut behind me. "Stop what?"

As she came out from around the corner, Jade let out a string of expletives that, after two weeks of Victorian speak, made me blush.

"What's *wrong*?" I asked.

"The inside doorknob is broken!" she said, storming over to me.

"What? Wait—what are you doing up here in the first place?" I asked.

She huffed. "I photocopied the changes last night, but then I woke up this morning with this pit in my stomach like I had made a mistake someplace, so I came up here this morning to walk them through."

"By yourself?" I asked.

"No," she said witheringly. "With stand-ins I invited over at five a.m."

"There's no need to—"

"I got inside," she interrupted me, "but when I tried to leave, the doorknob just spun and spun, and I couldn't get out. And now *we* can't get out. I've been in here for, like, forty-five minutes already. Is there another way?"

"No," I said, turning to the doorknob, "but I'm sure I can figure this out."

"Are you?" she asked, her steps toward me loud on the hardwood. "Are you *so* sure that there's some simple solution I overlooked but *you'll*—"

I whirled around and held up both hands. "Jade. Calm—"

Now she jabbed her finger into my chest. "I swear on the lives of both of your mothers, if you tell me to calm down, I'll—"

I leaned into her finger. "You'll what? You'll what, Jade?"

Our faces were very close together. My eyes flicked to that tiny mole on her nose again. Then to her lips. Why couldn't I stay focused on being furious at her? Her mouth moved closer to mine, and every cell in my body stood at attention. Were we—no. But she—

And then we were kissing again. She tugged on my shoulders

to draw me even closer, and I held her tight. Thank *god*. Maybe it *wasn't* too late.

But then she whimpered and pushed me back. "I can't do this."

I dropped my arms. They were made of lead now. "Oh . . . Oh."

"Look," she said, picking at the velvet cuff of her dress over and over. "I mean, clearly, we're very . . . But even though I—I mean—You're—"

I took a step toward her.

She held up her hands again and swore. "No! I'm so *pissed* at the way you're always sure if I've found a dead end, you can find some gleaming, shining path I'm too stupid to notice—"

"There is *no* part of me that thinks you're stupid. I'm just another set of eyes!"

"Well, that's not how you make me feel." She glared at me. "And you can't just kiss me and think I'll stop being angry."

I kind of thought I was following *her* lead just then, but I said, "Okay. I'm sorry. I won't." I didn't step toward her this time, even though I wanted to. "But . . . how about when we're . . . not angry?" This was it, wasn't it? "Jade, I like kissing you. A lot. I've been worrying it was too late to tell you, but if it isn't—"

"It is." She pressed her palms to her stomach. "Turner, I can't—I don't want to just mess around with you."

My voice sped up. "I don't want that, either. I didn't mean *just* kissing—"

"But I also won't be your consolation prize."

What? I had to step closer to her now. "Consolation? Jade. You're not my *second choice*."

She sidestepped me. "I absolutely *am*. Things failed with Alexa, so here you are. She was your first choice, I'm your second. We both know how linear time works, Turner."

My chest ached. "No. Liking you isn't *new*. I got distracted by Alexa, but my feelings for you were always there—just covered in seventh-grade hurt." How could I prove to her what I now knew in my bones? It had *always* been her. "Remember sixth grade? We were inseparable. We ate lunch together every day even though kids teased us for being boyfriend/girlfriend. And when you couldn't come over after school, we watched movies at the same time at our separate houses using the chat feature on Google Docs so it was like we were watching them together. And the treasure hunting. Jade. We were—"

"Things changed! And just because we've kissed . . . just because it feels—" She pursed her lips. "Whatever. I'm telling you, I can't do this. I'm saying no."

I wanted to tell her she was wrong. But I also didn't want to invalidate her feelings. I raised my palms in surrender as she marched off toward—

"Uh . . . Jade? Why are all the paint cans out of the paint can closet?"

"I promise I'll put everything back where I found it, *Dad*," she said, removing the last few.

"No—it's not—" I'd never seen the paint can closet empty. It had never occurred to me or my brothers to take everything out of it. I caught up to her and peered over her shoulder. "Is that—is that a *door*?"

"I saw a crack in the wall behind the cans, so I thought I'd check it out."

"I thought you gave up looking for the necklace."

"I did. But I hadn't given up on looking for another way out of here. And see? Definitely a door."

There was indeed a small door maybe four feet tall. A brass latch kept it closed.

"Wow! I always thought that crack was just boards meeting."

"Guess not," she said. She lifted the latch, and the door swung into the space under the eaves.

I gaped at the opening. My brothers and I had spent countless hours up here looking for secrets and never found anything. But put Jade in the attic—by herself—and forty-five minutes later, she'd found a whole hidden entrance. Because of course she had.

"It's dark," she said, peering inside. "Do I remember seeing flashlights backstage?"

"Uh, yeah." I zigzagged across the attic. In the wings, shelves filled with boxes and props lined the wall. I scanned all the backstage ephemera for the basket of flashlights and found it on the shelf directly above the blue settee Jade had asked about the first time she'd come up here with me. The first time we'd—

Biting my lips and studiously avoiding looking at the settee, I reached into the basket and retrieved three flashlights. I clicked each one on, discovering that only two worked.

"Find one?" Her voice was muffled. "Ugh. It's really gross back here," she called, and I hurried to the closet and followed her inside, flipping on both of the flashlights. The two together produced a strong enough beam to illuminate a large puddle.

A puddle? I directed both flashlight beams at the ceiling and swore. "*This* is where that water in the west servants' room was coming from!" I whooped in celebration. "Don't take this the wrong way, Jade, but I'm really glad you got stuck up here."

She laughed a little and took one of the flashlights from me. "Happy to be of service, I guess . . . Hey. Look!" She pointed her beam of light at a long, built-in shelving unit. My additional light revealed several crates labeled CHRISTMAS and a cherry-brown leather suitcase with MAJ in gold lettering by the handle. "Guesses as to who MAJ is?" she asked.

"Millie Jorgensen's middle name was Anna."

"Millie was the youngest daughter, right?" she asked.

"By nine years," I said. "Mrs. Jorgensen was forty-five when she was born."

"Geez." Jade picked her way around the puddle. "I bet *that* pregnancy was a surprise." She tucked the flashlight under her armpit, picked up the suitcase, and shook it a little. "There's, like, one thing rattling around in there."

"Like a necklace?"

"Don't think so. It sounds more solid. Let's get out of here and take a look."

Soon, we were sitting on the edge of the stage near the wings. Jade's hands smoothed the case balanced on our knees. "Well, Turner. Shall we?"

CHAPTER FORTY-FOUR

We each released one of the suitcase clasps and flipped the lid open to reveal a musty, rosy-brown fabric interior. A single book with a green leather cover lay inside.

Jade reached for it. Before I had a chance to read the title, she opened the book and thick paper fell out that had been folded into quarters. I plucked up the pages and flipped them over. In blotchy ink, someone had scrawled,

If you're tempted to give her the book, reread this letter from your "mother"!

"Huh," I wondered, shifting the suitcase onto the stage. I gingerly unfolded the pages.

Dearest Millie,

I regret your discovery of Elizabeth's journal. You would not listen last night, but I hope you will allow me space here to attempt some sort of explanation.

Elizabeth was a stubborn child. Unlike her older sisters, she would not learn a lesson until she had made the mistake herself. This was true of burning her fingers on the stove, of breaking both of her arms falling out of the oak tree, and of her dalliance with the ice delivery man.

When Elizabeth's courses stopped, she confessed to Margaret, who, naturally, confessed to me. Elizabeth wished to marry the ice man, but such an alliance would have been unfathomable. Papa had not climbed the ladder of prosperity for his daughter to marry a common laborer.

Margaret and I crafted a plan, and Elizabeth was brought to see reason. Papa had recently left on one of his long trips out West, so it was easy enough to write him and tell him the wonderful surprise that I was with child. When Elizabeth began to quicken and we knew for certain you were coming, we took Mrs. O'Reilly into our confidence. She has always been a most loyal servant. With her help, we told our acquaintances we were traveling to London for two months. In reality, we refuged with Mrs. O'Reilly's sister, a midwife in Milwaukee. I wrote to Papa after the two months had elapsed with fabricated news of balls and lectures and concerts in London. I said, with a little more time, I hoped to find titled husbands for both Margaret and Elizabeth. As Papa loved children, but did not have time for babies, I knew he would not mind over much waiting to meet his newest child, especially if it meant good matches for his older daughters.

Of course, the only men in our acquaintance were Mrs.

O'Reilly's husband and son, both brewers. To this day, the smell of malt and hops turns my stomach, remembering that terrible time.

When we returned home, the ruse was easily maintained. Soon, I nearly forgot you had not been born of my body. All this time, you have truly been my daughter, and I your mother.

Elizabeth was able to see the wisdom of our plan after you were born. While Bernard is perhaps not as handsome as the ice man was, his wealth and status and the opportunities they have afforded Elizabeth and their children certainly tip the scales in his favor.

Last night you accused me of a lie of such magnitude as to be an "unforgivable offense." Please consider, my dear Millie, that you, too, will find a Bernard of your own one day. Will that not be a better life than the one you might have had, living as the daughter of an ice man and his disgraced wife? Was not the secret of your parentage worth keeping if it prevented shame and embarrassment for our entire family?

I have made choices and kept secrets. For the life you have, and the lives protected by those choices and secrets, I regret nothing.

Please burn this letter after reading it. While your Papa will forgive me, I do worry whether his heart would survive such a shock.

I remain,

Your loving mother

I dropped the pages. "*Jade*," I breathed.

"Look," she said, nudging the suitcase upstage and scooting closer to me. It was clear she hadn't heard my exclamation. "It's recipes." She passed the book to me.

Stunned, I flipped the pages. The handwritten recipes had been set into photo corners with calligraphed labels pasted beneath them. "Mother's pancakes," I read out loud, "Swedish meatballs, krumkake, Willow Grove raspberry jam . . ." I gaped at her. "Willow Grove was the name of the Jorgensens' farm . . . Jade. I think these are their family recipes."

Jade gently flipped the book closed, then opened the front cover. "To Mother," she read out loud, "in celebration of your seventieth birthday. Love, Millie." She closed the cover. "She must have sneaked the recipes and put them together for this gift."

"But they've been famously missing for nearly a hundred years." I couldn't stop gazing at the cover. "Millie never gave her this present."

"How do you know?"

"Because the missing recipes were, like, a whole thing after Mrs. Jorgensen died. The daughters were all sure one of them had stolen them for herself. Lots of accusatory letters exchanged."

"When did Mrs. Jorgensen die?" Jade asked.

I did the mental math. "She was nearly eighty."

"So why didn't Millie ever give them to her?"

"I don't know . . ."

I flipped the cover open and reread the dedication: *To Mother . . .* Then I jumped. "You have to read the letter!" I handed the pages to Jade.

She read them, gasped, then read them again.

"*Elizabeth*," Jade whispered. "How old was she when Millie was born?"

More mental math. "Seventeen?"

"*Oh*," Jade breathed. "Poor Elizabeth."

I scanned the letter again. "Do you think she loved the ice man?"

"To risk everything like she did? Probably . . . And pregnant out of wedlock in the 1890s? Oh, honey. No wonder she went on to be a murderer."

"That's just in the play. It didn't happen in real life."

"But it sort of fits, doesn't it?" Jade said, letting the letter drift onto her lap.

This was all so amazing. The discovery of the recipes alone was wild. But the letter, too? The news about Millie and Elizabeth? Lula was going to freak out when she heard.

"Why was the letter tucked into the recipes gift?" Jade asked.

"Look at the back." I flipped the pages over. "I think Millie wrote it as a note to herself."

"If you're tempted to give her the book, reread this letter from your 'mother,'" Jade murmured. "Wow. It looks like Millie had this gift all set to go, but then she found Elizabeth's journal, who she *thought* was her older sister but who was actually her biological mother . . . I'd be pretty pissed at that lie, too."

"Yeah," I agreed. "And the things Mrs. Jorgensen says about Elizabeth being disgraced, that the child of an ice man would be somehow less than the child of wealthy people? It's pretty gross."

"Yeah . . . it really is." She took the letter from me and skimmed it again, her eyes growing darker as they darted back and forth across the page. "Poor Millie," she muttered. "I don't know what I would—"

Suddenly, Jade's face crumpled. Then she dropped the pages and stumbled to her feet, her skirts whooshing behind her.

"Hey, hey, hey," I exclaimed, scrambling after her as she headed stage right. "What's wrong?"

"Nothing." She waved a hand in front of her face. "I'm fine . . ." I caught up to her in the wings, a narrow black curtain behind me and another behind her. "I'm totally fine," she insisted, swiping at a few rogue tears.

"It's okay if you're not fine," I said.

"I know."

"I mean, it's a sad story."

She sighed. "I guess . . . I guess all that stuff about the lengths Mrs. Jorgensen went to—the things she had to change about Millie so she wouldn't be *embarrassed* by her . . . I mean, my parents . . ." Jade looked down at her hands. "It's a totally different situation. But they—" She shook her head. "I've been worried that if I don't get into an Ivy League school they won't be proud of me, but what if it's worse than that? What if I don't get in and they're *embarrassed* by me?"

I wanted to hold her. To make it all okay. But I knew that wasn't what she wanted from me. "No one could ever be embarrassed by you," I said instead. "There are laws against it that govern the universe."

She raised an incredulous eyebrow. "You were embarrassed by me."

"When?"

"Seventh grade."

"Seventh grade?" I scoffed. "No way. I mean, we were . . . competitive. But I was never *embarrassed* by you."

She coughed out a disbelieving laugh.

"Jade," I pleaded. "I'm serious."

"So am I."

"Then tell me."

She shook her head like she couldn't believe I was making her say it out loud. "You turned into Captain Sarcasm because you were embarrassed to be friends with a girl. Especially a know-it-all girl like me."

"Wait a second," I said. "The only reason I was . . . sarcastic was because you were mean to me first. Seventh grade is when you started calling me asshat."

She looked truly offended. "I walked into math class, day one of seventh grade, super excited to tell you about my trip to Bolivia with my parents—I'd bought you a T-shirt with a llama on it. But you took one look at me, called me 'Jack and the Beanstalk' and then bragged that Kendrick had taught you how to do the quadratic equation over the summer, and I'd have to figure it out on my own. And you were basically never nice to me again."

I stared at her. "*No.*"

"What possible reason did I have to cut you off as my best friend? Why would *I* have started it?"

I'd never been able to answer that question. Maybe because it was the wrong one.

"A llama T-shirt?" I asked.

"Yeah."

I'd started this . . . war? *I* had? Why? Why had I turned on her when she walked into class that day in seventh grade? I tried to remember. She was wearing purple jeans. I noticed because they were new. In fact, she had a bunch of new clothes because—

"You grew that summer."

"*Yeah*," she snapped. "I *know*."

"No, but, like. A *lot*—" It was coming back in waves. I stared somewhere in the middle distance, overwhelmed by the memories flooding back. "We were the shortest kids in our grade in sixth. Together. I didn't care that people called me Frodo, because I was Frodo with you."

"I remember," she said, her voice strained.

I looked up at her. "But then you weren't Frodo anymore. You were an Ent."

"I hate those books," she said. "You know that."

"But if you have Rob Inglis read them to you—" I held up my hands at her look. "Ents are tall. You were *so* tall . . . I guess . . . I guess I felt like you'd betrayed me."

"That's ridiculous."

"I was in *seventh grade*, Jade. Of course it was ridiculous."

"*I* wasn't ridiculous in seventh grade."

"*Everyone*'s ridiculous in seventh grade," I said. "It's part of being a person."

I waited. When she didn't respond, I lightly pushed her shoulder. She rocked back and forth on her heels.

"I'm sorry," I said. "All these years, I've been remembering this whole thing totally differently—that you got all snooty and competitive with me. But that's wrong. It's my fault, isn't it? It was totally my fault."

She peeked at me. Nodded once.

"I'm so sorry," I said again. "I don't want to fight with you. I want to—" I cut myself off. She knew what I wanted. And that kiss she'd shut down had shown me what *she* wanted. Or didn't want.

But then she asked, "You want to what?"

"Be . . . friends," I said, even though all I could think about was holding her. I forced myself to smile. "We're good together."

"At school," she said.

"At school," I confirmed, a little too loudly. "And in plays. We get each other. We know how each other's brains work. Our *brains* are really good together."

"Yeah," she said, but her heart didn't seem like it was in it. She took a deep breath and let it out. Examined her nails. "When do you think someone will come upstairs and find us?"

I fumbled with my watch, grateful for the distraction. "It's seven. Maddie said the run-through is at two."

"*Two?*"

"But interviews with PBS are earlier."

"When's earlier? Noon?"

My stomach growled, and I clutched at it. "Did you bring any food?"

She glared at me. Then she pulled an apple out of the pocket of her dress and thwacked it into my open palm.

"Ohh, thank you." I took a huge bite. "If only we had cheese," I said with a full mouth, trying to make her smile. "Or peanut butter." I swallowed and offered her the next bite. She turned the apple around, bit it, then handed it back to me.

"There are so many good apple snack recipes," I said, biting into it again. "In fact—"

She gasped, and I reached for her, worried she was choking. But she grabbed my arm. "Recipes, Turner. What if the *recipes* are the treasure?" She ran back to the edge of the stage and picked up the green leather book again. "What if Mrs. Jorgensen wasn't talking about her lost necklace at all?" she asked, striding back toward me. "What if it was these?"

I squinted at her. "Isn't that a little like friendship being the real treasure?"

"*No*," she said, opening the book. "Mrs. Jorgensen was nearly seventy when she wrote that her treasure was missing. And soon after, Mr. Jorgensen wrote, 'It's such a shame Anna cannot find her treasure.'"

"I mean, I guess it fits. For a family that had enough money to buy whatever they wanted, like more jewelry, something considered a treasure would have to be irreplaceable."

"Like handwritten family recipes," Jade said as she flipped through the pages. "But why didn't she just say 'my recipes are missing'? Why bother to call it a treasure?"

"I don't know. Victorian dramatics?"

"Maybe." She closed the book. "Well, it might not be a million-dollar necklace, but still, Finn. The recipes might be enough to push Mark Lester-Dean over the edge. They could have the recipe book published. Maybe in partnership with the Minnesota Historical Society. People stay here, love their Victorian weekend, buy the recipe book as a souvenir . . ."

I smiled. "And finding it makes a pretty great college application answer."

"Yeah."

I paused at the unusual note in her voice. "Are you disappointed we didn't find the necklace?"

"No," she said, hugging the book. "You're right. The recipes are a great story."

"Okay, so what is it?"

She shrugged. "It's pretty stupid, but when I told my parents my theory about Mrs. Jorgensen's lost necklace still being in the house, they got really excited. My mom confessed that she used to bury her grandmother's costume jewelry in the backyard and dig it up again because she wanted to be an archaeologist, and my dad said he dressed up as Indiana Jones for Halloween three years in a row, and then he brought out an *Indiana Jones and the Temple of Doom* movie replica whip and hat he bought in his twenties and we were laughing so hard and . . . it was . . . nice." Her lips trembled. "They're always pushing me to achieve—it's all we talk about. But for one little moment, I got this peek into my parents' joy. I think I thought if I found Mrs. Jorgensen's necklace, I would have a story to add to theirs, and feel like . . . I don't know . . ."

"You belonged with them?"

She pushed the curtain aside and headed toward the settee. "It sounds stupid when I say it out loud."

I followed her. "There's nothing stupid about wanting to fit in with your family."

We flopped next to each other on the settee and gazed out at the stage from the wings.

"Well, anyway," she said. "You held up your end of the bargain. You helped me find the treasure." She handed over the recipe book, and I set it on my lap.

"And you'll hold up your end and help me smash this mental block, and I'll audition for Acting Lab and—"

"Listen," she said, knocking her shoulder into mine. "If that's what you want, I will absolutely help you. But . . . you know you don't *have* to be in Acting Lab, right?"

I reveled in the pressure of her arm against mine. "But I want to be in Acting Lab."

"Why?"

I scoffed. "That's the next step."

"According to who?"

"Nomi. Lula. Andre. Kendrick."

"I doubt that very much."

"I don't know what to tell you. We're a theatre family."

"You aren't, actually. You're just a family-family."

"I'm going to audition for Acting Lab," I insisted.

"Then . . . I will help you."

Our chests rose and fell in unison. As much as I wanted to be with her, if we could be this—friends, on the same side—that would be more than enough.

She tugged the recipe book back into her lap. "So . . . why didn't it work out with Alexa?"

I stared at her shaky finger tracing the gold letters on the cover. "Why didn't it—?"

"Work out," she repeated, tucking her hand under her leg.

"I—I didn't want it to."

She flicked a glare at me. "Sure you did. An entire third of our agreement was centered around me paving the way for you and Alexa to—"

"Yeah, no, I know. And I appreciate that. It's just . . . things changed."

"Changed how?"

I could tell her the truth. But what if the truth smashed the delicate bridge between us?

"You don't have to tell me," she said.

"I mean, I want to, Jade. Just . . . promise me things won't be weird if I do."

"Weird?"

"Yeah. You've made it clear how you feel about me—about us. And I don't want you to think any of what I'm about to tell you is me trying to pressure you or—"

"Okay," she said, her voice quiet. She gripped the recipe book with both hands. "Just tell me."

"Okay." I blew out a stream of air between my lips. "When you and I kissed—"

"You can't start there."

"Why not? It's *my* story!"

"Don't care."

I rolled my eyes. "Where am I allowed to start then?"

She rolled hers back. "I'm sure you can find another entry point, Turner. You're never exactly at a loss for words."

I scoffed even though she was right. "Fine. Take two." I wiped my palms on my trouser legs. "Remember the night you sent Alexa to me under the stairs?"

Jade nodded.

"When she opened the door, I was disappointed . . . That's a pretty good indication of why it didn't work out."

"That doesn't make any sense. You were obsessed with her."

"I had a crush on her," I corrected Jade. "It's easy to crush on people when they're new and baggage-free. It's a lot harder to figure out how you feel about someone when you share a storage locker crammed with suitcases full of feelings."

She snorted.

"But . . . that night . . . before Alexa showed up under the stairs . . . I thought I'd sorted through them. And I was all set to tell you that I loved how close I felt to you during our conversations. That I couldn't wait to see you again when you were gone. That kissing you in the attic . . . hadn't felt like just practice to me."

Her face became unreadable, but I barreled on anyway. "But then you sent Alexa, so I was like, 'I guess I misinterpreted everything.' So when she asked if I wanted to make out with her, I thought, 'Why not?'"

"And?"

I shook my head. "I didn't feel anything. But she didn't like kissing me, either."

Jade squinted at me. "If it's your height, I swear to god—"

My lips twitched, pleased. "About thirty seconds in, she did back me onto a step stool."

"*She did not.*"

"She did. And the next night, we spent the entire time talking about Nomi's career. You were right. The minute she found out who my mom is, that was all she was interested in."

Jade let the recipe book slip onto the settee as she stood and took two steps away from me. "Are you disappointed?"

"*No!*" I scrambled to my feet, but I forced myself to stand still. "Seriously, Jade, no."

She spun around, and threw up her hands. "Then why did you keep meeting with her?"

"Because I needed her help in the show, feeding me my lines! I was scared of losing that. I'm not proud of it, but that's why!"

She tugged at her bodice and gritted her teeth. "You're infuriating, you know that?"

"*I'm* infuriating? *I* am?"

"You're saying you would have told me you liked me that night? Are you sure you're not reinventing the past because it didn't work out with Alexa?"

"No! Alexa and I were like . . . those tiny purple flowers that emerge for, like, ten minutes in the spring—crocuses. Pretty, but they don't last."

Her eyes furrowed.

"But you and I are like . . . for god's sake, Jade, you and I are like trees."

"*Trees?*"

"Yeah. They're solid. And they have those symbiotic root systems—"

"They're actually called mycorrhizal networks. They send each other nutrients and warn about insect attacks—"

I wanted to shake her. "—Because they're so connected. And I feel connected to you *all the time* without knowing how. Even when I'm furious with you, I don't know any other way to be around you but connected to you! And against my better judgment, I don't want it to be any other way."

She was quiet for a long time. When she finally whispered, "W-why?" I almost couldn't hear her.

"*Because,* Jade . . . you're my person."

It was so quiet in the attic, the only sound I could hear was my heart beating in my throat. I wished I could see her face. Guess what she was thinking. But she stood still. So, in one of the braver moves of my life, I waited.

CHAPTER FORTY-FIVE

When she finally turned around, her cheeks were wet.

"Jade—" I stuck a hand in my pocket for my handkerchief, but then she launched herself at me, and we stumbled backward onto the settee.

"I am going to kiss you now," she announced, taking my head in her hands.

Relief washed over me as I pulled her close, my heart beating a tattoo in my chest.

"But only because I want to kiss you," she insisted. "Not because you told me I'm your person, or because you somehow cross-pollinated *National Geographic* and Pablo Neruda. I am clearheaded—"

I grinned and made a mental note to find out who Pablo Neruda was as soon as possible.

"—I make my *own* decisions—"

And get a subscription to *National Geographic*.

"Plus—"

"Jade?" I whispered.

"Yeah?"

"I like you."

Her bravado dissolved. "Come here."

Our kisses were frantic—as if we had to hurry before everything fell apart again.

Then Jade's hands began to drift down my body, and before I completely lost all sense of reality, I had to know. "Jade—Jade. Hey—Just a second. *Jade.*" She pulled back. "Are we friends again or—are we—I mean—Am I also your—"

"Yes. And."

"And?" I gasped as she tugged my long Victorian shirt out of my trousers and traced the muscles on my chest, then my stomach.

"This okay?"

"*Yes.*"

"*And.*"

When I pulled the shirt over my head and tossed it onto the stage, and she laughed and said it looked like a parachute, I felt warm in the knowledge we were laughing together—not at each other. Not anymore.

I covered her body with mine and our kisses changed. These cleared away the hurt between us and all those years of misunderstanding.

Then, when she asked me to, I knelt behind her on the settee and unhooked her bodice, asking twice if she was sure before lifting her dress above her head. Even after it was on the floor, there were still so many layers of clothing between us, and we joked as I fumbled loosening her corset that it was a surprise anyone got together in the Victorian era with all these clothes. I stopped halfway through the unlacing when she said she wanted *this*, but just to be clear, she wasn't ready to invest in a jumbo box of condoms yet. I assured her I wasn't ready, either, but when I was, I wanted it to be with her. And together we removed her corset and added her chemise to the pile, and then she turned around, and I just looked at her and couldn't speak because she was too, too beautiful.

"What's wrong?" she whispered, covering herself when I jerked my head in the direction of the door. "Is it too much? Do you want to stop?"

"Never," I breathed, fumbling for clothes. "But I just heard the squeaky stair."

After grabbing my shirt off the pile, I hobbled across the attic as fast as I could. I pulled my head through the neck hole, but when I tried to jam my arm through the sleeve and found there were no sleeves to speak of, I realized I'd grabbed Jade's chemise instead of my shirt. Still. Any shirt was better than no shirt. Especially if it was Martin or Joan or Mr. Hoyt at the door. In the split second between the last footfall on the stairs and the door revealing who was standing there, I had a moment to wish for it to be Noah. Noah would understand.

The door swung open, and I caught it.

"Cute top."

"*Andre?*" I squawked. "What are you doing here?"

"I might ask you the same question," Andre said.

"He got his understudy to take the Saturday shows and flew home." Kendrick poked his head around Andre's shoulder. "He's only here for twenty-four hours, but we learned our lesson, Finn. We're together when disaster strikes." He frowned at me. "What are you wearing?"

I crossed my arms over my chest. "Uhhh." Someone I didn't know was standing behind Kendrick. "Hi! You must be Isaac!"

305

Andre and Kendrick parted, revealing a tall, gangly, pale-skinned guy with shocking blue eyes, dark-rimmed glasses, and auburn hair wearing a T-shirt that said, "You Matter! Unless you multiply yourself by the speed of light squared . . . then You Energy."

Isaac did *not* look like the guys Kendrick usually went for, who were conventionally handsome and did not have punny wardrobes. Or write heartfelt cards. I liked this Isaac guy already.

"Hi, Finn!" Isaac said. "Nice to meet you. K says it was your idea to call me." He beamed at Kendrick.

It gave Andre and I time to exchange a look. "K," Andre mouthed. I grinned.

"Yeah," I said, still blocking the door. How was Jade going to get dressed without my help? And with me wearing her chemise? "I did tell him to call you. It was a scary night. Thanks for driving all the way out here."

"Well, it was that or put up with him texting me every other minute." He directed this joke at Kendrick, whose shoulder bumped his, eyes full of bliss.

"Back to you, fancy pants," Andre said, nodding at Jade's chemise. "What's up with the lacy—" His eyes grew large and he thumped his chest twice. "Finn Erickson Turner! Is there—" He lowered his voice to a whisper. "*Sex* happening up here?"

I blush a lot. But this blush was next-level. "*No*," I insisted. "But—"

"But?"

"Look," I said, "the inside doorknob just spun and spun, so we got trapped—"

"Who's '*we*'?"

"Thanks for the rescue, fellas."

306

And there stood Jade, hair in place, dress back on. How had she managed the lacing without help?

My brothers exchanged a knowing look.

"Sorry to interrupt . . . whatever was going to happen here," Andre said. My face burned. "I do want to say, 'I called it.' But also, you're needed in the kitchen, Finn."

"And Jade, Mr. Hoyt has some questions about the revision," Kendrick added. "But more importantly, I called it first."

"No way," Andre insisted. "During *Blood Brothers*, I—"

Kendrick waved him away. "Yeah, yeah, yeah, but that was spring. In the fall, when they got in all those glow tape fights teching *Earnest*, I said, 'When they finally get together, it's going to get—'"

Andre punched the air. "'—super naked superfast!' Well done, Kendrick. Totally forgot about that—"

"Argh! What's wrong in the kitchen?" I interrupted at the same time Jade demanded, "Just tell me about the revision!"

"They're so cute together, aren't they?" Andre asked Kendrick and Isaac. "With their matching forehead worry lines and their mussed hair and their sex eyes—"

"Guys!" I said, raising my voice. "Please tease us later. *What's going on?*" All three of them laughed, and then Jade and I cracked up, and she plucked at the lace on my chemise, and I batted her hand away and said, "Finders keepers." She tucked her arm into mine as Andre and Kendrick caught us up, and I knew we both wished, despite everything, that we were still locked in the attic together.

CHAPTER FORTY-SIX

I was still grinning when I jogged through the kitchen door, the green leather book and the new script tucked under my arm.

"Finn! Where have you been?" Lindsey demanded as she waved a towel at fire blazing on the stove.

Letting the book and script fall onto the prep table, I pulled Lindsey out of the way and dropped a large pot lid on the flames, extinguishing them.

"Ugh, thank you!" she said. "Mrs. Dooley and Mr. Lord are being interviewed, and they told me to start separating eggs, but I didn't know what to separate them *from*, and then—"

"It's okay," I said, taking stock of the room. There were piles of random chopped things, and a pot of unrecognizable goop, but nothing else was on fire at least. "What's done?"

"Done?" Lindsey repeated.

"The soup should be simmering by now," I said, pointing at the plan that lay on the prep table, covered in food. "So should the sauce for the lobster."

"Well, people keep getting pulled out to talk to the PBS interviewers, and everyone has to re-memorize lines, and we also had to make breakfast. Seriously, Finn. Where did you go?"

I ignored her question. "Is there any breakfast left over?" I asked. My stomach growled so loudly Lindsey gaped at it.

She pointed at the pot of oatmeal next to the sink. "Brown sugar's in the bowl thing with the lid."

I grabbed a clean wooden spoon, crossed to the sink, dumped the rest of the brown sugar into the oatmeal pot and stirred, hauling it back to the prep table. "Okay, Lindsey. You go memorize lines." I took a bite. Lukewarm, but it would have to do. "I'll figure out what needs to be done here." She nodded and ran out the door.

"Finn."

Mouth full of oatmeal, I looked up. It was Mark Lester-Dean. *Oh, no.*

I swallowed hard. "Hi, Mr. Lester-Dean."

"Finn," he said again and strode across the kitchen. "Geoff Thatcher's husband just told me about your moms and sent me down here to 'get the plan from Finn.' What is going on?"

We faced off on opposite sides of the prep table.

"Um. I know it doesn't look good, but—"

"Someone should have called me last night when your parents left in an *ambulance*."

"We thought—"

"It's national television, Finn. And people are paying *a thousand dollars* a plate. That's a lot of money."

I gulped.

"You have no cook and no Mrs. Jorgensen. And unless you've got an airtight plan, I'm going to have to go upstairs and tell the PBS people this isn't happening and give an entire audience their money back. Without that last influx of cash, there's no way the Beauregard can afford to keep this house."

"Well—" I stirred the oatmeal, pretending it was progress on dinner. "I'm pretty sure—"

"*Pretty* sure?" Mr. Lester-Dean's phone buzzed. He fished it out of the pocket of his blazer and looked at the screen. "Hold on," he said, and stepped out of the kitchen.

I was sweating all over, and it wasn't just because I was standing by the stove. I dropped the oatmeal facade and leaned against the prep table. The pot of unidentifiable goop stared back at me. What the hell had happened down here? I'd left extremely clear step-by-step directions that I was sure anyone who could read could follow.

A bubble belched from the pot.

Apparently I was wrong. Maybe I'd written crappy instructions.

Or maybe there was more to cooking than reading after all.

Either way, food prep was already behind. How on earth was I going to memorize new cues and lines *and* supervise the most important meal of my life? Because without this dinner, Lula's dreams of this house would be over.

I rubbed my eyes with the heels of my hands. I needed to talk to someone. I took a step away from the prep table.

But I had to get started on the meal.

I stepped back. *I'll get the soup going first. Then the sauce. Then my lines.*

I reached for a fresh pot from the shelf over the sink. The pot in question should have slid into my hands. But it was stuck. I tugged at it. I had stacked the pots perfectly last week. It was a logical system that should have been easy to understand and keep up. I tugged again. Then again. *For the love of—*

When the pot finally jerked free, five others shot out after it— one banging hard into my elbow, the rest crashing like cymbals onto the floor.

I slammed the first pot into the sink, swearing over and over as the pain reverberated up my arm. A voice in my head told me to breathe and calm myself down, but why bother? There was no way this thing was going to come together. Sauces needed to simmer the amount of time they needed to simmer. Meat wasn't going to cook faster just because you needed it to. It had taken so much for me to prepare to play James, and I still had near misses every performance. But now? With new lines? My ears roared with the sighs of disappointed but unsurprised voices. Of Mark Lester-Dean informing us he was selling the house. Of Lula crying.

I gripped the edge of the sink. I was in way over my head. When Mark Lester-Dean returned—and holy mother of god, his phone call must have been pretty important not to come tearing in here after I made all that noise—I would tell him . . . what?

Noah jogged into the kitchen. "Hey, Finn. Silver's polished. Maddie sent me down"—he eyed the pots on the floor—"to help."

"Great," I said, my laughter bordering on maniacal. "How about memorizing my lines for me? Because I'm a disaster. Everything's a disaster. I don't know what I'm going to do—"

But Noah had disappeared into the pantry. When he emerged with a clean canning jar, he joined me at the sink and filled it with water. Then he handed it to me. "Drink, Finn."

I drank.

He put a hand on my shoulder when I was done. "Now breathe."

I breathed.

"I'll get Andre," he said. "He might have some tricks from when he learned James's lines in the first place."

I nearly burst into tears. "Oh my god, Andre . . ."

Noah offered me a small smile and waited for more.

Andre did not have my mental block. And we still had his costume. If being the cook was the only thing I had to do today, not only could I make the meal happen, I could make it something to remember.

I closed my eyes and leaned into Noah's hand. It was scary, thinking about giving up playing James. Mr. Hoyt would certainly see it as me giving up Acting Lab full stop. But I had to admit . . . giving it all up felt . . . light, too. If I was brave enough to let it go.

I thought about what Jade had said in the attic. Did I really believe my family would stop being proud of me—stop *loving* me—if I wasn't an actor?

"It's okay, Finn," Noah said, his voice soft.

I wasn't sure we were thinking about the same thing, but I met his eyes and nodded anyway. "Can you find Andre?"

"You got it, Chef." Noah squeezed my shoulder and jogged out of the kitchen.

Chef. The knots loosened in my neck.

Mr. Lester-Dean doubled back into the kitchen. "We're going to have to squeeze in four more people. Very, *very* VIPs. So start talking, Finn, because—"

I planted my hands on the prep table. "It's all under control. First of all, Jade revised the script. Mrs. Jorgensen's character has been written out of it."

"Okay . . ."

"And my brother Andre—"

"Hi!" Andre and Noah appeared in the door.

"I ran into him on the stairs," Noah reported.

"I thought I heard a crash and came running," Andre said. "You okay, Finn?"

Nodding, I gestured at my brother as he and Noah joined me at the prep table. "Second of all, Andre's home now," I told Mark Lester-Dean. "He's—" The words caught in my throat. This was it.

"He's what?" Mr. Lester-Dean prompted me.

I took a deep breath. "He's . . . come back to play James so I can focus on the meal." Andre's head jerked around, seeking my eyes, but I stayed focused on Mark Lester-Dean.

"Finn's a really good cook," Noah inserted.

Andre nodded. "His foods teacher said he was good enough to try out for Teen Chef Cook-off."

My chest warmed. Jade must have told him that. Or maybe Kendrick. Either way . . .

Mr. Lester-Dean's features smoothed. "Who did you say revised the script?"

"Jade Montgomery," I said. "She's the one you liked so much with the supersmart insights at the read-through, remember?"

He nodded. "All right then. Good start. But I still want to read the changes."

I pressed my rolled-up copy of the script flattish, then handed it to him.

Taking it, he glanced at the large watch on his wrist. "Make sure to account for those four extras, Finn. One of them is the governor."

313

The minute Mr. Lester-Dean was out of earshot, Andre took me by the shoulders. "Are you sure?" he asked.

"Absolutely."

"We can do a put-in rehearsal, the two of us, if you want, Andre," Noah offered.

"Thanks, man. Meet you in the library?"

Noah took the hint and, smiling, ducked out of the kitchen. He really was a good friend. I was glad I'd finally figured that out.

"Finn—" Andre began.

I closed my eyes. "Andre? Is it . . . is it okay if I don't audition for Acting Lab again?"

"Is it *okay*?" I peeked at my brother, whose eyebrows were drawn together in confusion. "Of course it's okay," he said. "Why wouldn't it be okay?"

"Because. We're a theatre family."

"Finn, we're a—"

"Family-family. I know. But—"

"And all it takes to make a family is—"

"People and love. But, Andre—"

"*People and love.* Please note the distinct lack of theatre in that equation."

I rolled my eyes.

He cupped my head in his hands and bent over a little, knocking our foreheads together. "Hey," he said. "You gotta say what's in that brain of yours more now than you used to when Kendrick and I lived at home. How am I supposed to beat down your weird-ass assumptions when you don't tell me about them?"

I snorted. He was right, though. Before he and Kendrick moved away, we talked a lot more, but we also communicated through looks and breaths and shoulder shrugs. No number of texts could replace the three of us living on top of each other in our wing.

He released my head and pulled me into a hug. "Finnster—"

I squeezed my eyes shut.

"Just be you. If that's a guy who's in shows, fine. If he's someone who's never in one again, also fine. Because it's you we love, numbskull. And you don't have to do anything to earn that."

Stupid, stupid tears. We held each other for a long time.

"We're a team, the five of us," Andre said, his voice thick all of a sudden. "And like it or not, you've got a limited-edition jersey."

"Costume," I corrected him.

He laughed. Then he took me by the shoulders and held me at arm's length. "Finnster. We've all watched you struggle onstage. But we thought you were struggling because it was something you wanted for yourself. That's one thing. But struggling for us? Because you think that's what *we* want?" He made a face. "Don't do that. Life's going to be a struggle anyway. So you might as well fill it with as many things as possible that make you happy."

My face was fighting with itself to smile or cry. "Cooking makes me happy," I admitted. "It makes sense to me. And I like learning about it."

"That's a great combination," Andre said. "Fill your life with stuff like that."

The pot of goop belched again. Startled, Andre dropped my arms. "What in the name of Mary Berry is that?"

I took the pot by its handle and inverted it into the compost bucket. "Nothing. Starting over."

"Better you than me."

"I feel the same way." We smiled. "I'm really glad you came back, Andre."

"Me too. Kendrick and I have been talking . . ." He sighed. "I give him a hard time for being so negative sometimes, but at least he's willing to examine problems. I mostly try to pretend they don't exist . . ."

That was true.

"So. You feel a little better?"

"Yeah. What about you? Need help working the lines back up?"

Andre scoffed. "No, I'll read them, like, twice, and—" He stopped and had the good grace to look chagrined. "I mean, no thanks, Finnster. I'll be fine."

CHAPTER FORTY-SEVEN

Alone at the prep table, I drew my finger down the menu.

In an effort to make it foolproof, I'd kept things super simple. (Though clearly not simple enough.) But I was back. And now the governor was coming.

I looked at the clock on the wall: nine a.m. There was still time to revamp. And Mrs. Jorgensen's book of family recipes seemed like a great place to start.

—··—

Ten minutes into writing up my new food plan, Isaac and his bright blue eyes strode through the kitchen door, a folded piece of paper held aloft in his hand. "Forsooth!" he said. "I cometh bearing news."

I smirked, forgiving the wrong century, and accepted the note. I recognized Jade's handwriting immediately.

Turner—
Mark Lester-Dean likes the revision, and he also
told me about Andre taking over James. I have a

million things to do right now between the lines and requests from Maddie, so I'm just dashing this off to tell you that I overheard Kendrick calling Andre to make plans for him to fly home. I figured once you saw Andre, you'd sacrifice yourself, give Andre the part, and save us all by cooking the big, fancy meal yourself. In fact, I was so sure, I made those changes to the script last night.

I frowned and looked up at Isaac, who handed me another copy of the script to replace the one I'd handed off to Mark Lester-Dean.

On page two, the cast list named Andre as James instead of me. Mouth agape, my eyes drifted back to Jade's note.

Call it a symbiotic tree root thing.

I smiled.

I gave you something else, though, if you want it.
Xo, J

I glanced back at the script's cast list and found my name. "Dead Cook?"

Isaac, apparently, had been briefed. "Jade said the play would be so much better with an actual person being the dead cook. So I have instructions to drive over to Costume Rental to get you a dress and a wig and a fake knife and some fake blood. You game?"

"I'd get to be the dead cook with a knife in her chest?"

He grinned. "Yup."

Suddenly, acting like a piece of furniture sounded pretty fun after all. "I'm in."

"Great!"

"But hey—while I've got you here, do you mind—"

"Also going to the grocery store? Jade said you'd probably need me to—"

"Because she thinks of everything."

He laughed. "Apparently."

<hr />

The rest of the day was a flurry of people in and out of the kitchen. I chopped and stirred and sautéed and baked and directed traffic, and everyone started calling me "chef" again, which felt better than any part in any play ever had.

Alexa stuck her head in the door midway through the afternoon. "Finn."

I looked up, then resumed stirring. "Alexa."

She stepped inside. "I was talking with Maddie . . . And maybe it wasn't supercool what I did after all."

"Oh . . . thanks."

"It's just—"

I scraped the side of the pot. "Oooh, the apology's going to be a lot better if you don't justify yourself, though."

She made an embarrassed noise in her throat. "You're right. I'm sorry. Full stop."

"And I'm sorry I didn't tell you right away how I was feeling." I took a dramatic breath. "It's just—"

"Finn!"

I winked at her. "Joke."

She put a hand on her hip and smiled at me. "Friends?"

We weren't going to get back to that breezy place we used to be in, probably. Then again—who knew? Jade and I had been mortal enemies, and now she was my girlfriend. "You bet. Friends."

At four o'clock, Maddie informed me each place setting was complete. "The china from prop storage is rimmed in gold," she reported. "We set goblets for water, champagne, red wine, white wine, and liqueur, plus dessert cutlery, a bread and butter plate and knife, three forks, three knives, and one spoon. Sound good?"

"Can we make it two spoons?" I asked, counting how many eggs I had left with one hand while stirring the boil down on a pot with the other.

"Copy that, Chef," Maddie said.

"I just hope everyone's super thirsty," Magnus said as the two of them went off in search of more spoons, "and really into silverware."

At five thirty, footsteps thundered down the stairs. I raised my eyebrows at the sight of Mr. Hoyt leading the entire cast into the kitchen. "Hey, Chef," he said. "Thought we'd preshow in here this time. Okay with you?"

"Yeah. *Yes.* Welcome to the kitchen, everybody."

Before the previous performances, we'd all met in the parlor upstairs for an in-character Mr. Jorgensen inspection that masqueraded as a pep talk.

This felt different.

"Circle up, everyone," he said. "Careful of the stove. So . . . how do we feel?"

As the cast nodded or muttered, "Good, ready," I smiled at this non–Mr. Jorgensen version of Mr. Hoyt.

"Any announcements regarding dinner?" he asked.

I stirred the sauce for the lobster Newburg on the stove. "There are snacks and finger foods in the servants' dining room to get you through the dinner and the show," I said, "but I have something special planned for our postshow party."

Whoops and hollers made me blush into the saucepan.

"Thank you, Finn," Mr. Hoyt said. "And let's take a moment to also thank Jade for excellent script doctoring, Maddie for organizing us all, and Andre for taking over James at the last minute."

"And Isaac," I called over the applause, "our lifeline to the twenty-first century!"

More whoops.

"All right, then," Mr. Hoyt said. "Ready to do this one more time? In the middle."

I removed the sauce from the heat. Pushing my way in next to Jade, our hands found each other's for a moment before putting them into the circle.

"For Laura on three," Mr. Hoyt said.

Then time slowed down.

"One!"

Everyone's faces were wide open.

"Two!"

They'd done so much for my family over the past two weeks.

"Three!"

My heart lurched as I realized: Love plus People.

"For Laura!"

They were family now, too.

Everyone hugged everyone else, Victorian rules be damned. When Kendrick found me, he said in a low voice, "Nomi called. It's torturing

Lula not to be here, but she's okay. They told me to tell you they're so proud of you."

Finding a speech-preventing lump in my throat, I hugged Kendrick extra hard.

Then Jade hooked my elbow and tugged me into the storeroom. Grinning, I kicked the door closed and pressed her against a shelf to kiss her, but when I looked into her stern face, I pulled back. "What's wrong?"

"Nothing's wrong. I wrote—" She eyed me up and down. "You look really cute in that apron."

I offered her a lazy smile.

She blew air out like she had a straw between her lips. "Just—hold your horses, Turner," she said. "Business first. I wrote up—"

I crossed my arms and stepped back to keep myself from touching her. Her eyes dropped to my biceps. "Oh, screw it. Come here."

Kissing her this time was even better, if that was possible. Being with Jade was another thing that made me happy, and made sense to me, and I liked learning about.

"Where's Finn?" someone's muffled voice came through the door. "Is this pot supposed to be on the burner?"

Jade pushed me away from her. "You have to get out there."

"I know," I said, even though the last thing I wanted was to let her go. "But more of this . . . later?"

She struggled to catch her breath. "I mean, my god, yes."

My face was starting to hurt from smiling so much. I reached for the door handle.

"Oh, wait," she said. "The whole reason I grabbed you—well, part of the reason—"

I laughed. "Come with me. I have to save that lobster sauce."

Hand in hand, we passed through the storeroom door and fielded knowing smiles from the remaining serving staff.

"So," Jade said as we grinned and hurried over to the stove, "I wrote a very funny version of the house manager announcement for you to do as the dead cook." I shot her a look over my shoulder as I pulled the lobster sauce back onto its burner. "It's an *announcement,*" she repeated. "You can read it from the script. Will you do it?"

I stirred the sauce and looked her in the eye. "Jade, I would do anything for you—"

Her face softened.

"—that doesn't involve delivering memorized lines."

She crinkled up her nose and leaned in close. "I'll give you something to memorize . . . asshat."

I mock-glared at her and indicated the pot in front of me. "You're lucky I'm so busy and important with this whole cooking thing—"

She pressed her lips together against a laugh. "Am I?"

"Uh-huh. Because I'm pretty sure we said 'asshat' was off the table."

"Hmm." She backed out of the kitchen, never breaking eye contact with me. "Don't remember agreeing to that. I guess you'll have to go back and—"

"Double-check my work," we said in unison.

She leaned against the doorframe on the other side of the kitchen. "I like you," she mouthed.

My heart surged, and I pushed the pot off the burner so she knew I was giving her my full attention. I faced her and tapped my chest. *Me too.*

CHAPTER FORTY-EIGHT

The next hour and a half flew by as I supervised seven courses marching up and down the stairs. The PBS cameras filmed B-roll footage of me adding oak lengths to the firebox, folding lobster meat into its sauce for lobster Newburg, and stopping Magnus to add a sprig of parsley to the mashed potatoes before he swept them away.

Finally, I handed Mr. Lord the dessert: something called "Dolly Varden cake." It was a multilayered, jelly-filled, frosted thing packed with cinnamon, cloves, and nutmeg that I'd found the recipe for in Mrs. Jorgensen's book. It smelled delicious, was beautiful to look at, and promised to be the showstopper I'd hoped for.

As Mr. Lord disappeared around the corner with the cake, I checked my wristwatch: forty-five minutes before the show began. I still had to get dressed and put on makeup. As I passed into the pantry, intending to climb the servants' stairs up to the second floor, Maddie and Magnus stopped me, holding my costume and accessories.

"We thought you might need help getting dressed," Maddie said.

We took the dress out of the dry-cleaning bag along with a petticoat, corset, chemise, bloomers, and a large pair of round bean bags. I held them, one in each hand. "What are these for?" I asked.

"They're your boobs, Finn," Maddie said. Magnus scooped them up from my stunned palms and weighed them in his own appreciatively.

"Realistic?" Maddie asked tightly.

I smirked. There was nothing Magnus could say that would be okay in this situation.

"I . . . have no opinion," Magnus said, setting them gently on a shelf.

For the second time that day, I wore a chemise. I tied the stockings over my knees, then stepped into my pantaloons. Corset next, which both nearly suffocated me *and* made me more fully appreciate what the women had been putting up with for the past two weeks, not to mention the centuries of women before them. After tucking my birdseed breasts into place, the petticoat went over my head, then finally, my navy tweed dress.

"Wait—we've got it on backward," Maddie said.

"No, we don't," Magnus corrected her. "Downstairs servants had to dress themselves, so their laces were in the front."

Maddie stared at him.

Magnus leaned back. "Right? Or am I not right?"

"No—" Her voice was raspy, and her eyes never left Magnus's. "You're right."

He cocked a smile. "I am?"

Oh god, I thought. *I've got, like, three seconds to escape.*

Maddie bit her lip. "What else do you know?"

"Uh . . ." Magnus grinned and dropped his voice. "The organ has one thousand and six pipes." Maddie started pushing him out of the room. "And when those gas-powered dragon wall sconces outside the art gallery are lit, they look like—"

They disappeared around the corner, but I heard Magnus say, "—they're breathing fire!" Then Maddie said something and their giggles and clacking footfalls echoed off the marble until they thundered up the stairs.

I yanked on the laces on the front of my dress. "I guess I'll finish by myself," I joked.

Mr. Hoyt appeared at the doorway, makeup caddy in hand.

"Oh, hi, Mr. Hoyt. I mean Mr. Jorg—" I felt sweaty all over.

Mr. Hoyt chuckled. "Hey, Finn. It's okay. It's been a pretty intense fifteen hours."

"*Yeah.*"

"I know you can do your own makeup, but I didn't think you had a lot of blood, guts, and gore experience, so I thought I'd see if you needed help."

Not long ago, I think I would have brushed him off and managed it myself, but instead, I said, "Thanks—that would be great."

"Should we go outside so we don't get fake blood in here?"

I led him out of the kitchen and into the hall, but as we wove our way around flats and props on our way out the door, I knew it was time to tell him I wasn't going to audition for Acting Lab anymore. But how? Unless . . . he was already assuming I wasn't?

We set up two chairs across from each other on the kitchen porch, and Mr. Hoyt opened his giant tackle box full of makeup.

"Foundation first," he murmured, and started dabbing a few different colors on my hand to find a match.

A warm breeze blew across the cool porch, and I stared at the rainbow of beige streaks Mr. Hoyt was making on my skin. *Ease in*, I told myself. "So . . . I just want to say thanks, Mr. Hoyt."

"Oh. No problem. Part of being an actor is learning a lot about makeup. I'm happy to help." Mr. Hoyt selected a foundation color and gestured for me to look up.

"No, but, I mean, thank you for that, too."

"Too?"

"Thank you for taking this part," I clarified, looking at the curved brick ceiling as Mr. Hoyt sponged the foundation across my forehead. It was a little easier to talk when I didn't have to make eye contact. "For helping out my family."

"Of course," Mr. Hoyt said. "I'd do anything for Laura. Close your eyes."

I tried to keep my face smooth for the makeup's sake, but I wanted to smile. I knew what being willing to do anything for Lula felt like. Mr. Hoyt swept the sponge with foundation across my ears, eyelids, cheeks, nose, and neck. Finally, I said, "You met in college, right?"

"We sure did. You can open up." Mr. Hoyt tucked the concealer and sponge back into the caddy. "We became friends when we both needed a good one at the same time."

"Oh. Sure," I said, thinking of Noah. "Why did you need a good friend?"

"Uh . . ."

I blushed. "Oh. Sorry, Mr. Hoyt. I don't mean to pry."

"No, no—it's okay." Mr. Hoyt selected a flat container of white powder. He flipped the container over, then back, then twisted off the lid. After loading the brush, he blew across it. "Close again." He patted the places on my face he'd sponged on foundation. "Let's just say my family has never particularly understood the theatre thing."

"That's the absolute *opposite* of my family. Theatre is everything to us." I sneezed a little as he powdered my nose. "Well," I said, thinking of what Andre and I had talked about, "almost everything. Still, it sucks that your family didn't understand."

"Open." Smiling a little, Mr. Hoyt replaced the brush inside the caddy and took out a wheel of makeup with dark purple, blue, olive green, and a brownish yellow. "You're an old lady who's been working long hours her whole life, so I'm going to give you some under-eye bags. Then we'll powder one more time and get that knife in your chest. Okay?"

"Okay."

"Look up."

I complied.

He dabbed layers of colors under my eyes. "Think about it from their point of view, Finn. The only certain things are death and taxes. So you make money to pay those taxes. And to take care of your family after you die. I like to think they disapproved of my choices out of love."

I laughed a little. "I know all about doing things out of love."

Mr. Hoyt leaned back and inspected his handiwork. "Yeah?"

"Yeah. I knew a long time ago this mental block was going to make it really hard for me to—" My breath caught. This was it. I dried my palms off on my skirt. "Um. Mr. Hoyt? I'm . . . not auditioning for Acting Lab again . . . but you knew that, right?"

He gave me a half-smile. "I love having you in shows, Finn. You have great energy, and you take direction well."

"But I'm not confident enough when it comes to lines."

He shrugged. "The thing is, Finn, you're so good at other things. Michael Shurtleff wrote one of my favorite books about acting, and he says if you can imagine yourself doing anything other than theatre, go do it. But I would say that's true for everything. Laura's always telling me, 'Drop yourself into the stream of the universe, Fletcher.' It's a little . . . out there for me, but I kind of like what it suggests."

"Yeah. I've heard her say that." I tugged at my bodice. "But instead of doing it, I think I've been trying to re-form the universe's riverbanks."

Mr. Hoyt considered this. "I'm not saying life is always easy. But when things get difficult, I think we have to ask ourselves: Am I making things unnecessarily harder for myself? And if the answer is yes, then my god, Finn. Get out of your own way."

"Yeah . . . I mean, I love theatre," I said. "But memorizing does *not* fill me up. If only there were something where I could have a script the whole time."

"I don't know," he mused, packing up his makeup kit. "There are things like that. Voice-overs. Audiobooks."

Audiobooks. Maybe I could join the ranks of my favorite narrators. Maybe someday Julia Whelan and Bahni Turpin could come over for a dinner I made, and we could all talk about our latest projects. I laughed. "Yeah. I guess it doesn't have to be all or nothing, does it?"

Mr. Hoyt smiled and shook his head. "I really wish there was a way that Lab would have worked out for you, Finn. But I have a feeling Ms. Pedina will be elated to have you join her Advanced Cooking seminar in the fall."

It was as if Mr. Hoyt had opened the door to a hallway I'd forgotten existed. "Advanced Cooking!" I exclaimed.

"Now, don't drop out of theatre entirely," Mr. Hoyt said. "You're a wonderful dancer. But only do it—"

"If it fills me up. I know. Thank you, Mr. Hoyt."

"Of course."

He wiped off his hands on his handkerchief, and we stood. "You seem taller suddenly."

"That—that's the first time anyone has ever said that to me."

Mr. Hoyt quirked an eyebrow.

"Short guy. No one thinks I'm taller than I am."

"Tell you what, Finn—I grew four inches my freshman year of college."

"Yeah?"

"Absolutely. There's still hope."

"That's what my parents say. But it's okay. Being this height sure weeds out the riffraff."

He laughed. "Let's get your wig on. I'm going to cover you in blood, then it's time to get into places. You look like a super dead old lady, Finn."

"Thanks for that as well."

CHAPTER FORTY-NINE

Right before the show started, Mr. Hoyt ushered everyone into the dining room, far away from the audience. Which was smart, because the cast couldn't stop laughing at my costume.

"The bags under your eyes!" Maddie cackled.

"And your wig!" Lindsey exclaimed from behind her hands.

"Dude. You're the ugliest lady I've ever seen," Magnus promised.

"Got it out of your systems?" I swung my torso from side to side to show off the fake butcher's knife implanted in my chest.

"Stop it!" Jade moaned. "I'm going to laugh-cry my makeup off!"

"One minute to places," Isaac called in his role as our new house manager.

"Thank you, one!" everyone called back. With last grins at me over their shoulders, the cast filed out of the room for the top of the show.

Jade pressed a sheet of paper into my hands and kissed my cheek. "Here's the new opening speech. Break a leg."

I had a moment to myself in the grand hall to give the speech a quick skim while Isaac was getting everyone settled. Then he passed through the curtains and gave me a thumbs-up.

I peeked inside the music room. Well-dressed audience members—including the governor of Minnesota and her husband—filled the two semicircles of folding chairs. I took a deep breath and pushed through the curtain.

The knife in my chest elicited several gasps and murmurs from the crowd. I wanted to smile but knew the woman I was playing would not be terribly happy about having just been murdered. I glared at them all instead before beginning to read.

"My name is Philamina Wintergarden—" *Good lord, Jade. What a name.* "And until last night, I was the cook here at the Jorgensen House. This morning, I was murdered. You look like stupid people—"

The audience laughed good-naturedly.

"So I don't expect you to be able to solve who did it. But I can't remember, and here you are, so." I made a *harrumph* sound in my throat. "Tomorrow, Mrs. Jorgensen is hosting a ridiculously large party. Today, two young potential suitors of two insipid Jorgensen daughters have been invited a day early to get to know the family. You, too, have been invited as an invisible, silent guest. Now if that isn't some highfalutin crockery, I don't know what is."

I read the rest of Jade's speech, delighting in Cook's crotchety attitude and insults to the audience. The laughter that ensued made me think that we should have been doing it this way all along.

Too soon, the speech was over, and I excused myself to die. I opened the curtains, Martin Lord as the butler appeared, and the play began.

I had time to think as I lay on the ground in the silver safe. Even after the Beau collected all the money, would it really be enough to fix the roof? I thought about how hard Lula worked and the toll it took on our family. And what Kendrick had said about spending all this time and money on a house that would never be ours. Did taking care of the Jorgensen House fill Lula up? Or was she making her life—and our lives—harder than they needed to be? Inside my head, I walked from room to room of the house. I loved it, but the only places outside of our wing where I felt like I wasn't just a caretaker were the attic and the gatehouse: two places where I didn't have to worry about not touching the walls and minding the furniture. What would it feel like to live somewhere I could just *live*?

Soon organ music filled the house, and I knew the cast was dancing. That meant it was time for me to come back to life so the audience could withdraw and deliberate.

"All right, stop staring, get back here," I said as Cook. I led the audience members back into the music room and folded my arms across my ample bosom. "So. Who killed me?"

Even with previous audience members signing nondisclosure agreements, I was surprised that the solution to both mysteries hadn't leaked out over the two weeks. So debate was raging in the room.

After a few minutes, they decided that Bridget, the scullery maid, played by Lindsey, was the killer and that Magnus's character, Jeremiah, had stolen the painting. They were only half right—it was Jade's character, Elizabeth, who was the killer.

I wasn't supposed to let them see the final scene, but it was our last performance. (The fact they'd all paid a thousand dollars a plate didn't hurt, either.)

"Something's coming back to me," I said, clutching my head. "It's a woman, yes, but she doesn't work here."

"Is that a hint?" the governor asked, clasping her hands together.

"Do I look like a nice person?" I improvised. "I'm not giving you a *hint*, I'm just telling you what I *remember*."

"It has to be a family member then," a tiny old woman in a seersucker suit said. "My money's on Elizabeth!"

My clue was enough to tip them over to the correct answer, and I made a show of remembering it all. Then I hurried them back to the dining room to see the final scene.

Before I collapsed back on the ground, dead, I found Jade's eyes, and she winked at me.

God, she was everything.

━━

After the final scene, we took our bows. With the PBS cameras rolling, we answered audience questions about the house and the process of putting on the show and living like Victorians for the past two weeks. Then Mr. Lester-Dean clasped his hands together.

"We are so proud of all the hard work that has gone into making tonight happen," he said. "Thank you all for coming to the Jorgensen House and supporting the Beauregard Theatre!"

I stared at him. No mention of Lula. Or that Nomi wrote the play. I cleared my throat.

"Oh," Mark Lester-Dean said, "and of course, a round of applause for our actual cook, who also played the dead cook, Finn Turner!"

Everyone applauded, but I held up a hand. "Thank you, but I'd also like to acknowledge three very important people. First, my mothers, Laura and Naomi Turner. Naomi wrote the script, and

Laura renovated this house and directed the play. Laura had a medical emergency yesterday, so she and Naomi aren't here tonight."

The audience murmured their concern, and I nodded to accept it. "Also, Geoffrey Thatcher, the former artistic director of the Beau, who recently passed."

Martin's hand fluttered to his chest, and Joan and Lindsey glided to his side.

"Geoffrey loved this house and loved Laura's passion for transforming it. Tonight is a perfect thank-you to him. It may have been a very irresponsible thing to do financially—"

The crowd chuckled.

"But my brothers and I have had a wonderful childhood here, and we thank him for his irresponsibility." The audience laughed again. I looked around. "I should have a drink or something to toast. Who's the chef around here?"

CHAPTER FIFTY

As the audience began to leave, Jade sidled up next to me. "Sorry for murdering you," she teased.

I chuckled and took her hand.

"You were really good tonight, Turner."

"I was dead!" I protested.

"No, you did that whole speech. And improvised a *lot*. Especially that great bit at the end. Maybe you should be in improv."

Another aspect of theatre that didn't involve memorizing lines. "I'll think about it," I promised. I tried to hug her but realized I still had the knife in my chest. "Oh, uh—" I cleared my throat. "Hey, everyone? Once you get out of costume, meet downstairs in the kitchen. I've made lemon meringue pie!"

Cheers.

Jade squeezed my hand.

"It's Mrs. Jorgensen's recipe," I told her. "It called for a huge number of lemons, though. I'm not sure if it turned out."

"Wait. Lemons are hybridized now. Did you use a million modern lemons? They used to be a lot smaller."

"They *did*? *No!* That pie's going to be soup!"

"You get to make mistakes," she laughed, "even at the things you're supposed to be great at."

"It's still embarrassing! If I had known you had so much knowledge about Victorian citrus, I would have asked for your help."

"Well, I can still help," she said, looping a finger through my bodice lacing. "You need *help* getting out of costume, don't you?"

I broke into a huge grin. "I *do*."

"Think again," Mr. Hoyt said, appearing out of nowhere behind us.

Jade and I blushed and separated.

For now. After all, everyone was spending one more night here, and it was a big house.

―――

After climbing out of my costume and washing my face, I descended to the kitchen, hoping against hope that Jade had been wrong and my lemon meringue pie was okay.

Noah and Magnus were leaning on their elbows on opposite sides of the prep table, eyeing the pie.

"Can we eat it now?" Noah asked.

"It might not have set," I warned him.

"It's still pie," Magnus said. "How 'bout now?"

"I'll get plates," Noah offered.

I poked at the pie, and the insides sloshed over the crust. "Better make it bowls instead."

Alexa, Jade, and Maddie arrived next, arms full of cell phones. "The twenty-first century has arrived!" Maddie announced.

I dove for my phone and switched it on.

Jade put her hand over mine. "You sure you're ready?"

"Ready for what?"

"To leave 1891."

"*Yes.*"

She cocked her head. "I'm not sure I am."

"Why not?"

"I liked who I was here. I mean, lots of problems for women and people of color for sure, but . . . as Elizabeth Jorgensen, I didn't see subtweets about me that made my stomach ache."

I set my phone on the prep table and interlaced our fingers.

"Plus, I got to find a treasure," she said.

"Was it me?" I joked.

She snorted. "Yup. The treasure was friendship after all, Turner."

But before I had a chance to see if my phone would even turn on, Kendrick tapped my shoulder. "Let's go."

I tore my eyes from the screen. "Where? Why?"

"The parents are home."

"They *are*?"

"Yeah. Come on."

"Jade, I gotta—"

"Go," she said. "I'll find some straws."

⌲

I followed Kendrick up two flights of stairs to our family wing. When we passed through the door, Andre was waiting for us.

"Hey, guys," he said in a quiet voice. "Leave the lights off, okay?"

Kendrick and I rounded the corner with our brother. Our moms were on the couch—Nomi on the end, Lula's head in her lap. Their faces looked like they hadn't slept much but were also relieved to be home.

"Hi, boys," Nomi whispered.

"Hi," Kendrick and I said, our voices watery.

"It's okay. She's fine," Nomi assured us, stroking Lula's hair.

I had held it together for twenty-four hours. I'd been brave and strong and resourceful. But now, seeing Lula there, in that same position of vulnerability I'd seen her in during her cancer fight, tripped something inside me. Tears spilled down my cheeks.

"Oh, honey," Nomi said. But she wasn't only oh-honeying me. Tears ran down Kendrick's cheeks, too.

I reached for him, and we held each other and shook from sobbing. Andre wrapped his arms around us both.

"Let it out," Lula said, her eyes still closed. "Let it all out. But it's okay. I'm fine. Just a big bump on my head. Some stitches."

"It's not just football players who get concussions," Andre joked. "Turns out we theatre people live dangerous lives, too."

"Come here, boys," Lula said, reaching out a hand. "Sit close. I missed you."

We knelt on the rug close to the couch.

"You sure you're okay?" Kendrick asked.

"No loud noises or bright lights or screens for a while," Nomi whispered.

"We have something to talk about," Lula said.

"We don't have to do that right now."

"Yes, we do. They need time to think. And they need to go back to the party. Kendrick—Isaac's here."

Kendrick huffed out a laugh. "Yeah. I know."

"Andre says blue eyes . . . refraction . . . what did you say, Andre?"

"She's overtired," Nomi said, smiling.

"They have to go back to the party," Lula repeated. "The refraction is waiting."

Now I laughed, too.

"You did so well, gentlemen," Lula said. "We all did so well. Except my cooking. It was ambisimal. Ambisimal. Naomi, I can't say—"

"Abysmal?"

"Yup. That word was my cooking. But we did it. The guy is going to do the house."

We looked to Nomi for a translation. "Mark Lester-Dean says Lula's plans for the house are a go."

"So," Lula said. "Whaddya think?"

"What do you mean?" Kendrick asked. "You do it."

"That sounded like Kendrick," Lula said.

"It was."

"No, but I mean it sounded like *Kendrick*."

Kendrick chuckled. "Mom. It's me. It's Kendrick. I think you should do the things you want to do here. The Victorian immersion. The fundraisers. The whatever. You believe in this place and what it can do. So . . . I believe in *you*."

"If you want to do them," I added, Mr. Hoyt's words in my head. "Do you want to, Lula? Just because you've sunk a lot of time and energy into something doesn't mean you have to keep doing it. Or do it because that's what you think people want you to do."

"It's not just about what I want," she said.

"It kinda is," Andre mused. "Well, you and Nomi. Kendrick and I don't really live here anymore. And Finn'll be gone in another year."

Now tears dropped onto Nomi's cheeks.

I reached up and held her hand. "What do *you* want, Nomi?"

She let out a shuddering sigh. "I want you all close to me forever."

"In the important ways, always," I said. "What else?"

"Well . . . I've always wanted a big garden."

"We can plant a big garden," Lula drawled.

"No, I mean—" Nomi swallowed. "I want my *own* garden."

"Like at your own house?" I asked.

She hesitated, then nodded.

"What did she say?" Lula asked. "My eyes are too closed to see."

We all looked to Nomi.

"I said . . . yes."

"You want our own house? Let's get a house," Lula said. "I didn't know you wanted a house. We don't have to live here. I can just work here. Do all the crazy here. And we live in a different house. Away from the crazy. Why didn't you tell me?"

"Because you've said a thousand times that this is the only place you've ever felt at home. I couldn't take that away from you."

"Baby," Lula murmured. "Home is where *you* are."

Nomi's chin trembled. Then she brought one of Lula's hands to her lips.

"I'm sorry for making you feel like you couldn't . . . want . . . house."

Lula's breathing changed.

"She's asleep," Andre whispered.

We all exhaled in unison.

"So," I said in a low voice. "Looks like we're moving."

Nomi regarded me. "How do you feel about that, Finn?"

"If you'd asked me two weeks ago . . . I would have freaked out," I admitted. "But . . . I don't know. I think I'm okay with it. Lula's

341

right—it's the people we love that make a home. But—oh my god, I can't believe I didn't lead with this—I think Jade and I found the treasure."

"Is that a euphemism for sex?" Kendrick asked.

I reached around and whacked him on the chest. "*No.* And *shut up.*"

"Finn?" Nomi asked as Kendrick and Andre cackled silently. "What—"

"Finn and Jade finally got together," Kendrick said.

"Got together?" Nomi repeated. "Okay . . . Um. Finn, did you use protection?"

"*Oh my god,*" I complained. "We just kissed. We're . . . dating, or whatever. *That's all.* Plus, I know—I've had health class. Forget about that for a second. Let me tell you about the treasure!"

"Jade," Nomi said to herself. "I like that Jade."

I tried, but failed, to push down a smile.

———

I explained about how we searched for the necklace, then found the recipes and the letter and the book.

"Wow," Nomi and my brothers breathed when I finished.

"Millie Jorgensen was Anna and Karl's *granddaughter,*" Kendrick mused.

"But raised as their daughter," Andre said.

"Poor Elizabeth," Nomi whispered. "I can't imagine being denied my child like that."

"Does it change how you feel about this house?" I asked Kendrick.

Kendrick blew some air between his lips. "I don't know. It changes how I feel about Millie, though. I mean, she never got married. I always thought it was because she thought she was better than everyone. But I wonder if she didn't ever get married because she wanted to prove Mrs. Jorgensen wrong. Being married to the 'right person' didn't have to dictate her happiness."

"Yeah," Andre said. He paused. "I always thought Millie never got married because she was gay. Do we have any evidence of that, or did I make that up?"

Nomi shrugged. "It's possible. It's also possible she saw her sisters' lives with men and decided she'd rather have the autonomy that being single afforded her. She certainly had the privilege of money to make that choice a possibility."

"What are we going to do about the recipes and the letter?" I asked Nomi. "Are we going to make them public? How does all of this change the Jorgensens?"

Nomi shook her head. "Millie was the youngest, and even after her entire family died, and she lived another thirty years, she never revealed what was in that letter. We have to consider that. But this is very interesting." She stroked Lula's hair again. "Lula will be *very* interested." She grinned at me. "You found the Jorgensen treasure, Finnster."

"Jade did, really. I found the flashlights."

Nomi chuckled. "Well. You three should get back to the party."

"You coming?" Andre asked.

"Oh, no," she said, pulling out her phone. "I've got an online date with some real estate listings."

<hr />

As the three of us clomped down the central staircase back to the party in the kitchen, Andre tugged at my shirt. "Hey, not to rain on your parade or anything, but are you sure the recipes are the treasure?"

"No," I admitted. "But the Jorgensens definitely treasured them if Millie went to all that work putting them together."

"I suppose anything can be treasure, really," Andre said. "It depends on what you value."

"I can see why *you'd* value those recipes, Finnster," Kendrick said as we rounded the corner on the landing. "You're such a good cook."

I beamed. "Thanks."

"And that you'd treasure Jade. She's—"

"Her name is *Jade*!" Andre interrupted him.

"Huh?"

"The gemstone? Jade?"

I stopped walking. "*Jade*—"

"I get to tell her!" Andre shouted, running down the grand hall to the servants' staircase. Kendrick and I tore after him. "Ja-ade!" Andre hollered.

"Andre!" I yelled.

Andre disappeared down the stairs, Kendrick at his heels. "Ja-ade!" they shouted together. "You were the treasure all along!"

And like I had my whole life, I chased after them, laughing.

Acknowledgments

Pulling off this rompy, unexpectedly personal book took an army. Thank you to all my parents and my sisters for loving me fiercely. Dan, Eliza, and Eleanor: The three of you make me feel like I've won the lottery.

Craig Johnson, the former site supervisor of the James J. Hill House in St. Paul, Minnesota, was an absolute godsend. I cannot thank you enough, Craig. Thank you also for Hill House help from Alex Weston, Mark Taylor, and docents Joe, Cynthia, and Stacey. While the Jorgensen House is a fictional place, I derived much inspiration from the Hill House. Give it a tour the next time you're in St. Paul!

Thanks to Kelsey Hokenson, the Ramsey House site supervisor, and ReNee, Mark, and Adriel, for teaching me about Victorian-era wood-burning stoves.

The Minnesota History Center! To the librarians at the Gale Family Library, curators Ann Frisina, Tom Braun, and Jenna Bluhm, and especially to my former student Hannah Novillo, thank you for being so awesome!

Nancy, the cooking and baking historian at Villa Louis in Prairie du Chien, Wisconsin, taught me about hybridized lemons and the time she mistakenly made lemon meringue soup instead of pie.

Much gratitude to Erika Kent for sharing her experience restoring Ten Chimneys in Waukesha, Wisconsin, and the tension between historic preservation and accessibility. I also loved hearing Erika talk about aspects of Ten Chimneys that "made the Lunts feel not so far away."

Katie McGlynn suggested I go see our college friend Ryan Reilly in Chicago in Windy Cindy's production of *Southern Gothic*. Thank you to stage manager Jenniffer Thusing, who let me shadow her, and to the August 2019 cast for sharing your stories of performing in such an unusual production! Special thanks to Ryan Reilly and Jay Geneske for putting me up and making me feel so welcome.

I owe much to my former colleagues in costume rental at Norcostco, but for this book, particularly Mandi, who loaned me a corset for a little "method" writing.

Thank you to Allison Hackenmiller, Dr. Liz Keeling, David Kundin, Julie Scullen, and Steve Slavik for helping me fight for my sabbatical as well as past and present members of the English Department and my principal Mike George for your unending support.

Thank you to my students. (Particularly all my CW II students, who know how I got the idea for this book.) I love every single one of you.

Nina LaCour's Slow Novel Lab class changed the way I will write forever. Nina's wisdom and cheerleading continues to guide me at every stage of my writing career. Thank you, my friend!

Thank you to Matt Goldman and students in Matt's Voice & Style class at the Loft Literary Center in Minneapolis in the fall of 2019.

Kristi Romo wisely suggested I get a lecture pass to Hamline's MFAC program during January 2020. Thank you to Brandy Colbert, Nina LaCour, Phyllis Root, Eliot Schreffer, Anne Ursu, and the rest of the faculty for welcoming me so warmly. Special thanks to Elana K. Arnold and Swati Avasthi for working with me on the Finn and Andre packing scene, alumni Justina Ireland and Tasslyn Magnusson for an encouraging chat about historical research, and Alex Fallgren for being Alex Fallgren.

Karen Estrada, Ricky Kubicek, Annika Williamson, and Meng Yang: Thank you for conversations that affected *Roof* in meaningful ways.

Jon Chelstrom generously answered all my firefighting questions. (Kerry, the named firefighter, is for my favorite firefighter/phys ed teacher. High five, Bogie!)

I wrote a lot of this book in Drew Brockington's office with Waffles the Catstronaut looking over my shoulder and Leroy the bulldog at my feet. Thanks for your friendship and encouragement, Drew.

Kathleen West and I became author friends as I wrote this book, and now I can't imagine my life without her. You're so smart, KC. Also so pretty.

Kristi Romo, my critique partner, the midwife to my books: You are singular, you care about every single word I write, and I'm so lucky you're in my life.

I am honored by everyone who was willing to beta read for me: Maame Opare-Addo, Chris Baker-Raivo, Jessica Edelheit, Karen Estrada, Alex Fallgren, Allison Hackenmiller, Andre Hardy, Craig Johnson, Sam King, Ricky Kubicek, Nina LaCour, Kristi Romo, Kristyn Seo-Taff, Dr. Kaia Simon, Mitchell Slattery, Kathleen West, Cassidy Wester, Katharine Woodman-Maynard, Meng Yang, and Laura Zimmermann. Thank you all for your keen eyes and perspectives in different stages of this manuscript.

My editor, Maggie Lehrman, can see into my soul. Thank you for pushing me and believing in this book, Maggie.

Everyone at Abrams is heaven. Special thanks to Jenny Choy, Penelope Cray, Emily Daluga, Deena Fleming, Mary Marolla, Erin Vandeveer, Amy Vreeland, and everyone in marketing and publicity!

Andrew Hudson is the artist behind *Roof*'s amazing cover. Thank you forever, Andrew.

Being a literary agent is half badass businessperson and half author caretaker, and Sara Crowe is 100 percent awesome at both. Thank you also to the rest of the excellent Pips!

Finally, thank you to all the librarians, teachers, booksellers, bloggers, bookstagrammers, and readers who put books into kids' hands.

This last part is for my school librarian: Here are my sources, Hackenmiller!

Making Victorian Costumes for Women by Heather Audin

Many YouTube videos by dress historian Bernadette Banner

Mrs. Beeton's Book of Household Management by Isabella Beeton

The Supersizers Go . . . Victorian with Giles Coren and Sue Perkins

Manners and Morals of Victorian America by Wayne Erbsen

Personal papers of Ceila Tauer Forstner

How to Be a Victorian: A Dawn-to-Dusk Guide to Victorian Life by Ruth Goodman

Personal papers of Mary M. Hill

The Essential Handbook of Victorian Etiquette by Professor
    Thomas E. Hill

James J. Hill House by Craig Johnson

Dining with the Victorians: A Delicious History by Emma Kay

The Victorian Tailor by Jason Maclochlain

A Victorian Lady's Guide to Fashion and Beauty by Mimi Mathews

Victorian Fashion by Jayne Shrimpton

The Essential Handbook of Victorian Entertaining by
    Autumn Stephens